D0210172

Books by Maisey Yates

The Carsons of Lone Rock

Rancher's Forgotten Rival
Best Man Rancher
One Night Rancher
Rancher's Snowed-In Reunion

Gold Valley Vineyards

Rancher's Wild Secret
Claiming the Rancher's Heir
The Rancher's Wager
Rancher's Christmas Storm

Copper Ridge

Take Me, Cowboy
Hold Me, Cowboy
Seduce Me, Cowboy
Claim Me, Cowboy
Want Me, Cowboy
Need Me, Cowboy

For more books by Maisey Yates,
visit maiseyyates.com.

You can also find Maisey Yates on Facebook,
along with other Harlequin Desire authors,
at Facebook.com/HarlequinDesireAuthors!

NEW YORK TIMES AND *USA TODAY*
BESTSELLING AUTHOR

MAISEY YATES

Rancher's Snowed-In Reunion
&
Claiming the Rancher's Heir

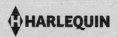

Recycling programs
for this product may
not exist in your area.

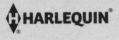

ISBN-13: 978-1-335-47532-9

Rancher's Snowed-In Reunion & Claiming the Rancher's Heir

Copyright © 2023 by Harlequin Enterprises ULC

Rancher's Snowed-In Reunion
Copyright © 2023 by Maisey Yates

Claiming the Rancher's Heir
Copyright © 2020 by Maisey Yates

For questions and comments about the quality of this book, please contact us at CustomerService@Harlequin.com.

Harlequin Enterprises ULC
22 Adelaide St. West, 41st Floor
Toronto, Ontario M5H 4E3, Canada
www.Harlequin.com

Printed in U.S.A.

CONTENTS

RANCHER'S SNOWED-IN
REUNION

Chapter 1

After

Flint Carson had to hand it to his brother. His recent move in life had inspired Flint. And he couldn't say that he was often inspired by his little brother. Not that Jace wasn't a decent guy, it was just that Flint, in general, didn't want what Jace had. He had settled down recently, and that wasn't in the cards for Flint.

But when his brother had become a part owner of the hotel that his fiancée bought, it had gotten Flint thinking. And then he had done more than think. He had been content for a long time competing in the rodeo. Working his family ranch, giving to them in a way that he could. His father recognized rodeo triumphs, and he took them as credits to who he was as a father, as the rodeo commissioner.

He also recognized contributions to the ranch. His mother appreciated that his father felt appreciated. He didn't do emotions, so that kind of physical involvement was what he had to give, so he gave it.

At least until a couple of years ago. It had started being profoundly not enough.

And after…

There was just so much anger in him. There had been, for a long time. For a lot of reasons. But after that song had come out…

He gritted his teeth. It infuriated him every time.

But what didn't infuriate him was his brand-new purchase. Pine Creek Resort. Nestled in the mountains of central Oregon, a couple hours away from his family home of Lone Rock.

He'd seen it and just felt drawn to it. He didn't give much credit to fate or feelings—not these days. But he believed a man ought to trust his gut.

So, he was trusting his.

It was practically off-grid, and solar panels, generators and other things kept it going with the iffy power running to the place. But it was pretty seamless, and he had done his due diligence on that. Because while he thought it was great that Jace and Cara were running the hotel at the end of the main drag of Lone Rock's main business center—which was just a few businesses, surrounded by mountains—he wanted more. Bigger.

The thought made his mouth curve into a smile as he looked around the highly polished lobby area. It was all logs and wooden beams. Rustic sort of luxury.

He could remember back when he'd said he didn't have ambitions or dreams at all.

But that was before.

Back then, everything he'd done had been to burn the rage out of his blood. To push himself to the edge so that he could ride out the simmering hatred that turned his blood to poison.

He'd chased adrenaline because it made things feel clear. Pure. Clean.

Could have been worse.

Could have been heroin.

Maybe it wasn't all that different now. Maybe this wasn't all that different. Maybe he was still trying to climb impossible mountains, just with more financial risk than physical.

With the weather being what it was, almost every guest had canceled their reservation for the weekend. There was a huge storm coming in, and while usually the hotel was accessible year-round, there had been some warnings and questions about whether or not it would be possible over the next couple of days. He didn't mind. A little bit of quiet in his newest acquisition while he looked to the next one was fine by him.

And since there was only going to be one guest, he'd let the staff go as well. The guest had declined maid service, and there was enough food that all he would have to do was heat and deliver. And he didn't mind that.

A little bit of manual labor didn't bother him at all. In fact, he thought it was good. Another way to burn out that rage. He had to do it.

And as if just thinking had brought it all to him, he suddenly became aware of the fact that there was music playing in the lobby. And not just any music.

You were the cowboy my mama warned me about
And I thought I listened, I thought you were dif-
ferent
I gave you my heart, and you gave me good-luck
charms
I gave you my body, and you kept my scarf
I gave you my body, and you kept my heart

For God's sake. Was it destined to follow him everywhere? Even when he quite literally owned the damn
place?

He growled and stalked toward the reception desk.
The guy had told him how to control the music, but as
his own personal level of hell played around him, he
couldn't quite remember how.

I gave you everything to the sound of crashing
waves
You knew you were the first one
I wanted you to be the only one

It made him think of her.

The song always made him think of her.

The way she'd looked at him, like she was searching
his eyes for the answers to all of her questions. Word-
less questions he'd wished he hadn't understood. Questions that still echoed inside him.

In the end, she'd said that he was right. She had said
that they needed to finish the whole damned thing.

She was the one that had called it a fling.

She said she loved you too.

Yes. She had said that. And then she had taken it

back. She had said that it was just because of the sex. And he'd been more than willing to believe it because hearing her say that she loved him had done things to him. Terrible, intense things that made him feel like his chest was being cut into.

He needed to find the volume. Or a sledgehammer. Before the next part.

But then it was the next part, and it was in his head, his heart, his soul.

You took the clothes off my body
I gave you my yes and I love you
You took the skin off my bones
You gave me nothing at all
I prayed for our sin to disappear
But I didn't mean for it to end in blood

He found the speaker right then. He found it just a lyric too late. He crouched down, reaching for the knob on the speaker behind the desk. And as he did, he heard the door to the lobby open. He hit the off button on the speaker just as the next part of the song started.

He couldn't explain the way it made him feel.

He could remember where he was the first time he heard it. The first time he'd heard his ex-girlfriend — was she his ex-girlfriend? He'd never had a girlfriend in his life. And they weren't supposed to be that, but he'd also never ended a physical relationship with someone and felt like their connection was still there. And yet.

The simple truth was, he'd gotten in deeper with her than he ever had been with anyone else. Much deeper than he'd intended to. And he wasn't going to say he'd covered himself in glory at the end of all things. But she had seemed to accept it. He'd been up-front with her, from the beginning, about what they were, about what they could be.

So imagine his surprise the first time he'd heard that song. Documenting everything. The most personal, deep feelings he'd ever had in his whole life turned into a sing-along.

Even if no one else had ever heard it, it would have felt too raw and personal for him to listen to.

But people had heard it. So many people.

To make matters worse, her fame and his own niche notoriety in certain circles had made it so there were theories out there on the internet about who the song was about.

Her fans were nuts. They spent all day weaving together theories about what every lyric meant. And he knew that because he'd googled it, because he'd wanted to know what the lyrics meant too.

Dammit.

The terrible thing was, her fans made points. Points he didn't like, but points nonetheless.

That would have been bad enough. But it didn't stop there.

Strangers sometimes accosted him on the street and asked him how dare he break Tansey Martin's heart? Country music's sweetheart. Barrel-racer-turned-overnight-singing-sensation.

She was beautiful and beloved, and he was the expertly cast villain in her narrative. Set to music, which meant that people could hum his humiliation as a catchy tune.

He could remember clearly the way that she had

looked up at him. The way that she had looked up at him when he'd said all those things. The awful sort of things that he'd warned her he would say. As everything had broken apart inside of him, the walls that he had erected around himself beginning to crumble, she had looked up at him, and she had said that he was right.

That he was right, and they shouldn't be together. That he was right and they should forget everything.

Yeah. He knew that. Because he knew his limitations. And then... And then four months later, completely and totally blindsided by this song. And he'd known it was about them. That it was their story

It was like she had crawled beneath his skin with those song lyrics. Like she had described his own pain. Like she'd dug into his soul and carved clear arrows to his own motives. To things he'd denied even to himself.

He'd pretended that he wasn't hanging on to her scarf for any particular reason, and she had immortalized it in song and made it impossible for him to pretend.

But it was the pregnancy scare.

That was what destroyed him the most, because it shone a light on the way that he had fallen apart most profoundly.

The worst, cruelest way he'd failed her.

When something like that happened, you had to take a good look at yourself. Even though there hadn't been a baby in the end, it had been a come-to-Jesus moment. A look-hard-at-the-man-he'd-become moment.

He didn't like that man.

It was one reason he'd changed everything. One reason he'd started...working. Really working. Not just on his father's land, not just on being rodeo champion yet again. But building something that was entirely his.

And he couldn't let that song into his head. Not now. Because it was the only thing that could get beneath his skin, just like *she* was the only thing that ever could.

He was pretty good at staying stoic in the face of difficult things.

It wasn't the fans yelling at him. That was actually fine. That made him *mad*. Anger, he had found, was fantastic fuel.

It was the pain.

The pain he wasn't supposed to be able to feel anymore. The pain that ambushed him when he didn't expect it. When he was alone. The pain that took him right back to the place that he'd been when he was a boy, a place he couldn't even think about, much less fully remember or relive.

And so he pushed the song to the back of his mind, and he stood up. But then he froze. The predator spotting prey. That was what it felt like. Like everything in him went quiet. And the edges of the empty lobby blurred.

Her.

There she was. Standing there at the center of the room, strawberry blond hair curling and cascading past her shoulders.

She looked like he remembered her.

Not the way that she dressed up for the public. All fake eyelashes and red lipstick.

This was just her.

The way that he had seen her that first day. Coming in from barrel racing, her cheeks bright red, her smile exuberant. Though she wasn't smiling now. She looked storm tossed, her hair full of snowflakes, and a couple of twigs. Her face was wet, likely from melting snow, and it forced him to remember how hot her skin could be when he put his hands on it.

She looked just like she had the first time...

Before

She wasn't his type.

Flint Carson had interacted with more than his fair share of the sort of women you met at a rodeo. From rodeo queens to buckle bunnies, and everything in between. He tended toward the queens and the bunnies. Soft, pretty rhinestones. The sort of glamour that wasn't necessarily subtle or classy, but he liked it. He was a man, dusty, hard and full of grit. He liked a woman who was the opposite of all that.

That was the point of women, as far as he was concerned.

Bring on the glitter, the lip gloss, the long fingernails. Flashy, maybe even bordering on what some would call trashy. He didn't think it was trashy.

He liked it.

Now, some of the barrel racers had a little bit of flair to them, but they still weren't his thing. Felt too much like coworkers, really. He didn't like it.

He was also very careful to choose women close to his age and level of experience. He didn't have forever in him. Hell, he didn't even have more than a couple of nights in him, so it didn't do any good to go after a woman who was expecting something more. To go after the kind of woman who wanted something more.

He needed the women that he hooked up with to want exactly what he wanted.

Which was why, when the pint-size, barefaced barrel racer tripped on unsteady legs on her way out of the gate after a ride, and landed right in his arms, the first thing he told himself was, she wasn't his type.

She had freckles all over her face. Her eyes were green. Her hair was strawberry blond, curly, he could tell; even though it was in a braid, there were wispy tendrils that had escaped. She was thin but athletic, wearing a plain white tank top and a pair of torn blue jeans. She was young.

And something in him burned.

He set her back on her heels.

"Careful there."

"Thanks, Ace," she said, brushing some dust off of her jeans. "I'll do my best to be more careful."

"Darlin', I just saved you from doing a face-plant, and you're going to get sassy with me?"

"A face-plant never hurt anybody."

"Neither has spending a few minutes in my arms. You can ask around."

She laughed. But it wasn't a particularly kind or warm laugh. "Of course. Somehow that doesn't surprise me."

"What's your name?"

"Tansey," she said. "Tansey Martin. You're Flint Carson."

She knew who he was. He supposed he shouldn't be surprised. She was…young. He was sort of an elder statesman of the bull-riding circuit, and in addition to that, his dad was the rodeo commissioner. Practically everybody around these parts knew the Carsons.

"Guilty," he said.

"Of quite a lot of things if the gossip is anything to go by."

She could walk away. That was the thing. She could walk away, but she was antagonizing him instead. *He* could also walk away.

Neither of them were doing that.

It would almost be interesting except she wasn't his type.

She wasn't his type, and wasn't charmed by his whole facade. Which made him wonder if there was any point to the facade at all. Made him tempted to drop it. And he never dropped it, not ever.

"Now," he asked, "did your parents ever teach you not to listen to gossip?"

"My mom taught me that gossip could be useful. If something is said often enough, there's probably some truth to it. And maybe a person should listen to it. All my daddy taught me was the way 1999 Ford pickup taillights look going out of the driveway."

"Sounds like a country song," he said.

She smiled, and it was unreadable. Not flirtatious. Not friendly. He wanted to know what the hell it meant. "Yeah. It kind of does."

She was standing with her horse. He had kind of only just noticed. The big animal that was right next to her. Funny.

It was like she took up all the space.

"Nice," he said, patting the animal on the flank.

"Thanks. Cinderella has a thing for cowboys that are too charming for their boots."

"I take it her owner does not."

"No, she doesn't. Like I said. Taillights. I'm familiar. With cowboys. Do you know what they're good for?"

"What?"

"Leaving."

That made him want to do something. Surprise her. Climb a mountain.

Stay.

"That is true. We are very good at that."

Except, he didn't leave. Neither did she. Neither of them pointed that out. They just stood there and marinated in the irony.

"You want to get a drink?" he asked.

Her lips twitched, like she was pondering that. "Sure. I'm not having sex with you. To be clear."

The way she said it was a gut punch. And good thing she wasn't his type, or his mind might have wandered somewhere it shouldn't.

"I'm not asking," he said. "To be clear."

Her face went scarlet. Well. He'd succeeded in getting something other than a cool, snarky reaction out of her.

Though, he had no idea why he was asking her for a drink. Except they were standing there, right near the gates, cluttering up the space, taking up too much room.

So, obviously they needed to move to another venue. It was the last night in this particular stop on the rodeo tour, and he didn't know how he hadn't noticed her before. He didn't really stand around watching all the other events. He had once, when he'd been new to the game. When things had been shiny and bright and he'd been excited.

At least, in his memory he was excited. It was entirely possible that he was painting the whole thing with a varnish that had never actually been there.

Always easier to look back on the glory days.

Mostly, he had been young and angry, and the adrenaline had felt good.

Now he was old and angry, and the adrenaline made his muscles hurt.

Okay. He wasn't old. He was thirty-four, but that was getting on in rodeo years. And that was a fact.

Especially when you'd been doing it since you were eighteen years old. It was a lot of years of abuse. More than not.

"Are you old enough to drink?"

Her face went red. "Yes."

"Okay. I don't want to be out there buying alcohol for a minor. I don't have a criminal record, which is a miracle to be honest. So I'd rather not get one now."

"That's kind of a surprise. I thought all you guys had a slew of DUIs."

"Sorry to disappoint."

"Well. I'm happy to be surprised. I didn't think your kind could surprise me."

"What exactly is my kind, Tansey?" He started to follow her out of the arena area and toward the stalls where the horses would be kept until they were ready to load up and head to the next event.

"Smooth talker. Probably never met a woman you couldn't con out of her clothes."

"Now, that sounds vaguely predatory. This here being the modern era, I am a huge fan of consent. I don't con anyone out of anything. Now, if they get a look at me and decide they'd like to take their clothes off, that is another story altogether."

"Good to know. A respectful womanizer. But a womanizer nonetheless."

"You do have my number. But then, I don't go around claiming to be anything other than a bad bet. I assume your daddy did."

"He thought he'd try to be a family man for a little bit. Didn't work out."

"Well. There's a difference between me and your father, right off the bat. I'm never going to pretend to be a family man."

"Well, I suppose that's something."

He watched as she took all the tack off of her horse—he didn't figure she was going to accept any help from him. She probably had a million reasons for it too. Something about being independent, he was sure. And while it would be fun, maybe, to engage in that banter, he figured he would keep going in the direction of the unexpected banter. Because he liked it.

He liked talking to her.

And hell, he'd had a great idea how this night was going to go. He'd won his event, kept his top spot on the leaderboard, and he'd been planning on going out to the bar with all the other guys, including his brother Boone, and having drinks. Which would probably devolve into taking shots, which would inevitably end up with him finding a woman to hook up with…

He'd go back to his motel room, they'd have sex, she'd go her way and he'd sleep for a few hours before getting on the road the next morning.

He could see it all play out in his mind. And it bored him.

Tansey didn't bore him.

And anyway, she wasn't his type.

So it wasn't like it was going to be anything but a conversation. He couldn't remember the last time he'd wanted to engage in a conversation with anybody after an event.

He didn't engage in a lot of conversations, really. He did a lot of drinking, a lot of physical things.

Didn't talk all that much.

This felt like a novelty. And… Hell. He was in the market for one. Hadn't known that he was until she'd fallen into his arms. But then, maybe that was a sign.

Not that he believed in that kind of thing.

Still, he found himself jerking his head toward where he parked his truck. "Want to take a ride with me?"

"I'll drive myself," she said. "Which bar?"

"Cactus," he said. "It's right across the street from the Okay Motel. That's where I'm staying."

"Me too," she said.

"How about we drive there, park across the street. Then nobody has to watch the drinking."

"I don't get drunk," she said.

"Why not?"

"Because. I like to have my wits about me."

"Well. There is the difference between you and me. I prefer to make my wits a bit blurry."

She looked at him, for a long moment, and he had the uncomfortable feeling that her green eyes could see more than just his face, his shirt, his jeans. He had the feeling that she could see something deeper in him than he even knew was there. And he didn't like it.

And still, he wanted to go get that drink with her.

"Okay. Meet you there."

After

She was standing completely still. Like she was the prey. Like she knew it. Like she knew that she had been scented.

Like she knew exactly what he felt.

Because hadn't she always?

Until that last moment.

And hadn't he always? Until then.

When they had both pretty spectacularly lied to each other's faces and broken down the world.

He stood by it.

Because the fallout had proved that he was right. His own behavior after the fact, and hers.

He would never have said he was sensitive. Far from it. He was a man who didn't do feelings in the slightest. But he felt like she had taken a layer of his skin and peeled it off with a paring knife, pulled it back and showed the world everything that was inside of him. And he didn't even like to look at all the things that were inside of him.

Hearing the pain in the song was like being stabbed through the heart.

Because as much as it was about her own pain, it was about his. As much as it was about him breaking them up, it was about him breaking himself. As much as he was the villain to her...

He'd been that for himself too.

If he believed in fate, he'd have been certain it had come for him today.

He didn't believe in fate.

It was just that life was a bitch.

So he had to be a bigger bastard.

He put his hand up to his head, and reflexively, without thought, touched the brim of his cowboy hat, and tipped it. "Howdy."

"What are you doing here?" She looked around, shocked, and he realized that she had gone as white as the snow outside.

He slowly moved from behind the counter, and began to walk toward her. She was the only thing. The only thing. "I might ask you the same question. Because I looked at the books, and your name is not on them."

"I don't check into hotels under my real name," she said.

"Oh right," he said, "because you're fancy now. Because everybody knows who you are. Everyone knows everything about you, don't they, Tansey?"

"Yes. I know you're trying to be mean, and trying to make it sound like maybe I'm above myself, but it's true."

"It seems there's something else you don't do. You don't look to see who owns the hotel you're staying at."

Her mouth dropped open. "I've been here before. You've *never* been here."

"I just bought it. It's mine. And you're the only guest." He spread his arms wide. "Looks like it's just the two of us."

Chapter 2

*R*un.

That was all Tansey could think. She needed to run. Because she'd never, ever wanted to come face-to-face with Flint Carson ever again. Not in her whole life.

But there he was.

Maybe if she closed her eyes, she could be not in this moment. Maybe if she concentrated really hard, he would disappear.

Maybe this was a dream.

The whole drive up here had been a nightmare, and maybe it hadn't even been real. Maybe that was the thing. Maybe the whole drive, with the intense, freezing snow, the white stuff piling up on the road and making it slick and almost impossible to keep her tires on the road, had been part of a nightmare. Maybe the branches falling across the road, the tree that had fallen down after her on the soft ground, and the lack of cell phone service, had all been an elaborate nightmare.

Ending with Flint. Standing right there in the lobby of the hotel.

Like it was *The Shining*. Except, it wasn't a crazy groundskeeper; it was her way-too-hot-for-anyone's-own-good ex-boyfriend, who had absolutely destroyed her and broken her into tiny pieces.

Ex-boyfriend. He was never your boyfriend. He was a guy who had sex with you. And you were an idiot.

Yes. She had been an idiot. And she'd had grace for that young idiot. That young idiot who had known better, whose mother had told her better, who had purposed to not act out her daddy issues in that way, but had done so because Flint was just so charming. Because she hadn't actually had any experience.

Because she had told herself that she knew getting sexually involved with a man who wasn't going to fall in love with her could hurt her, but she hadn't really understood it. Because she had told herself she could handle a fling, and then she had let herself believe that she had been convinced on some level she could change his mind about it being a fling.

She had been like every other dumb twenty-two-year-old who didn't want to believe that she was, in fact, like all the other girls.

Well, she'd made her peace with that, because she was more than two years past all that, and a heartbreak sure offered a lot of clarity. She didn't waste her time being outraged at that girl.

No. She knew where to put her outrage. It was on him. And there he was.

If this was a nightmare, she could take an umbrella out of the umbrella stand by the door and start whacking him with it.

She pinched her arm. It hurt, even through her heavy coat. But he was still standing there.

"What the hell are you doing?"

"I'm trying to see if I fell asleep on my way up here. Or maybe hit a tree and I'm unconscious in a ditch, so I'm hallucinating the ghosts of back-when-I-was-stupid past."

"Well. If you're hallucinating, then so am I."

"Great." And she had fantasized about running into him before, even though she had never wanted to see him again.

That seemed like a pretty normal thing.

In her fantasies of seeing him again someday, she had imagined herself in a beautiful designer dress—not looking soggy from her tramp through the snow up to the lobby, and being caught off guard.

No. She had always imagined they would run into each other at some soiree, not that Flint would have any reason to be at a soiree, but it was her fantasy.

Realistically, she hadn't thought it would happen, so she could imagine whatever scenario she wanted.

She had imagined that she would be dressed meticulously, looking every inch as wealthy as her music had made her, maybe with a handsome man on her arm—forgetting the fact that she hadn't been on a single date since she and Flint had broken up—and the look of regret that would wash over him would be profound.

But she would be happy. And she would drink champagne, and she would *show him*.

Because the best revenge was living well.

She had written it into the song because he had said it to her. He had said that to her about handling her own father's abandonment. And when she had written the song, she had hoped that he would hear it and appreciate the irony.

And now she found herself horrified by the realization that he had undoubtedly heard it.

Because all the self-protection that she had engaged in when he had broken up with her suddenly didn't matter. Because she had put it all in a song.

She had known that, but knowing it and coming face-to-face with it were two very different things.

And this was in no way what she wanted. This was way too real. She preferred the glossy fantasy.

This was him. And it felt like the first time…

Before

She had no idea what the hell she was doing. She didn't do this kind of thing. Didn't go out and have drinks with extraordinarily handsome cowboys. He was extraordinarily handsome. She'd known that, though. Ever since she first started riding with the rodeo two years ago.

She'd gotten into it hoping to see her dad again.

It was so stupid. All of it.

Her little pursuits to try and make a connection with a man who didn't give a shit about her at all. But she'd thought… Their paths would have to cross. Even when he wasn't competing in calf-roping events, he was often doing odd jobs around the rodeo. It was his whole life.

Plus, she'd figured… He paid attention to the rodeo circuit; he was bound to see her name.

Those were the two things her dad loved. The rodeo and country music. She was bound and determined that she was going to reach him through one of those ways or the other.

Funny that Flint had mentioned the taillights thing sounded like a country song.

She already knew it. She'd already made it one.

Of course, it wasn't the demo that her manager was shopping. It felt too personal. She hadn't played that song for anyone.

The frothy little love song that she'd recorded a couple of months ago when she'd found somebody who wanted to take a chance on her and push her to the labels was easier for her.

Not that anyone had shown any interest in it. But she did all the open mics that she came across while traveling for the rodeo, and that worked out pretty well for her.

Everything she did had a purpose. She'd joined the rodeo to find her dad, being in the rodeo let her travel, traveling helped her get her music out. That was how she did things.

But this… Having a drink with Flint Carson accomplished nothing. She didn't know why she had kept talking to him. Didn't know why she had stood there, unable to drag herself away. And she did not know why she'd said yes to this. But when she pulled up to the motel at the same time he did, and got out, crossing the dusty, two-lane Arizona highway to the little dive bar across the street, she stopped questioning it.

He opened the door for her, and she looked up at him, at his chiseled face, square jaw, strong chin. He had dark stubble over that jaw, and it looked rough, and she couldn't deny that she felt her fingers itch slightly with the urge to touch it.

Which was very stupid. She liked to think that she was smarter than that. That her body was smarter than that. Because it knew the memories of what it felt like to be abandoned. Remembered what it was like to crumple down on the ground, on her knees, with the gravel biting into the denim as her father's truck got farther and farther away and she gave in to her anguish. That was embedded into her soul. It was more keen, more real, than any desire to touch a handsome cowboy's stubble could ever be. That moment of it being the last time she ever saw her father would always be more burned into everything she was than…than the dark blue of his eyes. Like worn denim. So compelling and enticing…

She took a deep breath and pressed on into the bar.

The floor was rough wood, and there were neon cactus signs all over the place. And also a pink flamingo. She admired the commitment to tackiness, even if it wasn't totally following a theme.

There were a lot of cowboys and cowgirls already in there, people that she knew. She felt slightly embarrassed to be coming in with Flint, because why would anybody be with him unless they were going to sleep with him? She had never known Flint to hang out with a woman that he wasn't going to hook up with.

Well. Allegedly.

Maybe she had sort of noticed him from across the bar before, and that was what some of the girls she was with had said about him… And maybe she had committed some of that to heart a little bit more than she ought to.

Maybe she had gone back to her room and scribbled down a few song lyrics about unobtainable men who were nothing but bad decisions wrapped in dust and denim.

Maybe.

She was an artist, though. She often wrote about things that she had no desire to experience. She often wrote about things that she would never do. Things she didn't even want to do. She wrote about the human experience. Not necessarily her own.

The love song she'd recorded was a prime example of that.

She'd never been in love.

She thought about the song she'd written about her dad again, and shoved all that to the side.

"What will you have?"

"Uh. Beer?"

She just really wasn't a big drinker.

"Sure. What kind?"

"I don't know."

"Okay. That helps me make a decision."

He went over to the bar, and she sat down at one of the little tables in the corner. He came back a few moments later with two beers, one in each hand.

"How did me not knowing tell you anything?"

"I got you something easy. Something friendly. Since clearly if you don't know what you're drinking, you don't have a lot of experience with the drinking. So… mainstream it is."

"Are you insulting me?" she asked, drawing the glass toward her.

"Not at all. I'm giving you something accessible."

"Out of deference to my inexperience?"

He cleared his throat and took a drink of his beer. And far too late she realized the potential double entendre with that. Of course, he didn't know how inexperienced she was. Anyway, her experience, or lack thereof, when it came to things other than beer was immaterial to this moment and this conversation.

"What exactly are we doing?" she asked, lifting her glass up and taking a sip. Damn him. It was good.

"Having a beer."

"It's just… You have a reputation."

"That I do. Though, you're going to have to tell me which one you mean. Because I have a reputation for being a very good bull rider, as it happens. Maybe you missed it, but I'm in first place right now."

"I didn't miss it. And that isn't the reputation I'm referring to."

"You mean that I like to have a one-night stand. Many, many of the people who travel with the rodeo do."

"Right. Well. I don't."

"Great. Good to know."

"So why are you talking to me?"

"Why are *you* talking to *me*? Because as you said, I have a reputation. You seem to know it…"

"I don't know why I am talking to you. It's just that I wanted to."

"Well, I wanted to talk to you too. I can't say that I know why either." He huffed a laugh and took another drink of his beer. "I'll just tell you, I've known what I was doing for a long damn time. I joined the rodeo when I was eighteen. I knew that I wanted to be the best. I knew I wanted to win. I *have* won it all. Several times. I knew that was my goal. I achieved it. On a smaller scale... I tend to know what I want out of a given day. I knew what I was going to do tonight. I was going to leave the arena, I was going to come to this bar. I was going to go over there," he said, gesturing to the corner where there was a jukebox, and a gaggle of women dressed to the nines, their hair done up, their best push-up bras doing admirable work.

"I was going to strike up a conversation with one of those women, and we would've both known from the very beginning exactly where that conversation was going. We'd have had sex. Sorry. But it's true. I would've said goodbye, and she would've been on her way." He shrugged. "Yeah. I usually know exactly what I'm doing. I have no idea what I'm doing right now. No idea what's happening here. And I guess maybe that's part of why I like it. Why I'm interested. Because you ran into me... And changed the course of my evening. I think I'd have to be a particular kind of fool not to see where that went."

"It won't be bed."

"You've been very clear on that. And I have no interest in pushing."

She sat with that for a minute. Did that mean that he would have liked her that way if she'd said she wanted it? She had never been particularly flattered by the attentions of cowboys. In fact, just the opposite. Her mother had always made it very clear that cowboys had absolutely no standards. *"Darlin',"* she'd said. *"Men will stick it in the hole of a hollow tree. Don't you ever let yourself feel flattered because they want to put it in you."*

She knew that it came from a place of protectiveness. A little rough around the edges though it was. Darlene Martin was rough around the edges. It was part of what Tansey loved about her.

Her mom had taught her how to arm herself, protect herself, where she hadn't been able to do the same. Tansey was appreciative of that. She learned all of her mother's lessons, so she didn't have to learn her own.

If she wasn't careful, a man like Flint Carson could be a very difficult lesson.

But you know better. And this is just a conversation.

"What are your dreams?" he asked, leaning back in his chair. "You want to win it all in the rodeo?"

"I wouldn't be opposed. But… My dad is Huck Jones."

He frowned. "I know that name."

"Yeah. He's done roping and a few other events, plus general setup and teardown work, with the rodeo for a long time. I got into the rodeo to be closer to him. To find him again. Because I was a kid when he left and…"

"Taillights," he said.

"Yeah. And I guess I thought that I was going to change something. Redeem something, fix something by finding him. But you know what? He's never around. Even though I tried coming to him, I haven't ever encountered him. He hasn't been competing. I… I thought at least he would see me, and he would want to get to know me. If I was doing something that interested him.

I thought that I would matter. I thought that I would matter more. I really did. I guess I thought maybe the hearth-and-home thing wasn't for him, but if I took myself out on the road…"

"Right. Well. What a prick."

And that made her laugh. "Thanks for that. I think so too."

Except it hurt. It hurt a lot. And there was a reason she didn't go around just talking about this, but it was such a strange thing. To be sitting here like this with him. She had felt like she didn't want to leave his side from the moment she fell against him. This felt natural. And maybe that was why she felt compelled to ask him what it was they were doing. Because it shouldn't feel natural. Not to her, not to him.

They shouldn't just want to sit and talk to each other with no ulterior motives. In this world, in any world, it didn't seem to be a thing as far as she could tell.

And yet.

"What else? You didn't say that your dream was to win big here."

"I enjoy barrel racing. But no. It's not my dream."

"What's your dream?" he asked.

"I… I just recorded a demo. I… I want to be a singer. Well, I'm a songwriter. Really. And if what I end up doing is selling songs, that's fine too. It's okay if I don't actually end up being famous or anything like that." Except she kind of did want to be famous. She kind of did want to show him. She wanted to buy her mom a big house and end up on TV. She wanted to force him to see exactly what he'd walked away from. He acted like she was an anchor. Something that was dragging him down, holding him back.

She wanted to prove that she would've been the thing that got him ahead.

Better than he could do for himself.

Maybe that was bitter and toxic. But she couldn't help herself.

"Well. They do say the best revenge is living well," he said.

That was like balm.

He understood. He got it. She hadn't even had to say any of those dark, ugly things that rolled around inside of her chest. He just knew. He understood.

"Yeah. Well. That would be about the favorite revenge, I have to say. Especially because that version of revenge involves some pretty nice cowgirl boots."

"If you win the overall prize barrel racing this year, I'll buy you some boots."

"I don't need a man to buy my boots," she said. "That's the point."

"I get that. But maybe it would be nice if there was a man who wanted to buy you boots?"

"Sorry. I don't think that's a very good goal either."

"Why is that?"

"My mama raised me to be independent. At the end of the day, the only person you can depend on is…you."

She felt sad for herself just saying it, and she waited for him to look at her with pity. But he didn't. That was the interesting thing about him. He looked her straight in the eye. He looked at her like an equal.

He was a strange sort of man. Not exactly what she'd thought.

Though she was wary of him all the same.

"Can't you depend on your mom?"

She hesitated. "Yes. Though she is also an independent woman, so she has her own life. We stand for each other, but we mostly stand alone."

"I see."

"You have a lot of family, don't you?"

He nodded. "Yeah, I'm lousy with brothers." He hesitated for a moment. "And you probably know my sister, Callie. She was barrel racing until pretty recently."

She nodded. "Yeah, I do know her a bit. We're close to the same age."

He winced. "Right."

"You must never be lonely."

He chuckled. "I didn't say that."

"Oh."

"I respect that you want to stand on your own feet," he said, his tone switching abruptly. "But you can't stop me from buying a pair of boots for you to stand in if you win."

"I'd have to win," she pointed out. "And I'm not number one right now. Or did you not notice?"

"I didn't notice. I was too busy catching you when you tripped."

He met her gaze for too long. She looked away.

"Okay. So tell me how to win."

"You have to love nothing more than the moment you're in. Think about nothing more. Care about nothing more. You didn't ask me what my dreams were."

"Okay then… What are your dreams?" she asked.

"I don't have any."

"Oh."

"But that's why I win. Because it's very easy for nothing else to matter to me. Nothing but the moment. Nothing but the ride. Nothing else tugging on my attention. Nothing splintering my focus. There's not a single damn person out there that I care about more than I care about that moment. Not a single thing. Not a truck, not a house. Nothing. That's how I do it."

"You don't… You have a really big family…"

"Yeah. I mean… I love them. I do. But… I'm very good at putting a wall up over my emotions. In fact, I'm not entirely sure that I could get to them now if I wanted to."

He said it so casually. But she had a feeling that it was true. A deep truth. And one that he probably didn't go around speaking out loud. And he told her because… because they were able to talk to each other. Because it just worked.

If he wasn't going to question it, then neither was she.

"I'm not sure that I can do that. I care about too many things. Sometimes I feel like I care about… Everything," she said.

"You just have to learn to shut it off. Don't burn so bright with passion that you let it smoke you out." He snapped his finger. "You have to remember it can work for you. It can get you where you're at right now. But don't let it sabotage you either."

"Thanks."

She finished her beer. And the two of them stood.

They left together, and she was keenly aware of the fact that people were watching them. She made a show of putting a lot of distance between their bodies as they walked through the parking lot, and across the street.

"Bye," she said, waving.

"See you at the next stop."

"Yeah. See you then."

After

"So we're the only two people here?" she asked.

"That's about the size of it. And I don't know what's going on, if a tower got knocked out or something, but there's no cell service. We've got a landline, as long as that holds."

"Are you letting me know how easy it would be for you to kill me and bury me in a snowbank?"

His lips quirked up on the side. "I wouldn't do that. You're famous. Too many people would miss you."

It was the edge to him that surprised her, though.

Does it? If he's heard the song... You know him. You know how private he is, how protected.

Yes. And on some level, she knew that if he ever did hear the song, he would probably view it as a betrayal. And maybe part of her wanted that. Had wanted to pour out her own pain and anguish, to make everybody understand the intimacy of it. What he had taken from her. Not her virginity, it was deeper than that.

She had never slept with another man before, and she hadn't slept with one since, because she had been afraid of being hurt.

That was the part that got her.

That he knew what it had meant to her to give herself to him.

Yeah, she could see how maybe he would be upset that she had advertised that. But hell, people didn't know that it was him. Well. They did know that it was him. There were entire online forums dedicated to analyzing every single part of the song. If her scarf was a metaphor, or if it was real. If she was writing about the bull rider that she had been seen with on the coast that summer she'd gotten famous. Or if it had been a whirlwind affair in the studios with Harry Styles.

She had never met Harry Styles. But somehow, there were rumors about the two of them. Imaginary Tansey had a way more interesting love life than actual Tansey, who had one lover and a broken heart.

Your heart is not broken anymore. You just feel fragile because you are facing down your problematic past.

But yes, there were a lot of rumors. And many of them were true. It had been especially jarring to read a thread about lyrics where somebody had correctly identified the blood was about a miscarriage or a pregnancy scare. And it wasn't like it was subtle; it was just reading people trying to get deep into her words, rather than just applying their own experiences to it. Because to an extent, she had imagined that the song itself and what it could mean to people would be more interesting than what it had meant to her.

But somehow, she herself had become an object of fascination and… And that meant that people had wanted to know what the song meant for *her*.

But she had never said his name out loud. His name hadn't passed her lips once since they had parted that last day.

All that to say, she felt like she didn't fully deserve

his rage, but she also couldn't deny that she had known it would be there.

Deep down, she had known, because she knew *him*. If he hadn't thought she would write a song about it, then he had never really known her. Hadn't been paying attention. Not even when she had played him the song about her dad, the first song that had made her famous. The one that he had encouraged her to record. He had been an audience of one the first time she had ever played a song that had come so deep from her heart like that. And he had been the one who had said it was the key to her fame.

He'd been right.

As famous as the song about her dad had made her, the one about her heartbreak had taken things into the stratosphere.

That forced her to think about why she was here, and she'd rather not do that. So she focused instead on the blazing blue of his eyes.

She'd seen those eyes look a lot of ways.

But never angry. Not like this.

"Well. Good for me then. Because yeah, it would be kind of a bad idea for this to be the last place that I was headed, with you being the owner and all. That is a totally traceable murder. I wouldn't attempt it."

"Lucky for you, I'd rather have the notoriety of having you have stayed here, than I would getting rid of you."

His voice was hard, and it was like some of the anger was slowly beginning to subside. There was something flat there. Something unreadable. Except… She didn't trust it.

"What?"

"You're going to make sure that everybody knows that you stayed here. Wrote a song here or some shit."

"Right. So I'm going to tell everybody that I stayed at my ex… Sorry. Is it better if I just keep your name out of everything? Because we can go ahead and address the number-one hit in the room if you want."

"I don't want to talk about that shit. Except to say that you and I both know that whether you ever confirmed it or not, people know it's about me. I'm the one that gets yelled at by crazy fans walking down the street. You can deny it, you can refuse to address it, but the best thing you could do is show everybody that we're fine."

But they weren't fine. Nothing in her was fine. She felt utterly and absolutely rattled. And this was her retreat…

And it was never going to be again after this. Because he owned it now. She could never come here again.

If this was fate, fate was a bitch.

Or maybe this was all balancing the cost of what she'd been given. Maybe poor country girls didn't get to have fame and money if they weren't also given heartbreak and exes they couldn't forget.

"You know, that's quite the weird, blackmail-sounding thing that you can't make me do, but I think I would rather just leave."

"You're welcome to try. But the weather has picked up. Everybody else was smart and didn't come up. All my staff left. Because it was the smart thing to do. You were the only fool that decided to make the trek up."

"And I can make the trek back down." She turned around and started to head for the door. She pushed it open, and the wind just about blew it back. She shoved it, and headed back out into the night. Fuck all this, and him too. Him *specifically*.

Maybe there was a song in this.

That was the real problem. She couldn't think of a song. And she didn't want anyone to know that. She was completely dried up. She had written the greatest breakup album of all time. With a song that had reached into people's souls and taken hold of them. Had taken on a life of its own. She had done the same writing the song about her dad. She knew how to grab on to pain. She knew how to grab on to pain and turn it into something real and relatable.

And now she was famous and successful and...

And she was still sad. Because it had given her money. It had let her buy a house for her mom. But it hadn't given her a relationship with her dad.

And she was alone. And she couldn't figure out how to trust people any more than she could before.

Hell, it was even worse. Because the only person she had ever trusted was Flint. The only person that she had ever hoped might be more than he seemed was Flint.

And he had proved that he wasn't. And then she had gotten famous. And her ability to trust people had become even more compromised because people could actually get things from her. They actually wanted things from her, and that? That made everything feel fraught. It made everything feel impossible.

And now it felt like there were no more songs. Because all she had was old, lingering pain that she didn't want to keep writing about, and the thrill of a success story that she couldn't quite access. It made her feel ungrateful. It made her feel small and sad. To be standing in the spotlight and still feeling like she was shrouded in darkness. She was beginning to feel terrified that it would all go away. Because the only thing worse than the idea of staying in the spotlight, bombarded with all the fame, was what would happen if it went away.

Because one thing was sure. It was exposing to write a song like she had about her and Flint. But it gave her a way to expel some of that pain. It gave her a way to talk about it. She didn't have anyone in her life that she could talk about it honestly. The only person had been... Flint. And then it had ended. So she had written songs about him instead. And talked to the world about how he had let her down. There was a catharsis in that.

She battled the wind and walked down to her truck, forced the door open. All of her bags were still inside. The door to the hotel opened, and she saw Flint, up the stairs, looking down at her, backlit by the lights from the inside.

And he came down the stairs, heading out after her, the wind whipping the T-shirt he was wearing, tightening it over what she knew was a very firm body. And she did not need to be looking at him right now; she was trying to run away from him.

"What the hell do you think you're doing?" he shouted. "You were lucky to make it up here okay— you are not driving back down in this."

"You lost any right to have an opinion on what I do," she yelled back.

"Did I lose it, or did we agree to dissolve it?"

Well. There was the rub. With the wind and the snow blowing between them, and ferocity and fear burning in his blue eyes.

"I was protecting myself. If you were worried about anything other than your own feelings in that moment, you would've known that."

"You should've said it all to *me*," he said.

The song. That was what he meant. That she should have said all those things to him, and not the world.

It hurt, because it wasn't unfair.

"What would it have changed?" she asked.

She was breathing hard, and so was he.

"Nothing," he said, his voice rough.

It was hard to hear. For one moment she'd forgotten. For one moment she'd hoped. But this was the reality of it, of them.

"Okay then. Don't lecture me. Don't lecture me on what I should've done. Don't lecture me on what the right thing to do would have been when I told you that I might be having your baby and you looked back at me and said you didn't want it."

"If you had…"

"You never even texted me back."

"Because you said that you weren't."

"I wasn't. Or maybe I was. But I lost it either way. I never took a test."

"I'm sorry. If you had been…"

"Is this what you do? Tell yourself if I'd been pregnant you would have handled it well? You didn't handle anything about it well. What makes you think you would have been better if there was a baby? You're rewriting the story."

"We all get to write our own stories, Tansey, you of all people should know."

The words hit hard, and he stood there, blue eyes blazing.

"I'm leaving."

"Don't," he bit out. "It's too fucking dangerous. You're not leaving just because you don't like me."

"I have to leave."

She just had to. She couldn't stay, not with him. It was too much, too real.

Nothing had been real like this since him.

And she couldn't stand it.

Chapter 3

She got into the truck and started the engine, and he stood there in front of the vehicle, the headlights pouring over his body. She found some joyful irony in that. That she was the one driving away. When she had written a whole hit about the taillights on her father's truck, and watching him leave.

This should be a triumph. As soon as she started back down the winding road to the main highway, she regretted trying to leave.

There was snow all over the road, and her tires were slick. She had four-wheel drive, but this was solid ice. The temperature had dropped with the passing of time, and the movement of the storm.

Her truck was slipping and sliding, and her heart was pounding. She tried to drive slow, tried not to put herself in a position where she would have to brake suddenly, which would cause her to slide right off the road and over the edge of the embankment. Her palms were slick. She rounded the corner, and had to slam on her brakes, because there was a giant tree down in the middle of the road. Stretching from end to end. Her breathing was ragged, and she could barely hear it over the sound of the wind whipping against the side of her truck.

Shit. What was she going to do? She couldn't even turn around. The road was too narrow. And she would have to…to walk back up and…

There was a pounding on the door of the truck. She jumped, and turned toward the passenger side, and saw Flint standing there looking in the window. "Come back to the hotel," he shouted.

He was shouting because of the roar of the wind; she knew that, except he still sounded angry.

"No, thanks."

"Fucking hell, Tansey, don't be suicidal because you don't want to see me."

He didn't understand. It felt like suicide to see him. To be sharing air with him. To be sharing the same space with him. Because the problem was, he was still beautiful. And no matter how she had rewritten him into the perfect storybook villain, no matter how she tried to make herself remember only that terrible moment when he had shut all of his emotions off, and had been a blank wall she couldn't see through, couldn't reach through, couldn't get through, when she saw him, she had to remember that he was a whole human being. A man. Flesh and blood.

A man who had kissed her, touched her, given her pleasure.

A man who had held her, and cared for her, and given her things that no one else ever had before. And then taken them away from her.

Yeah. It was easier to remember him as the collection of truths she had put into that song. Because every line had been true. But he was right. It had been a story. Carefully chosen details designed to create a neat narrative. One that highlighted the things that had been so good they were painful, the things that had cost her. The risks she had taken. But none of his.

She hadn't put in all the ways he'd helped her, respected her, listened to her...

Hadn't put any of his risk, any of his vulnerability into it. Because even though he'd never opened up to her, not all the way, even though he'd never told her why he was the way he was, she'd seen how he was. That being with her scared him sometimes.

All the fear, the vulnerability in her song... It had all been hers. And so in the end it had been about her pain, because she hadn't given any credit to the idea that he might have had any.

But looking at him now, she knew the man. The whole man. Not just the one from the song.

And it made her ache.

It was why her little fantasy about running into him and coolly walking away could never actually happen. Because it wasn't really Flint in that fantasy. Just a hollow stand-in that looked like him. Not one that embodied his heat, his life. Everything he was.

"Come on," he said.

"I can't turn around," she said.

"I know," he said. "If you get in the ditch right now,

you're never getting back out of it. And it's too slick to try. So just get out of the truck and leave it here. No one else is getting past that tree either. We are going to have to get a chainsaw out and cut it into pieces to move it. And we could do it now, but to what end? There's just going to be more obstacles down the road. There's a hotel a quarter of a mile back that way."

"We have to…walk back?"

"Yes. We both have to walk back. Because you were playing the part of idiot in a horror movie. Congratulations."

"You're being such an asshole," she said.

"You too."

And it was only then that she realized they were literally shouting at each other over the howl of the wind and through the window of her truck. And her own voice was ringing sharply around her, and she didn't like it.

Reluctantly, she got out of the truck.

"Where are your bags?" he said, his voice hard.

"Just behind the seat…"

He reached back there and grabbed her duffel bag, and her guitar, slamming the door shut with his elbow.

"You don't have to carry…"

"If I were you, I would give it a rest. You can stop telling me what I can and can't do, and what I should and shouldn't do, because people who run off into blizzards don't get to make proclamations."

He wasn't wearing a coat. He had come after her in only that T-shirt, and she was so aware of how the wind was biting at him, but he just put his head down and kept walking forward.

It made her feel small, and strange. She was walking

directly behind him, and she realized that she was using his body to help shield her from the wind.

And that was sort of a humbling realization. She couldn't say she cared for it.

She was freezing, and she was wearing a coat. His arms were bare.

And this was the problem with Flint. There were these moments. Because this was exactly who she'd begun to believe that he was. The man that would shield her from everything. The man that would carry it all on his shoulders. And that was more, and different, than the sharp heartbreak she had been carrying around all this time. It was a deeper, more fully realized regret.

All that she didn't have because of what she had wanted him to become.

Because she hadn't been wrong about everything. Because that was the problem with a heartbreak anthem. It didn't give credit to the good things. And it was the good things that made losing love sad.

It was the fact that he was the man who would chase her down in a snowstorm, block the wind and carry her bags, while he was wearing only a T-shirt.

There was good in him, that was the issue. When things were wonderful, they were just amazing. But when he shut down, it was like he was a blizzard all by himself.

She couldn't reach him.

When he was cruel, it cut deep.

There was something in him that made him like this and she didn't know what it was. Didn't understand what had shaped him into this man who was so perfect in so many ways, until he wasn't.

Of course, the fact that she didn't know what his issues were was his fault. He could have shared with her. He could give her something. He could tell her more about himself. But he had never wanted to. He had told her what he couldn't give, but he hadn't told her why.

Maybe there was no *why*.

Except, she had one. Her reasons for not being able to trust were specific, and ample. And he'd added another layer to it. It was neat, explainable. Easily written into songs, and easily folded into stories.

Him? He hadn't given her those pieces. But she knew enough about people to know they must be there. And to know that he wasn't sharing for a very specific reason.

But she didn't actually want to feel charitable toward him. And even though he had just saved her from a storm, he had also been the reason that she had run out into the storm. Because he hadn't even bothered to not be a jackass to her.

He did ask you to stay.

Fine. He had. But it was much too little, too late, and it wasn't when she had wanted him to ask her to stay.

The walk was icy and cold, and her boots were not equipped for the task. She slipped as she tried to get up the hill, and a squeak came out of her mouth, and he whipped around, dropping her duffel bag and grabbing her arm, keeping her from falling. She looked up at him, and their eyes met. And she was brought right back to that first time they'd met each other.

When she'd stumbled coming out of the gate.

And everything in her went still.

The terrible thing was looking up at him and knowing exactly what she'd seen in him. Knowing exactly what she'd been thinking. And knowing that if she had been put in that exact same position all over again, she would've made the same mistakes. Over and over again.

Because there was something about him. Something about him that was her own personal brand of favorite mistake.

It was horrifying.

"I'm fine," she said, pulling herself out of his hold.

"Right."

Words bubbled up inside of her. Ones she shouldn't speak. But... They had been apart for two years, and there were endless wells of unspoken words between them.

Why should she give him the benefit of leaving it all unspoken anymore?

"It might make you happy to know I don't need my mom to warn me about cowboys anymore. I have my own warnings."

"Good. Listen to them," he said. "Because God knew mine weren't enough."

"Excuse me?"

"It's not like I didn't tell you." He picked up the duffel bag.

"We were...whatever we were for how many months? You gave me warnings, but you never gave me reasons."

"Why do I have the feeling that's going into a song?"

"It already is," she said.

"Wow. Quoting your own song lyrics at me. That's something."

She growled, and went ahead of him. She didn't need him to shield her from the wind. She didn't need him to shield her from anything. She didn't need anything from him.

"You don't know your way around here as well as I do," he said.

"You don't even know how many times I've been here," she said.

Three. But she didn't need to tell him that.

"Yeah. But I've actually been staying up here for the last couple of weeks," he said. "Making sure the transition went smoothly. There are some changes that I'm going to make."

"What are you…? What are you doing, anyway? You never expressed any interest in owning hotels."

"Yeah. Well. My brother and his fiancée bought a hotel in Lone Rock. He's more of a silent investor, but I found the whole thing really interesting. So I started looking around for properties. And this came up. I thought it was perfect. But I'm also looking at a hotel in downtown Portland. And considering something in Nashville."

"Right. Why Nashville?"

He shrugged. "Music city. Exciting."

"You know you don't have to tell me that."

"I do know," he said, his voice heavy with irony.

"Why would you buy something in a place where you might actually be in proximity to me? Since you hate me so much. Apparently."

"Why do you sing about the end of our relationship every single day?"

Ouch.

"Because it makes me a lot of money." He didn't say anything after that. Neither of them did. Finally, the lights of the hotel came into view.

"I'm surprised there's still power," she said.

"There's a backup generator, and some backup solar as well, with energy stored that we can feed off of. Because this is so rural, these kinds of things are a problem, even when the weather isn't this bad."

She huffed, and pushed through the lobby door. It wasn't a huge hotel, but it probably had about one hundred rooms. All in a big, gleaming log-cabin-style structure. The furniture was made of rough-hewn wood, with big geometric-patterned rugs over every surface.

She had always found the place restful. And had also found that nobody here was overly impressed with celebrity even if they did realize who she was, so she enjoyed the peace that came with it.

There was no peace now, though. There was Flint.

"What brought you to Oregon? Because you know this is where I am."

"Weirdly, Flint, I didn't think of you at all." She had enjoyed staying in Oregon when she had come with him, and they'd done quite a bit of traveling around the state with the rodeo. The Pendleton Round-Up and the big event in Sisters were both huge, and she had enjoyed being there every time.

That was all. She didn't necessarily think of Flint when she thought of the state.

Liar.

"Right. Fair. So maybe I didn't think of you when I thought of Tennessee."

"Except you sorta said you did."

"Maybe it was because a certain song came on the radio. Tough to say."

"Which room am I in?"

"Well. You can take your pick," he said. "The one we have you down for is the suite, though, and I imagine, given how fancy you are these days, that's what you want."

She scoffed. "What do you mean how fancy I am?"

"Don't tell me those aren't six-hundred-dollar jeans."

She blushed. Because yes. Her jeans were expensive. She had never imagined she would become that person. It was the weirdest thing. The way her money meter had adjusted. How she had gone from spending thirty dollars on a pair of jeans to one hundred, to more. And each incremental increase, as her income had gone up, hadn't really seemed like much of anything at all.

And to think, she'd once been so disdainful of people she thought of as excessive. But she hadn't done much to keep herself from enjoying certain kinds of excess that had come with her success.

She didn't drink, she didn't do drugs and there had been absolutely no sex since parting from Flint, so surely expensive clothes and a new truck were reasonable. Also a new house. And a house for her mother. *Of course* a house for her mother. That had been the most important.

"There's no reason for me to not take the suite," she said.

"Full-service. I'll walk you there."

"You don't need to," she said, holding her hands out for her bag and her guitar. "I'm going to go get settled in."

"All right. Do you want some dinner?"

Her stomach growled. And she really wished it hadn't, because she would like to say that she didn't need dinner, but she had been planning on eating here. The food was wonderful; she remembered that from her last visit. Except…

"Where is the food going to come from?"

"There was a certain amount preprepared by the chef in anticipation of the weather."

"Great. I'll have some of that after I get settled in."

"Well, let me get you your key."

He went behind the counter, the counter that he had been behind when she had first walked in, when he had stood up and nearly given her a heart attack. He took out a key card, and ran it through the device that programmed it before handing it to her.

"Thanks," she said, but his fingertips brushed hers, and she hadn't expected it. And all of the air in her lungs felt like it had been removed. Evaporated.

They just stood there for a moment. And memories swirled through her head. Memories she'd rather not have.

She took a step back. Decisively.

She needed a shower. She needed to get her head on straight. This was all unexpected, and a little bit too much.

She walked up the big, curved staircase—made of the same sort of log as the rest of the big lobby area—and headed down the hall toward the room she had stayed in before.

She unlocked the door, and let herself in. There was a large four-poster bed at the center of the room, done with plush bedding. There was a window seat, which she had spent a lot of time in last time. And a desk in the corner. She set her things down, and opened up her bag. She found her writing notebook, well-worn, but not used recently, and set it on the desk. Then she took her pen out, and...

She pulled out a little neon cactus key chain. It didn't light up anymore—the batteries were dead, and she hadn't been able to bring herself to replace the batteries, because that would be admitting that it mattered to her.

She ran her fingers over it, staring. And then she set it down next to the notebook.

This was the situation she was in. So she might as well embrace it. Might as well live in it.

What else could she do?

Chapter 4

He waited an hour, and then he went into the kitchen and dug around for one of those preprepared meals. There were strict instructions on how to reheat the steak without overcooking it, and how to plate the meal and all of that. He ignored a good portion of them, because he didn't care about whether or not it looked fancy. But for some reason, he did feel compelled to serve her something that tasted good. Hell, if he was too petty, she'd write a song called "Overcooked Steak" and he'd never hear the end of it.

He stopped for a second, and simply stood there. Tansey was here.

Tansey Martin. The only woman who had ever gotten under his skin.

The woman he had told himself he was outraged at for the last two years.

Outraged because she reminded him of all of the things in himself he hated.

And she was still beautiful.

Hell, it was no mystery why he'd gotten involved with her.

Remember when you didn't think she was your type?

Yeah. He remembered it vividly. He also remembered the first time he had tried to hook up after he and Tansey had parted ways. And hadn't been able to muster up even the tiniest bit of interest in the beauty queen he was chatting up. He had ended up going home alone. As he had every night since then.

Two years. It was a hell of a dry spell.

But he was too filled up with demons to want sex. That was the problem.

What you need is an exorcism.

He tried not to think about her, or how beautiful she was, or the fact that they were alone here, and it was pretty much prime time for the sort of exorcism that he was thinking of.

No way. Never again. Not her.

He already knew how that ended.

But you can only ever have relationships that end. So why not?

The carrots finished reheating and he put them on the plate, not caring at all how they were arranged, and then he covered the plate with a big domed lid, and started up the stairs.

He knocked on the door, and a few moments later, she opened it.

Her hair was wet, and she was wearing a white plush bathrobe. It covered everything. From the base of her throat down to her ankles. It was huge on her. But he was so very aware of the fact that she had just been in the shower. He could remember showering with her.

His hands moving over her slick curves… "Dinner," he bit out.

"Oh. I didn't realize it was room service," she said.

"Yeah. This is a fancy ass establishment, Tansey. I figured you knew that. Since you're the resident expert on the place."

He walked in, and looked around, then he saw that the desk had space. But he stopped when he got over there, because her notebook was sitting there, and beside it…

Beside it was the cactus.

Before

He didn't know what possessed him to buy a little neon cactus, didn't know what possessed him to stick it in the cab of her truck before they departed for the next stop. But he did.

And when she came to find him when they got to Sedona, with the little light hanging from her finger, and a strange expression on her face, he felt something expand inside of him. "What's that?"

"A reminder," he said. "A talisman. Stay prickly. And remember to put a wall up when you get on that horse. Don't think about anything but the ride."

"What does a cactus have to do with a wall, Ace?"

"Because we were in the Cactus when we talked about it," he said.

"Okay. Your symbolism sucks. But I'll hang on to it."

He watched her ride that night; she won. He went

to find her after, and gave her a high five. "It was the cactus," he said.

She rolled her eyes. "It was not the cactus."

"It was the damn cactus. You can't prove that it wasn't."

That was how he found himself asking her out for a drink again. This time, they had two beers. Not just the one.

And she didn't put quite so much space between the two of them when they left.

They had three nights in Sedona. She won every single one.

On the last night, it was three beers.

"Okay. So now I'm in the second position. But that doesn't mean you're going to buy me boots," she said.

"The hell I won't," he said, jamming his finger on the table. "Have you not figured out that I don't let anyone tell me what to do?"

"I don't know. I haven't really pondered you all that much."

"Liar," he said. It was a little bit more flirtatious than he had been with her.

She wasn't his type.

That was the thing.

But she was awfully damn pretty in the bar light. And just after she finished her ride, even with those fluorescent lights shining down on her. She was pretty in every light—that was the thing.

But not his type.

"I never lie," she said. "Not ever."

"Because your daddy was a liar?"

"I assume he still is. He's not dead, and his mouth is still moving."

"Fair."

"What about you, Flint?" She rarely called him by his name. She usually called him Ace. He didn't know why. He liked it, though. "Are you a liar?"

"I try not to be."

"That's not very definitive."

"How about this. I don't know if I'm a liar or not. Because I don't get close enough to anyone to need to lie."

"I'm not sure I follow."

"You lie to protect yourself, right? You lie to make people think better of you, mostly. I've never needed to do that, because I've never cared enough to do it."

"Well," she said, and suddenly, the bar seemed quieter. "I guess that's about as honest as a person can be."

"Like I said. I try."

He downed the last of his beer and they both got up, walking out the door. This time, it was a little bit farther of a walk to the motel, but they'd decided to walk so they could drink. They took the walk back kind of slow.

For some reason, he stopped. But she seemed to have the same idea he did. He turned to her. The sky above was lit up only with stars, and he could see them reflected in her eyes.

He couldn't remember the last time he'd wanted to kiss a woman. Just kiss. That was what he wanted to do then. He wanted to reach out and cradle her cheek in his hand and feel how soft her skin was. He wanted to lean in and press his mouth to hers, but slowly.

He just wanted to kiss her.

He didn't want to take her back to his motel room.

He didn't want… He didn't want anything but to kiss her. She hadn't said that he couldn't kiss her.

"Ace," she whispered. "Please don't."

He took a step back. "Okay."

They started walking again.

"Did you only stop because…because I asked you to stop? Were you going to…?"

"Yeah. To both."

She nodded. And then they reached the motel parking lot. And she beat a hasty retreat toward her room, which was at the opposite end of the complex. And he wondered if he had ruined whatever this was. And for some reason he felt…torn up with regret over that.

He didn't want to lose her.

He knew that much. So he wouldn't let himself be that stupid again.

After

"You still have this," he said.

Tansey looked at him in horror. She hadn't meant to leave that there. But then, she hadn't known that he was going to come here. She hadn't realized that he was actually going to come to her room to bring her dinner. And she felt exposed. She felt unmasked in some strange way.

"Everybody needs a good-luck charm," she said, her heart pounding hard.

"I would've thought that this wasn't a good-luck charm to you anymore."

"Well. That's the thing. You don't know me. Maybe you never really did."

"I think I did," he said, his voice rough.

"Well. Well." She took the lid off the food. "I'm actually not… The thing is, Flint. That was the first relationship that I ever had. You know that. Because I told you a lot of things about myself. It was the first relationship that I ever had, and the first heartbreak that I ever had. Of course I wrote about it. I'm…" She was trying to decide if she was going to outright lie to him or not. "I'm sorry. I didn't consider how it would make you feel when I released the song." That was partly true. Because if she had considered it at all, she'd hoped that it would make him *see*. She'd hoped that it would upset him.

She had hoped that it would show him.

She'd hoped that it would hurt him.

"I only thought about how I felt." What she had felt had been the only thing that mattered. "And I'm not actually invested in people yelling at you on streets. I've never asked anyone to do that, and I've never confirmed that the song is about you for that reason. I don't like any of that. I never asked anyone for it."

She sat down, and took a bite of her steak. "Do you want to have dinner?"

"What?" he asked.

"Let's just have dinner together." She didn't know why she felt compelled to do this. Except…here they were. Thrown together for a reason.

There had to be a reason, right? Fate, or Christmas magic or something.

She did still have the cactus. She needed…something. She needed something to jar her inspiration loose. Being with him these past couple hours she'd had more complicated feelings than she'd had in the past two years.

She felt more alive.

And she might be angry, that was for damn sure, but at least she felt something.

That feeling of wistfulness that she'd had when she'd been watching him walk in front of her—the feeling he might be a better man than he'd been when they'd broken up, but the man that she had always imagined he *might* be—was the beginning of a song. Was the beginning of something.

It was what she was here for.

And anyway, she knew better now. She wasn't in love with him anymore. Yes, she was still kind of angry. Yes, the hurt was still there. And yes, he was still beautiful. But she knew better now. Intensely, and wholly.

"We can eat downstairs," she said.

She resolutely picked her plate up. "Come on."

"Do you want to get dressed?" he asked.

She suddenly realized she was still in her robe.

"Oh. Yes. I do." She set her plate down. "I'll meet you downstairs?"

"Yeah," he said.

By the time she'd gotten her sweats on, she was resolved. Determined. She was going to use this to find a new angle on their relationship. She was going to use this as a way to heal.

And maybe it would also heal whatever was happening with her music.

Because she needed that. Otherwise that would really mean that the most exciting and wonderful part of her life was over. She had fallen in love and lost it. She had success and it was slipping away...

She pushed those thoughts away.

There was more for her. There was.

Flint Carson was not the end of her road.

But he might be the key to her reclaiming some of her creativity. And she was going to run with that.

Except thinking like that forced her to think back, and the whole time she headed down the stairs, she was thinking about him. And about how tonight paralleled another moment he'd come to her rescue.

Before

She felt like a coward leaving the motel as early as she did, a coward for avoiding Flint. But he'd been about to kiss her. Or he'd at least been *considering* kissing her.

And she'd...she'd panicked. Because she wanted to kiss him. She wanted to kiss him so much it consumed her every waking moment. She couldn't do that. Because...

He's not just a cowboy, though. He's Flint.

He's your friend.

Yes. He had become her friend over these last few days. It seemed improbable and strange. But she liked him. He was the highlight of every day. She...

She was headed down the highway when her truck started to overheat. Persistently.

"Shit," she shouted. She hit the steering wheel with the palm of her hand. "Shit."

Smoke started to pour out the top of the engine and she pulled to the side of the road.

She sat there. And she looked at her phone. No service. No damn service. What the hell was she supposed to do? It was Arizona, and it was hot.

She squinted and looked up ahead. There was a call box, blessed be. She got out of the truck, panic making her move quickly. It was hot, and she had Cinderella in the trailer, and she needed to get gone.

She was halfway between her truck and the call box when she heard the sound of another engine. She stopped and looked behind her. It was a sleek, shiny Chevy pickup, and it pulled sharply off the road behind her.

She ran back toward her truck, ran back… And realized exactly who it was.

"Flint," she said, not knowing if she sounded scared or relieved… Relieved. Overly relieved.

"What happened?"

"I overheated. It's this…this shitty truck. I need a new truck. It's fine."

"Well, if you win…"

"Do not offer to buy me a truck, Flint Carson," she said.

She stuck her finger out toward him, and he grabbed it, and shook it, the contact of his skin against hers making her tremble. She pulled it away, and took a step back.

"Okay, I won't offer," he said.

"Flint…"

"I have an idea. I'll unhitch your trailer, we'll get it hooked up to my truck, and we'll call someone and have them get yours. Then we'll get on the road together so you and your steed aren't sitting here in the heat. How does that sound?"

There was no way to argue with this. She'd tried to avoid him, she'd broken down. He was the one who'd found her.

Maybe it was fate.

"Thank you."

About half an hour later, they were driving down the highway in Flint's truck, with his superior air-conditioning keeping them both cool.

"Lucky I happened down the road when I did."

She could argue. She could say that it wasn't lucky, because there was a call box, and while it would've been a whole thing, she could've handled getting out of there herself. But this was better. And not just because she had been rescued sooner. Because she was with him.

"Yeah. I was lucky. Look, I… I'm sorry." She wanted to fix what happened last night. The way that she had freaked out and overreacted.

"You don't need to apologize to me for anything."

"I was weird about last night. And I was avoiding you. It's why I tried to leave really early today. But apparently we both had the same idea. And thank God," she said.

"It was my mistake. You made yourself clear. I was trying to give myself a loophole. You know, a kiss isn't a one-night stand."

"Now that's a song title," she said.

"It would be a good one."

There was nothing but the sound of the tires on the road. "You really just wanted to kiss me?"

"Right in that moment, yeah. Now, what I would've wanted thirty seconds after that..."

She leaned across the cabin and pushed his shoulder. He was solid and warm, and she could smell soap and his skin, and she regretted all that a little bit.

The touching. It was dangerous.

Why?

She shoved that to the side. She shoved that ridiculous question right to the side, because she knew that it was dangerous. She wanted to be friends with him. He had helped her; their friendship was valuable to her. She enjoyed talking to him, and he had given her the cactus, which now—against her will—seemed to function as a good-luck token.

He had rescued her from the side of the road.

It didn't have to be dangerous, this thing. It didn't have to be wrong or bad. It could be good. But she had to be... It had to be *not* kissing. It had to be friendship.

"I really like you," she said. And she felt so stupid with those words coming out of her mouth. He was a man. A man who had one-night stands. A man who probably didn't have silly girls saying that they liked him.

And when she had said it, she hadn't meant to be confessing that she *liked* him. It had started out as a speech about how he was a really good friend. But the truth was...she liked him. In all the middle school glory that it implied.

It was just that she wanted to be his friend more.

"You're the only real friend that I've made on the circuit," she said. "You're the only friend I've had in a long time."

"Same," he said, his voice sounding rough.

"It just matters a lot to me. This."

And he didn't say anything for at least an hour of the drive.

Chapter 5

After

When she came down the stairs, he had his own dinner ready, and had sat down at one of the tables in the dining room. He was still wearing jeans and a short-sleeve shirt, and she was in sweats, no makeup on her face.

He wondered what her adoring fans would think of her now.

They would probably love her for this. Classic Tansey. So down-to-earth.

If he happened to look at the things that people said about her, well. He was only human. He didn't have an endless amount of resistance and restraint where she was concerned. But then, he never had. It had always been... It had always been fraught. She had always been someone that he couldn't look away from. No matter how he couldn't explain it.

"Why exactly did you want to have dinner together?" he asked.

"Because this is ridiculous. Because…because you were an important part of my life, Flint. And now we don't even talk."

"As far as I know, that's how breakups go. Admittedly, I'm not an expert."

"Oh. So you admit that it was a breakup?"

"Yes," he said, his voice rough.

There was no point denying it. Because there was no point denying that they had been entangled in each other in a way he wished they fucking hadn't been. In a way they *shouldn't* have been. In a way he never had been with anyone else, and never would be again.

But here they were, and somehow it was like something entirely different and something altogether the same. Because he hadn't been charming for a single moment since she'd walked into his hotel, and he had no intention of being charming.

He didn't put up the performance for her.

But then, he never had.

She'd never believed it. She didn't buy into the facade that he had put up to interact with the world.

What he knew about himself was that he was a bigger bastard than most people realized.

Boone knew.

Boone knew better than anybody else, and seemed to forgive him for it, but that was kind of what younger brothers were for, he supposed. They had to see you better than you saw yourself. They had to see you better than anybody else did.

Didn't mean that *he* should.

Because Boone knew the truth, and he was still the brother that Flint was closest to.

And Tansey knew the truth.

Without even knowing any of the details of his life, she knew the truth.

Because he had shown her. He had shown her what he did when the chips were down.

Even with all that discomfort, there was something... undeniable about it. His connection to her. The same way there always had been.

Because he was himself when he was with her. Unvarnished and raw and not even bothering with the face he tended to show the world. And it was true now too.

Except she took that and she wrote a song about it. And she might do it again.

"I want... Do you want royalties from the song?" she said, as if she read his mind.

Everything in him rejected that. Everything in him was disgusted by the offer. Outraged by it. "No, I don't want to make any money on that shit," he said. "I don't want to make any money off of the things that you told everybody about us."

There they were, eating really good steak, and not getting along at all, and he had a feeling that wasn't at all what she had expected out of having dinner with him. Or what she had wanted. But here they were. And he was committed to the lack of facade. Because why couldn't they just be honest? Because he had been telling his brothers for two years now that the song wasn't about him. He'd been telling anyone who asked that it wasn't about him.

Part of him had told *himself* that it wasn't.

That she'd made it up. Because she hadn't fought him. She hadn't said any of those things *to* him. So maybe there *had* been another man.

Except he knew he was the first. Except he knew that he was the one.

And he knew that he had her scarf.

He had it here.

Just like she had the cactus. So whatever other stories they told, whatever they had told each other the moment that it had all ended, there were lies buried in there. And that much he knew. Even if he didn't know himself well enough to know what the hell all the lies were. Or what he was supposed to do about them. Because he hadn't known what to do then, and he knew even less of what he was supposed to do now.

Except his feelings were carefully kept behind the wall in his chest that he normally kept them behind. She was here and he was angry. She was here and he thought she was beautiful.

She was here, and they were having dinner in this fancy dining room, with her in sweats and him in his mud-covered boots, and they were fighting.

Whatever it was…it was real, and it was them.

So he was just going with it.

"Is that how you feel? That it was wrong for me to make money off of it?" she asked.

"Yeah. I fucking do. Because it was…"

"You told me it was nothing, Flint."

"And you told me it was fine. So are we going to be angry with each other now for a lack of honesty?"

"That was never why I was angry with you."

"Why *are* you angry with me then?" he asked.

"Because you ended it. I didn't want it to end. And you know what, I was too afraid to tell you that. Because I knew it wouldn't make a difference, and I knew that it would just…expose me. But now here I am sitting with you, and you might be mad at me about the song, but I'm kind of mad at myself about it too, because now you *know*. All the things that I didn't say, all the things that I couldn't say, you know what they are now. The song is the truth."

"The song is *part* of the truth," he said.

She winced. "The song is *my* truth. My feelings. It isn't yours. Only you could write that song."

"Good thing I'm tone-deaf."

"Can I at least do what you…demanded, asked, me to do first? I'll promote the hotel. I'll tell everybody how much I loved it, and that it's under new ownership and… I can make a big song and dance about the fact that I was here during the snowstorm and it was wonderful."

He shrugged. "Yeah, because I might as well get something out of it. And maybe if people know that you were here with me, they'll stop yelling at me on streets."

"Yes. Fine. That seems fair." Silence lapsed between them, and she stabbed the carrot with her fork and took a bite of it. "You're going to quit riding rodeo, aren't you?"

"What makes you say that?" he asked.

"Because of what you told me. About focus. About goals. About how you couldn't want anything else as long as you were trying to win. So this is what you want now? This is what you're trying to win?"

"Yes. You know, I have a trust fund. But I wanted to make sure I didn't use it for this. I don't want my dad's success. I want my own. And inescapably, my success is going to be built on some of that. I can't erase the advantages I got from him. Because my winnings that come from the rodeo... I was in the rodeo because of him."

"But you won because of you."

He didn't know quite what to do with that. With that kind word from her, because it was as real as any of the mean ones, but he wasn't sure why she had bothered to give it to him.

"I didn't really choose it, though. So now I decided to have something that I chose. I decided to make sure that it could be something that I wanted. That I was..." He was going to say that he was proud of. He wasn't sure that he was proud of a damn thing. Because what everything came back to was... This was something he *could* do.

He was fine enough at doing things.

It was why he'd worked for his family all those years. Because he could.

Feeling? Being there for someone emotionally? That was beyond him.

Something had broken inside of him a long time ago, and he didn't even have the desire to fix it. If something could have, it would've been Tansey.

But he hadn't wanted her to fix it then any more than he wanted it fixed now.

So maybe proud was a bridge too far for anything that he was going to do.

"I wanted something that was mine," he said.

And that much was true.

Because a man had to have land. His own. And his own achievements to stand on.

She nodded. "I understand that. You know…you know that I joined the rodeo to show my dad. And you know that I… I wanted to be successful and famous to show him. He doesn't care, Flint." She swallowed hard, and looked away. "He asked me for money. He found me, of course, not when I was barrel racing, no, nothing like that. He found me when I was really successful. When I might have something to give him. And you know… I couldn't figure out what I wanted to do. If I wanted to hold the fact that I had money and he didn't over his head and deny him. Or give it to him so that he would need me." She wasn't looking at him. She was looking past him. "Neither reason was very good motivation. Both make me…kind of a terrible person."

"What did you do?"

She swallowed hard. "I gave it to him. But not so I can hold it over his head. I gave it to him because… I just wanted it to not mean anything. And for him to not matter. If I withheld it, it was admitting I was angry. There was no way for me to really win. So I gave him money. Payment for the emotional scarring that produced the music, except I didn't say that. I didn't want to give him any credit for it. He never mentioned it. I think if he had known that the song was actually about him, like if he had known that it was autobiographical, he wouldn't have asked for money."

"He knew you were famous, but he's never listened to your music."

"No."

"Well. He's a special kind of asshole. Even I listened to my expert takedown."

"You thought *he* deserved it, at least that's what you said when you heard the song."

"I didn't say I *didn't* deserve it, Tansey," he said. "I said I didn't like it."

And that was the truth. It was a strange thing, this conversation. These honesty pitfalls. The fact that he remembered too keenly how much he had liked her.

It was easy to let all the pain that had come after that erase the friendship. His genuine affection for her. It was easy to tell himself it had all been some kind of sexual fever dream, followed by an immature tantrum on her part.

That was a lie.

He'd been in too deep with her. And it had not been his imagination. He couldn't deny it. Not now.

It was way too easy to remember the good times. To remember that friendship as the foundation, and the way that had shifted. The way it had shifted under his feet without him making the decision to let it.

Because he knew better. That was the thing. He had never in his life let himself get drawn into a relationship with a woman because he knew he didn't have the capacity to give a woman what she needed. He had always known that marriage and children weren't for him. He had known that since he was fourteen years old. And he had never, ever crossed those lines; he had never done anything that he was ashamed of with a woman. Not until her.

But he knew why it happened.

Because of her. Because there was something about her. And in the end, he supposed it wasn't all that surprising that she'd ended up famous. If he couldn't look away from her, it stood to reason the whole world couldn't look away from her.

He gritted his teeth. And he tried not to remember. He really did try to not remember.

Before

It turned out that her truck was effectively blown up, and while she absolutely refused to let him buy her a new one, she did concede to the fact that while she sorted it all out, she was going to need a ride. And he offered to be that ride. They would be driving from Utah to Nevada over the next few days, and they'd be taking the road trip together. All that would be fine if he didn't still want to kiss her. And if she hadn't been very clear that it wasn't going to happen.

I really like you.

He couldn't remember the last time a woman had said that to him.

I want you, sure.

But not *I really like you.*

He liked her too.

It was a hell of a thing.

He took his position back behind the gates to watch her event, and his heart was pounding harder than it did when it was his turn to ride.

When she rode, she rode spectacular, and it put her right up in the number-one spot.

When she got off, and came out of the gate, he pulled her in for a hug, lifting her up off the ground.

"Easy there, Ace," she said, her arms wrapped around his neck. He put her down, and kept holding on to her. She kept holding on to him.

"Tansey…"

She looked around, then stretched up on her toes, and kissed his cheek.

It was so innocent. A butterfly kiss. A whisper.

And it made him hard as a rock, instantly.

She was not his type.

He would do well to remember that.

She turned beet red, then ducked her head and extricated herself from his hold.

This time, when she went back to put her horse away, he did help with her tack, and he didn't accept any argument. He was driving her back to the motel. Because they were riding together. And once they were safely ensconced in the truck cab, all the tension that bloomed between them felt like too much to handle.

What was this? He had no idea what the hell it meant. No idea what the hell was happening. He wasn't…

Did he have a *crush* on this woman?

That was the weirdest damn thing.

He couldn't accept that.

They pulled into the motel parking lot and he put the truck in Park, then turned the keys off and pulled them out of the ignition.

"Wait."

Tansey put her hand on his. He froze. And looked at her.

She scooted across the distance of the truck cab, and put her hand on his cheek.

He just sat. Perfectly still. And he let her decide what to do next. He let her choose.

She leaned across the space, and she pressed her mouth to his. Tentative. Soft.

He sat completely still. And waited. She lifted her other hand, held the other side of his face and pressed more firmly against him, and that was when he wrapped his arms around her waist, pulling her closer to him, angling his head and deepening the kiss.

She made a muffled sound, wrapping her arms around his neck.

She kissed him back, all enthusiasm, no skill. He slid his tongue between her lips, and she returned fire, kissing him like she would die if she didn't.

It was all he could do to keep his hands still. To just keep holding her, rather than letting his palms move over her curves, not pushing his fingertips up beneath her shirt.

It was a temptation. It was a real damn temptation.

But there was something beautiful about letting the kiss just…be a kiss.

He thought he might drown in it. Thought he might die. He had no idea how long it went on. Just kissing her. Holding her. Lust was a drumbeat through his whole body. But the moment…

The *moment*.

He lifted his head. "You don't happen to have that cactus on you, do you?"

She laughed. The press of her breasts against his chest as she giggled making him groan.

"Why did you ask about the cactus?"

"Because nothing mattered but the moment."

She let out a long, slow breath. Her eyes looked a little unfocused, her lips swollen. And they were very close to his motel room. Normally, that would be the assumption. He didn't kiss a woman just to kiss her.

But he had to let the kiss with Tansey just be a kiss. Because it needed to be. It just did.

"You did good tonight," he said. "The barrel racing. I'm not grading you here. But that was good too."

She laughed and lowered her head. "Thank you."

He leaned in and kissed her. Shorter this time. "I need to tell you good night," he said.

"Why?"

He gave her a meaningful look. "Because I need to. I'm trying to be good."

"Oh," she breathed.

"I'll see you tomorrow."

And he didn't know how any of this had happened. How they had gone from friendship to this.

They might be… Hell. He might be dating her.

He didn't know what he thought about that.

But he also knew that he wasn't willing to let her go. And that told him quite a bit.

After

Yeah. That was the problem. He had known. He had known that he was getting in too deep. He had known that he was walking into something he had no right to walk into.

And there was no excuse for him. There was no getting older and wiser. Because it was about him. It was about what he had to give.

And sitting across from her now, he could feel the echo of unfinished business inside of him. Except it wasn't. They'd drawn a line under it because that was what they'd had to do.

Maybe that had always been one of the issues with the song. Maybe one of the issues with the song had always been that it showed him the line hadn't actually been drawn where he thought.

Because he'd been convinced that he got out of it before he devastated her. And it was a lie; he knew that. But that was part of the problem. He thought that he had a pretty good handle on who he was. But it turned out he wasn't as strong as he thought when it came to his resolve. And he'd been convinced that he just knew himself. That his resolve was what had kept him from those relationships, when in fact his resolve had had nothing to do with it. There had never been a woman that compelled him. And the minute she'd been there…he turned away from everything he knew. Everything he knew that he had to do to keep someone safe from him.

Maybe the real issue was that as much as she hated him, it had made him hate himself even more.

"I keep waiting," she said. "To feel triumphant. I keep waiting. I had pretty great revenge on you, you have to admit that."

"I thought you said you didn't think about how I would feel."

"I did. I wanted to hurt you. I wanted to find a way to hurt you, because I looked at you in the face and…

I didn't hurt you. I couldn't hurt you. And I hated that. I wanted to."

"That's the problem," he said. "You can't get to me like that."

"That's what I don't understand. I don't understand why."

"Let's just call it a night," he said, pushing his plate back to the center of the table.

"Why?"

"Because the point of this wasn't to rehash what we were. I thought the point of it was to find some common ground now."

"Yes. I guess so. But I… I gave you everything, you know that. I gave you everything. And…" She swallowed hard. "I guess it just doesn't matter, does it? But part of me wanted to hurt you. To take even half of what you took from me away from you."

"If you want the fucking scarf, you can have the scarf."

"I don't care about the scarf," she said. "It was never about the scarf."

"Are you going to tell me the scarf is a metaphor, because I *literally* have your scarf, so I think you know it isn't."

"No, the scarf doesn't matter. It's just part of a lie that you told. That I didn't matter, because if you do have it, if you can really give it back to me, then why? Why do you have it at all?"

Rage welled up inside him. And other emotions he didn't want to examine.

Couldn't.

"I have it," he ground out. "Because the idea of getting rid of it feels like cutting my arm off. Are you happy about that? Is that what you want to hear?"

She sat back, and he just stared. He didn't know why the hell he'd said any of that.

"I will go get you your scarf."

He pushed the chair back, and stepped away, and he didn't look back at her.

Chapter 6

Before

She held her breath while she watched him ride. She always did. But he was always perfect. But last night she'd kissed him, and somehow things felt…really tangled up now. But that kiss had been…everything she'd ever imagined a kiss might be. No, she had never kissed anyone before that night. Before him.

She hadn't wanted to.

Was that really all she was going to do? *Really?* Was she *really* just going to…kiss him?

She couldn't afford to be distracted. Not right now. She couldn't afford to be derailed.

Maybe she was even on the verge of something with her music. And the last thing she needed was…

All the dire consequences her mother had ever told

her about what happened when you got with men who were far too pretty for their own good rolled through her.

She knew better. She did. They opened the chute, and the bull with Flint on his back tore out of there.

She held her breath, but he didn't make it eight seconds. It was only four. And he was on the ground.

"Oh shit," she said, her hand going up over her mouth.

Sure, he got another chance. Another ride.

But she'd never seen him fall.

He got up and shook it off, went back and got back on. The gate opened again, and out he went. This time he stayed on, but only barely. And his score was… It wasn't good.

It hadn't been a clean ride.

She greeted him at the back of the gates, right when he came through. "What happened?" she asked.

"I was thinking about something else," he said.

And everything in her went still.

They just stood there and looked at each other. There was space between them, but it felt filled. With something. Something big. Bigger than maybe the two of them.

"Oh," was all she could say.

"You better win," he said. "One of us has to."

She did win.

It didn't really matter that much. And maybe that was the thing. It didn't matter; he did.

They ended up in his truck again, kissing like they might die if they didn't.

This time, his hands moved. Rough, up under her shirt, moving along the line of her spine. She arched against him, and when he pushed his fingertips beneath the band of her bra, she stopped. "Flint… I have to… I haven't done this before."

He froze. "You haven't done what?"

"I haven't had sex. I'm not… I'm not ready."

He slowly released his hold on her. "Okay," he said slowly. "I didn't… I didn't realize that."

"I know. Because I didn't tell you. Can we still kiss?"

"Yes," he said. "Definitely can."

"Okay. I don't… Just not yet."

She just needed to be more sure. Of her feelings. Of his. Of everything. She was just afraid.

"My dad really hurt me," she said. "And yes. I get that I'm a cliché. I get that it's like…a whole lot of daddy issues. But I'm aware of them. I'm trying to not…"

"Okay. It's okay."

But they didn't kiss again. Not that night. Instead, he walked her to the door of her room, gave her hand a squeeze before he left her there.

But the following night, they were right back in his truck, and just before his mouth met hers, she tried to lighten it. "No sex yet, Ace."

"Noted."

But the kissing was hotter this time. Longer. A wild-fire that seemed like it was on the verge of burning out of control.

She wasn't aware of when she had pulled his shirt off of him, but at some point she did, and was moving her hands over his chest, down his back, and that was how she found herself laid across the bench seat in the pickup truck, her legs parting easily for him to settle between, and she could feel the hard ridge of his arousal up against her. She rocked herself against him, and then shook her head. "I'm not… I'm not ready for…"

"Okay," he said, breathing hard. "It's okay."

"I'm sorry," she said, terror warring with need. She wanted him so much, but she already cared about him far more than she was able to deal with or admit. If she actually let him inside of her body…

She just had to be sure she knew what she was doing. Sure she knew how she was…arranging all this inside herself.

And what if…?

What if she got pregnant? That was what happened to her mother.

It had just been an endless stream of heartbreak not only for her, but for Tansey as well.

There were consequences to this, and for the very first time, she felt somewhat sympathetic toward her mother, and her place in all of this, because apparently, charming cowboys were a lot harder to resist than she could have ever imagined. She had thought that *knowing* was enough.

But knowing *about* cowboys was different than knowing Flint.

"Do you want to come?"

It took her a second to realize what he was asking. His voice was hard like gravel, and she was desperate. Sensitized all over.

"Do I want to…? Oh. But I can't… Flint, I'd… You…"

"Not about me. I want to make you feel good. But only if you want me to. We don't have to have sex. But do you want to come?"

"Yes," she said.

"Can I?" He put his hand on the button of her jeans. She shivered. "Yes."

He undid the button, then the zipper, and moved his hand slowly beneath the waistband of her panties. She wiggled as his rough fingertips made contact with her very, very slick flesh. She moaned as his skin made contact with hers. As white-hot desire rolled through her. He began to stroke her. Her hips moved in time with his fingers, and she let her head fall back. "You're so pretty," he said.

And that was it. It sent her straight over the edge. She cried out as her climax slammed into her. She found herself immobilized by it, as wave after wave pulsed through her.

She was left spent and breathless in the aftermath.

He buttoned her jeans, zipped them back up. And then moved away from her, straightened up, there in front of the steering wheel, and put his face in his hands.

"Flint…"

"Just a second." He let out a slow breath. "You might kill me," he said.

"I don't want to kill you."

"I don't think you're going to have to try." She pushed herself into a sitting position. "Are you okay?"

"I'm great. I'm…" Her voice came out unsteady. She felt like she was going to cry. But she was good. She felt good. Well. Her body felt good. She felt like she needed to go lie down on the floor and curl up in a ball and wail about all these emotions that she didn't fully understand. That was what she felt like.

"I've never had sex with a virgin. I mean… Not saying that's what... I just don't want to do anything you don't want. I don't want to push you."

"You didn't push me. You didn't push me at all. You... I wanted it."

And she felt weird about it. And like she should've maybe offered him something. Except she knew that if she did, he would get irritated. It would sound like a transaction. She knew that he didn't want that.

"I'll walk you to the door."

They got out of the truck, and her legs still felt like Jell-O. She still felt unsteady.

And so she turned to him, and just pressed her body against his. He wrapped his arms around her, and just held her steady. And she had never felt quite so safe in all her life.

And she pushed against the emotion that was rising up inside of her.

"What is this?" she asked.

He shook his head. "I'm not really sure."

"We should call it something."

"Wilbur?"

"Oh, shut up."

She punched him in the shoulder.

"What did you have in mind?"

"A fling," she said, her heart pounding.

"I'm not sure you can have a fling without sex," he pointed out.

"Well...well, I'm not saying we won't. But maybe we should agree that it...that it will run its course and when it does, we're both okay with it. You said you don't... And I mean, I have all those goals."

"And you don't want to depend on a man," he reminded her.

"No, I don't," she said.

"Then it's a fling."

She nodded.

"Good night," she whispered.

"Good night."

After

She just sat at the table, immobile. Frozen. Her mind caught in a cascade of memories from the past. When things had been easy with him. When things had been beautiful with him. When they had kissed like it was inevitable, and she had hoped.

But he had her scarf.

It doesn't matter. None of it matters. Because you know where this ends.

Yeah. And she was beginning to feel like one of her favorite genres of country song. The one where you felt tempted to sleep with an ex that you shouldn't touch. But...

Yeah. It was tempting.

Not that he'd made any kind of gesture that indicated he was interested in doing that. She had to make sure not to confuse the intensity of the feelings that she felt around him, and the way that it picked at her creativity with actual desires.

She was smarter than that. She knew better than that. She was not the same girl that she'd been the first time she met him.

She heard footsteps and looked up. He was standing

in the doorway of the dining room, and he was holding it in his hands. And it was the weirdest thing. Because she had actually forgotten what the scarf looked like.

Because it didn't really matter.

It wasn't the point. It had been literal, but it had been a metaphor.

It was the one thing she had put in the song that held hope.

She'd hoped he'd kept it. That he hadn't just thrown it out. That it was everything he'd said. That he hadn't been able to throw it away because it had felt like finishing something.

Ending it.

And yes, they had ended it.

But it wasn't over for her. Not really. And she wondered if it wasn't really over for him either.

"Here," he said. He extended his hand and she stood up, walking over to him. Her footsteps were somehow muted and loud at the same time. And she reached out and took hold of the edge, but he didn't release his hold on it easily. Or quickly.

Until he did.

"Feels better to give it back to you than to get rid of it."

She studied this man, and tried to figure out…who he really was. Because he claimed he didn't do emotions or connections. And he claimed he wasn't sentimental. And God knew she had experienced the destruction of what it was like when he was finished with the relationship.

Yes.

She had been destroyed by that.

But this man… The one standing there holding on to

her scarf like it meant something. The man who had it with him on… He didn't live here. He had packed it to come here. For this day. For this business trip.

And you have the cactus he gave you.

Yes. And everything else.

She wondered how many women he'd had. How many women he'd kissed since he'd last kissed her.

There hadn't been anyone for her.

Suddenly, it was far too easy to remember all those old feelings. Far too easy to feel them. Far too easy to simply exist in them. Like no time had passed at all. Like he was still her lover, and not the man who had broken her.

She had tried so hard to turn it into a kind of complicated destiny. That if she hadn't been with him, she wouldn't have the song. She had turned it into an integral step in her life.

But it didn't feel like that here. It just felt like regret.

And like unfinished business.

Except maybe that was the story she was telling herself now because he was there and he was beautiful. And she still wanted him, no matter how much she tried to tell herself she didn't. It was painful. It immobilized her. She suddenly ached with it. Was on fire with it. And thought that it might burn her alive.

But it wasn't the kind of heat that they'd experienced when it had been new. When she'd been terrified and trembling, but so in need of it.

She knew. And she wanted it anyway.

Wanted *him* anyway.

So she took a step back, clinging to the scarf. "Thank you. For this." She wanted to forget everything. Everything that she knew.

About him. About heartbreak. About pain. She wanted to forget all of it. And jump into something she knew she shouldn't.

But she kept remembering all those times back then. When he'd made it very clear when she brought up sex that he wasn't offering.

Except he had wanted it.

No. Don't go there.

"I'm tired," she said. "I'll go… I'll go to my room now."

"Yes. See you tomorrow."

"See you tomorrow."

Chapter 7

He couldn't sleep. He couldn't sleep because all he could do was think of her. He couldn't sleep because everything kept rolling through him like a thunderstorm. Memories, things from the past, and need from now.

He got out of bed quickly, and went over to the window, looking out at the snow falling below. It was coming down thicker and harder now, and the wind was unforgiving.

They could be stuck up here for days. And he...he didn't know what the hell he was supposed to do with that.

He didn't know why he'd shown her the scarf, except... Maybe it was the penance that he needed to make. Because he could see that he hurt her.

Not that he didn't know that. He'd known that ever since the song had come out.

You knew it before.

But the fact was, this was another of those moments. Where he could turn back, or he could take a step forward, a step into something he knew wasn't a good idea.

Just like he'd done back then.

Before

They did a little more talking than kissing after that. It was a good thing. Because she needed to take it slow, and he understood that. He still wasn't quite sure what was happening between them. Not really. What the point of it was. Where it was going.

He didn't want to think about it. He was good at that. *Not* thinking about it. He hadn't lied to her when he'd said he was very good at putting up walls.

He was so good at it, he didn't quite know how to take them down. And he figured that was all right.

They both ended up winning top spot in their events for the season.

And he bought her the boots. Before they ever left the final event in Vegas.

"I told you not to do that," she said.

"Yeah. Well, I did."

"What are you going to do now?" she asked.

"I'm headed out to the coast for a few days." He always went and stayed in one of his parents' properties when the season was out. A little time to breathe between going and working the ranch and all the hard traveling and riding that happened all season long. "You should come with me."

He didn't know why he asked her to do that any more

than he knew the why of anything from the past couple of months. Why he was making out with this girl who wasn't his type. Talking to her for hours every night. Thinking about her all the time.

"Yeah, all right. But I'm still not having sex with you, Ace."

"Didn't ask you to." A smile tugged at the corner of his mouth. He wasn't even upset about it. He was a little physically frustrated, but he wasn't mad. Not even a little.

Because like everything else with her, the fling was unpredictable.

And he liked that best of all.

After

She couldn't sleep. She paced around the room, and then for some reason, opened the door. She crept down the hall. It was silent. The building was huge. She didn't even know where he was sleeping. And the odds were, it wasn't anywhere near her.

It was strange to be in such a big place like this with nobody in it.

Nobody but him. And somehow she felt his presence looming large as if they were staying in a tiny house.

She huffed. And continued down the stairs, into the lobby. The lights were off.

She looked around, up at the tall, arched ceiling with beams extending across it. The dim chandelier. And then she continued on toward the large windows that faced out over what she knew was a beautiful view in the daylight.

She could hardly see anything, it was so dark. But she could make out the swirling of snowflakes coming down.

She touched the window, and felt that it was freezing cold.

They had never been in snow together. They had spent the summer together. A summer that had been full of heat and longing.

A summer full of lies that she had told herself. But the truth was, he'd never lied to her.

She'd broken her own heart.

Even after two years she couldn't quite figure out how to make it beat normally again.

She sat down on the couch by the window, holding her notebook in her lap. And she started to write.

A prayer, really, more than a song. For what she wished could have been. For who she wished he could be, and who she wished she could be for him.

Somebody, someday would be enough to tear down the walls in his heart. She was only sorry that it wasn't her.

A tear slipped down her cheek. She had really thought that she was done crying over Flint Carson.

She'd thought that it had scabbed over.

That she had come to a place of reconciliation with it.

But he was here. And the problem was finding out that her feelings weren't anywhere near as different now from then as she would like them to be.

She closed her eyes, and she let herself remember. Because maybe that would jolt her back to reality. Maybe that would remind her.

It was so easy to remember that summer. To remember the beginning. To remember the end.

Chapter 8

Before

The house was beautiful. They had driven separately, so that they could go their separate ways after, because it made the most sense, after all. They still weren't claiming to be a couple or anything like that. They were friends who kissed a lot.

And she was still trying to sort through her feelings for him. Or rather, trying desperately to come up with something to call him that wasn't as terrifying as the word that seemed to echo inside of her whenever she thought of him.

She'd brought her guitar, and she was looking forward to spending a little bit of time working on her music. They'd reached pretty much a dead end with her demo, but she knew that was just how it went. They had gotten a couple of completely unknown internet radio stations to play her songs, but nothing big. And definitely no interest from labels.

She wasn't used to being on the coast. She got out of her truck and looked around: there were big, tall pines surrounding the house, and it was up on the edge of a sheer rock face, overlooking the great, pounding sea. The roar of it was intense, beautiful.

The front door to the house opened, and Flint stepped outside. Barefoot. She didn't know why that was notable. Only that it was. It felt intimate. She was wearing her boots. The ones he had bought her. She hadn't been able to help herself. But at least she hadn't let him buy her a new truck. She just fixed the old one. That was reasonable.

"Glad you're here."

She smiled. "Me too."

Her room was on the second floor, and had a breathtaking view of the ocean. It was also not his room. Which was fair. Because she had told him that she wasn't having sex with him. So of course he'd given her a separate room.

But she was starting to feel like holding on to her virginity was more of a habit than anything she actually wanted.

She wanted him.

And it was so difficult to figure out how much of that was weakness or giving in to something, or being just like all the people who didn't know better. When she was supposed to know better.

Know better than what?

He was a good man. He'd been nothing but a good

man to her. He hadn't pressured her into anything. Quite the opposite. He was being so respectful it was… It wasn't like anything she'd ever been warned about; that was for sure. Her mother had told her that men only wanted one thing. But Flint seemed to want to talk to her, buy her cacti and boots and kiss her. Let her stay in a beautiful beach house. Share meals with her. Share drinks with her. Flint seemed to want a lot of things from her. And he gave a lot of things to her.

There was no map for this. Not in her experience. And maybe not in her mother's experience either. It was okay that her mother would be wary. Upset about this. There were reasons she hadn't told her mother that she was here. Reasons that she had never mentioned Flint to Darlene Martin.

But she had never known a man like Flint. Tansey never had before either. She couldn't compare him to dire warnings that had nothing to do with him. He wasn't just a cowboy. He was Flint Carson.

And he was everything.

But he couldn't be what she stood on, what she leaned against. That didn't mean he couldn't be everything for right now.

For their fling.

She wanted to laugh and cry.

By the time she finished putting her things away and came downstairs, he had set a beautiful dinner out on the terrace. Right over the ocean waves.

"Did you cook?"

"My parents had this house for a long time, and knowing what to do with fresh seafood is awfully helpful. So yes. I did. But doing a crab boil is pretty basic."

"This does not seem basic. This is extremely fancy."

He poured her a glass of wine, and she felt like this was a life she had never even dreamed of. She wanted to know more about him, though. He was very good at asking her questions about herself. And he certainly alluded to certain things about him. But he didn't open up all that easily.

"So you won," she said. "Does that mean you'll be back again next year, or...?"

"Most likely. I don't really have anything else to do. What about you?"

"Well. Since nobody was all that interested in my demo song, and it certainly isn't going to pay the bills, I guess I'll keep riding for another couple of years." She shrugged. "It's okay. Wanting to get into the music industry is... It's very unlikely. I don't have any connections or anything like that. So... I don't see it as something that would be terribly easy. And definitely not something that's just going to happen."

"I've never even heard you sing."

She didn't want him to turn it around on her. Not just yet. "How come you're so good at hiding your emotions, Flint?"

"Practice?"

"But why? I guess what I don't get is... You don't really tell me that much. I mean, you're vague. You like to ask me questions, and you let me talk about myself, which is... It's nice. Sort of like therapy. But with a really good-looking man. But what about you?"

He lifted his wineglass and looked out at the ocean. It was strange to see him like this. The sun setting out on the sea, at a family home. They weren't in a cheesy motel or a bar. Or the cab of his truck. There was no one around. It was just different. And she felt different.

"What about me?"

"You never talk about yourself."

"There's not much to say," he said, and there was something in that smile that seemed false. It seemed very clear now, that the man she had met that first night, and the man she was looking at now, was a character. She had seen real pieces of Flint in the time since then. But this…this was a put-on.

The whole charming thing he did. The whole devil-may-care thing. She had seen moments of real emotion in him, but they weren't accompanied by revelations. The way that he gave her advice, that was real. The way that he listened to her, the way that he cared for her.

The care that he showed by respecting her boundaries, all of that was real.

But it also kept them protected and safe.

She wanted to find a way to get through those walls. But she was at a loss as to how.

Because here they were, theoretically temporary, so why should she be able to get through those walls? Why should he give her anything? She didn't know the answer to that.

And she didn't know if wanting to break them down was particularly fair.

She had plenty of her own defenses, so she understood that. She might not do such a great job of repressing her emotions, but the whole thing with him… Not sleeping with him… Holding herself back from him… Well, that definitely had to do with her dad.

With being afraid.

Because they'd said it was a fling, but now things felt different for her, and she wanted to be blasé and sophisticated and basically the most okay with the fact that this would have an end, but she didn't know if she could be.

It didn't make her want to leave, though.

She wanted to do something, give him something. To find a way to make him open up to her the way she had him. She wanted to know him. Know him like he knew her. But she didn't know what to do. So she just sat with him. There was a firepit out on the deck, and he started it up, and they sat on the couch there, and just sat together.

Not speaking.

They did that a few nights, things getting fairly hot and heavy in front of the fire more often than not.

It was harder and harder to not just join him in bed every night.

But she just wanted to be sure.

Do you? Or are you just scared?

Well. She didn't really have an answer for that. Because she was scared. She did know that. She just didn't know if that fear was smart, or if it was holding her back.

She got out her guitar that night when they sat by the fire, and started to pluck the strings.

"Play me a song."

And she knew exactly which one she wanted to play. The one she had never played for anyone.

"All right. This is some… This one's called 'Taillights.'"

The thing I remember most of all is the taillights on your truck

When you drove away from me and Mom, you
said we weren't enough
I remember the taillights most of all
If you were ever there on birthdays, it doesn't
matter now
If you ever sang me to sleep, I really can't recall
It's the taillights, from when you drove away

Her heart ached as she sang the song. As she poured
everything of herself into the phrasing. Because when
she'd written those words, she'd bled for them.

It was the very end that flipped it.

Someday, I hope you're sitting in a crowded bar,
and you look out the window
And you'll see my taillights
In a car that's way fancier than anything you could
ever afford
And you'll think of all those times
Of those missed birthdays, and when you
should've said good night
Every time you see taillights, you'll think of me.
And I won't think of you at all

She stopped, and wiped a tear off of her cheek.

"You need to record that," he said.

"I don't have anything I'd…"

"No. Just like that. Just you and the guitar. Send that
to your manager. And have them share that. It's amazing, Tansey."

"I don't know about that…"

"No. It really is. You should do it while you're here. We've got another week."

"Okay. I'll do it."

She did that night, and uploaded the file for her manager to grab. It wasn't professional, there weren't other instruments, it wasn't as good production-wise as the other song they had sent out, so she really didn't expect anything to come of it. And it wasn't what she was focused on right now anyway.

The next day they went to the local coffee shop, and as they walked down the street, he held her hand. And that was when she knew. It was when she really knew. That it was right. That she was ready. Because it wasn't just kissing, or fraught moments in the cab of his truck. It was holding hands. On the street. For anyone to see, and yeah, neither of them lived here, and no one knew who they were, but it was the principle of the thing.

It was the gesture that was just about touching. Just about being linked. Not about anything else. And she loved it.

Because she loved him.

It terrified her to think that. It broke the rules to feel it.

And she was willing to throw every last bit of caution that she had held in her chest into that coastal wind, and let it fly out into the sea. Because the world could keep all that, as long as she could keep him.

They had dinner out on the deck like they had done every night, kissed by the fire, and then he excused himself to go to bed. And she sat there.

For one breath. Two. Three.

And then she went after him. She took a deep breath and opened the door to his room, crossed the space and got into bed beside him. He sat up, looking at her. And she curved her arm around his neck and leaned in, kissing him on the mouth.

"Tansey," he said. "I am all about not pushing you to do anything. I am very committed to not pressuring you... Getting into my bed is maybe a bridge too far."

"I'm actually here for sex, Ace," she said, pressure and need building in her chest until she thought she might die of it.

"Well, that's something," he said.

She kissed him, his mouth that was so familiar now, but it was like falling. Knowing that it wasn't going to stop here. Knowing that it was going to keep on. That every desire inside of her would be answered tonight. That he would be inside of her tonight. It made her shiver, shake. He was already wearing nothing but boxer shorts, and he drew her up against his body, taking her shirt and stripping it up over her head. He made quick work of her bra, and he had already touched her between her legs once, so she wasn't really embarrassed.

And...why should she be?

They cared about each other. They had built to this. This wasn't a one-night stand with a stranger; this man had sat and talked with her.

He knew her.

She couldn't feel embarrassment in front of him. Not when he was...he was the one.

It made her feel jittery and strung out to even think such a thing, to believe in something she had told herself she didn't. Except maybe the problem was, maybe the issue all along was that she had always imagined that she would be one and done. That when she felt comfortable enough with a man to be with him this way, it would be love.

And that losing it would be devastation.

Would be something she would never be able to recover from.

He moved his thumbs over her nipples, and she gasped, arching her back, pressing her bare breasts to his chest. Oh, his chest. And suddenly, a surge of excitement went through her, because she had been thinking about being naked in front of him, and processing whether or not she was going to be embarrassed. But she hadn't thought about seeing him naked.

And that…

She hooked her thumbs in the waistband of his boxer shorts, and pulled them down. Throwing the covers back, and exposing his body to her gaze.

"Well, holy shit," she said.

"That's not exactly a song lyric," he said, his voice gruff.

"You're really hot," she said.

"Glad you approve."

She reached out tentatively, and wrapped her fingers around his thick arousal. He was glorious. Beautiful.

She squeezed him.

"Fuck," he said.

"See, it is a song. Just one only we're ever going to listen to."

He chuckled, and pulled her against him. He kissed her neck, down her collarbone, taking one nipple into his mouth and sucking hard. And it was better than just putting her fingertips on his cheek so that she could feel his stubble; his whiskers burned all over the tender skin of her chest.

It was intimate. Real and intense in a way she had never imagined this could be.

She felt like all her desires were somewhat childish. Or something she didn't quite understand. She got it now. She didn't know why the Tansey before this moment had been afraid. That girl hadn't understood. How right it would feel. How perfect.

She hadn't known just how wonderful it could be. She hadn't understood.

How easy, how right it was, when it was the person. The one.

But he knew her. The dark and ugly things. Her petty little heart and how much she wanted revenge on her father, how profoundly she'd been hurt by him.

How afraid she was. He knew those things. He knew those things and he seemed to just like her anyway. The way that she was.

And when he took the rest of her clothes off, and put his hand between her thighs, she cried out, not just because of the pleasure, but because of the overwhelming sensation of the emotion that was flooding her body.

Because it was deeper than desire. More than arousal.

He pushed a finger inside of her and she flexed her hips, trying to acclimate to the unfamiliar sensation. She liked it; it was just not…not something she'd experienced before.

He put a second finger in and began to thrust in and out of her gently, allowing her body to get used to him.

And then, very suddenly, she felt pleasure break over her like a wave, her internal muscles pulsing around him. She cried out, and he withdrew from her, then put his fingers in his mouth, sucking on them, slow and leisurely, like he was savoring the taste of her. And she shivered. "I have been waiting for this," he said.

He moved down her body and grabbed hold of her thighs, then he pushed them out wide, lowering his head to her center and tasting her deep. Long. She clung to him, forking her fingers through his hair and holding him there. Arching her body against him as she writhed with need. He pushed his fingers back inside her again as he teased her with his lips, his tongue. She couldn't breathe. Couldn't think. Couldn't do a damn thing but submit to the onslaught of pleasure.

She lost herself. In the absolute wave of need. In the wildness of her desire. And as she lay there spent, he moved away from her, going into the adjoining bathroom for a moment and returning with a box of condoms.

She was torn between…indignation, a lot of questions and relief.

"I'm an optimist," he said, by way of explanation. "And anyway, it's better safe than sorry."

"Well. I guess that is true."

He chuckled, tearing the box open, and then taking a strip out, tearing an individual condom from the strip. And then opening it quickly. He took care of the necessities, and then joined her back on the bed. He pressed his forehead to hers, and kissed her, deep and long. "Ready?"

She nodded, words deserting her entirely. He pressed himself inside of her, inch by inch, filling her. And the emotion that swamped her was almost too much to bear. It was beautiful. Wonderful. And so much more. This wasn't just about pleasure. Not just about satisfaction. Flint was inside of her. And she felt like something more than she'd ever been before. Complete in a way. In touch with parts of herself that she had never given a whole lot of thought to.

She had been right to be afraid of this. It was too much. It was transformative. She had been right to be afraid of it, but now, she embraced it. Wholly. Completely. With all that she was.

He began to move, deep, decisive thrusts, and she clung to him, until she began to feel the rhythm, find it. Arching her hips against his each and every time he moved against her.

She surrendered to it. To him. And when her climax hit, she could scarcely breathe. It was too much. And not enough all at once. Overwhelming, leaving her storm-tossed and just right where she needed to be.

With him. She was wild, and fractured, but safe all at once, because she was in his arms, and she knew that she could trust him.

And when his own climax hit, when his control fractured, his movements becoming hard and erratic, a growl rising up inside of him, she thought it might almost be better than her own pleasure. This man's pleasure. This man coming apart because of her.

Because he might be her first, but he'd had any number of women. And that he could still fall apart over her mattered.

And she didn't think of her mother's dire warnings then. Because it was different. He was different.

And they were different together. Maybe different than anyone had ever been.

The euphoria of it all carried her off to sleep. And she just let him hold her.

And she felt…like she was home.

She was still in a euphoric haze the next day when her manager called and said that a major radio station had picked her song up for airplay as part of an indie artist showcase. She wasn't really going for being an indie artist, but if it got her radio airplay… Well, it was more than anything else had ever done.

It felt exposing, that song. And yet… It was what she wanted her dad to hear, wasn't it? What he had done to her.

"It's going to be on a radio station," she said to Flint.

"That's amazing," he said. "And fast."

"I guess… When they know, they know. I just kind of can't believe that… Something I just kind of threw together like that…"

"The song was from your heart. It didn't need anything other than your voice."

And she held that close. That confidence. That simple belief in her.

Her manager decided to distribute the song online, which she hadn't done before, mostly because she didn't see why anybody would want to hear the song if none of the radio stations wanted to play it, but he was adamant that they get it out there before it played so that people could look it up after. Which was a good idea.

So within two days, the song was published onto various streaming platforms. And then something very unexpected happened.

The song got picked up on a popular app when a

viral "daddy issues" challenge happened, and people played the song in the background while listing terrible things their fathers had done. Making light of it, and using dark humor, but it pushed the sound around, which pushed it up various streaming charts in a way that no one expected.

Least of all Tansey.

"It's number one on the country streaming chart now," she said, shaking as she walked down the stairs into the living room.

Flint stood up and picked her up and swung her in a circle. "Does that mean I get to buy you a truck now?"

"You can't buy me a truck."

"Well, you won *something*, surely."

"You did," she said. "You're the one that told me I had to record that song."

"I think you gotta go with your feelings."

That was when she got a call that a morning show wanted to interview her, because she had gone from unknown to number one streaming thanks to the viral nature of the hit.

And she really had no idea how to process the fact that all of this had happened in a couple of weeks. The nature of the internet, she guessed, but it was just so far outside her comfort zone, and she was dealing with the fact that she was in love for the first time in her life, and having sex.

The morning show bit was short, and they didn't fly her out or anything; she just did an on-camera interview over the computer.

And when she asked the local bar that night if she

could play, it was a resounding yes, and what she couldn't believe was how the place packed out. For her.

And Flint sat in the front row, watching her, the pride on his face doing something to her insides.

When they got back to the house, he kissed her. Rough and intense, and she let herself get caught up in it. Let him hold her close. Tear her clothes off of her. He lowered her down onto the bed, and their need for each other was a whole tornado. He was inside of her before she could think, and even though it was fast and furious, she came twice, dizzy in the aftermath.

He kissed her throat, her jaw. "You're amazing," he said.

And she just felt it. Welling up inside of her. The need to say it. The need to think it. To really get it out there. "I love you."

His withdrawal was immediate, and she felt horrified. How had she said that; how would she even let herself feel it? That wasn't what this was supposed to be. And she knew it.

It was a fling. It was supposed to be a fling. And yes, she had started to fantasize about it being more. Of course she had. But… But she wasn't going to tell him like this. She was going to… She was going to feel out how long he could see this going. She was going to do it differently. That was all.

"Forget I said anything," she said.

"Tansey, I'm not sure that I can."

He looked grave. He sounded even graver.

"You have to," she said. "I know… I know that's not what this is."

"Do you?" he asked seriously.

"Yes," she said. "Yes, I…"

"Because if you can't…"

"I'm not done yet," she said. "Are you?"

"No." He shook his head. "I'm not done."

"Good. Then we don't have to talk about this. You can forget I said it. It was… You know. Post-sex euphoria, or whatever."

"I need you to listen to me. I can't give you that. I can't give it to anybody. Don't take it personally."

"No, I know. I… I listened to you. I did."

But she couldn't ignore the fluttering of her heart. The vague hope there.

She just felt like… She felt like maybe there wouldn't be grand declarations or anything like that, but like they might settle into something that was a little bit more long-term. That was all she wanted. Just a little longer.

She didn't need for him to love her.

And she didn't need to say anything like that again. She didn't.

She just wasn't ready for it to end.

And she would do whatever she had to do to keep him with her. For now. She would do whatever she needed to for now.

A week later, she realized that her period hadn't started when it should have. And she had no idea what to do. She was usually pretty regular, and she knew full well that they'd had unprotected sex the night of the open mic.

She wasn't stupid. If you spent your whole life not having sex, and having regular periods, then you started having sex and the period didn't come…

She knew what that meant.

She was terrified. Trembling. But she couldn't risk going out and buying a pregnancy test. People were already starting to take pictures of them. There were weird rumors online, a lot of speculation about her personal life. People treated her like she was a fictional character. There were so many stories about who her dad was, and what he had done, and it was like what she shared about herself had taken on a life of its own.

And if anybody took a picture of her buying a pregnancy test… How did actually famous people handle that? She had one song, and was having some kind of a moment on the internet. She didn't know how anybody stood this for years on end.

But before she did any of that, she would tell him. Tell him what she suspected. Because she wanted to have a deeper conversation with him about…about the fact that this wasn't a fling anymore. That much was clear. It had become something so much deeper. So much more serious. They actually talked. They shared things. And really, it had always been wrong to call it a fling.

They had been friends first. And it mattered.

A baby.

She wasn't ready for this. And she was afraid. What if he rejected her? What if he rejected the baby?

This is why you can't depend on anyone else.

No. Because she was shaking. Because it felt like he held her life, her future in his hands.

It was horrible.

She walked downstairs, into the kitchen, where he

was preparing dinner. It felt domestic. They felt domestic. They felt like something special and perfect.

Except for… Except for all the walls. He had told her about those walls from the beginning.

To see what he says, you have to tell him. You can't keep it a secret.

"I need to talk to you."

"We talk all the time," he said. "Does it require an announcement."

"This might," she said. "I'm late."

She looked at him, full of meaning. And waited for him to get it. She watched as about ten emotions cycled over his face. More than she had maybe ever seen him express in their time together.

"Well… You need to find out."

"I'm just… I don't know how. I'm afraid of what will happen if I go to a store here. Because people know that we are here. You saw that stuff pop up online. It's… It's a little bit unnerving."

"You need to find out," he said, his voice hard.

"I know," she said. "I will, Flint. I promise… And…"

"I don't want a baby," he said.

She blinked. "Well… I don't know that I was really planning on…"

"No. We said this was a fling. That was it. I told you, I am not up for this."

"I…"

Everything in her started to shut down. She didn't know how to handle this. Because he looked like a stranger. His eyes had gone deadly flat, his body language so distant… So…

"Are you saying that you would want me to get rid of it?" she asked.

He shook his head, decisively. "No. I'm not gonna tell you what to do. I just…"

"So you would just not have anything to do with it?"

"I didn't say that either," he said, his voice hard. "I said I didn't want a kid. And I don't. But I would be responsible. I would make sure that you had everything you needed. I'd be there. Physically. But I don't have anything to give, Tansey. Not emotionally. This… This was nothing. We hung out, we ate, we talked. We fucked. It wasn't real life. It wasn't really me. It was… It was something different. It's not my life. It's not who I am."

"So you… What? You would be in your child's life, begrudgingly?"

"Like a kid is going to know the difference."

"I… I can't have this conversation. I can't…"

"This has to end," he said. "Whatever the outcome. It can't keep going on like this. It's already too much."

"What?"

She didn't know how she had gone from telling him that she might be pregnant, to him talking about how he didn't want a child but he would be there in the child's life, to him wanting to end things.

"We've been careless, and this was supposed to be short-term. If you're not pregnant…"

"Right," she said, everything inside of her dissolving, breaking apart. And she could see herself, the little girl that she'd once been, collapsed on the gravel driveway, watching her father drive away. And if he had looked at his rearview mirror even once, he would've seen how badly she was devastated.

She wouldn't let Flint see it. She pushed the rising dread, the awful pain down. She cut it off; she didn't let herself feel it. She didn't let herself show it. She couldn't. She couldn't give him that. Because she would be different this time. She would push it down.

She would handle it.

She would stand upright, because she knew who she was.

"I should go," she said.

"Right now?"

"Yes. If it's done, then it should be done. I... I'll let you know. I'll let you know what happens."

"I don't want you to leave until..."

"You said it was finished. And you're right. Of course you're right. It was getting to be too much. And this is just... It's proof. I promise I'll tell you."

She packed up her things, and everything was numb. It wasn't until she left, until she drove all the way to a roadside motel six hours away that she let her chest break open entirely. That she let everything dissolve within her.

She cried until she thought she would be sick with it.

Curled up in a ball in the middle of the bed, weeping.

She didn't find a pregnancy test. She didn't know whether or not to pray that she was or pray that she wasn't.

Five days later, she started bleeding. And she was angry at herself, because now she would never even know if it had been a fluke, or if she had one of those early miscarriages that were far too common. Maybe it was better. Except nothing felt better.

She texted him.

Not pregnant.

He didn't respond. And she tried to heal. She tried to write music. She tried to move on. But the only lyrics she could write were about him.

And finally, during one session, she gave in to that. All the anger, all the pain. All the brokenness. The most scathing, personal lyrics that had ever come from her.

She couldn't stop them.

"It's perfect," said her manager. "It's the best song you've written."

"I don't know if I can put it out," she said.

"It's your pain," he said. "You can do whatever you want with it."

She held on to that. It was her pain. He was the one that had said they needed to be finished, and she hadn't fought him, because what would the point have been? She didn't want to show him that she cared more than he did. She refused to show him that.

And it had to go somewhere. She had to put it somewhere. It was her pain; her manager was right. Didn't she deserve to get something from what they had?

"Yeah," she said. "You're right. Let's…let's make that the next single."

Chapter 9

After

He didn't know what had drawn him downstairs. And he didn't expect to see her sitting there, her face in her hands, and notebook in her lap, and her elbows resting there.

Her shoulders were shaking, and he found that no matter what, he wanted to walk to her. He wanted to go and pull her in his arms, even though he had no right to do that. Even though he had no right at all, because it would just be more promises he couldn't keep.

"Tansey?"

She looked up at him, her eyes wide, tears streaming down her cheeks.

"I didn't expect you down here, I'm sorry. I'm just…"

"What's wrong?"

"I was just remembering," she said, her voice watery.

She swallowed hard. "And maybe...maybe it's okay that I'm letting you see it. Because I didn't let you see it then. And I told myself that I didn't feel it anymore. And that's why it's been easier to snipe at you. But that's how it was in the beginning too, wasn't it? I was mean to you because I wanted to push you away."

"You were never all that mean," he said, something sore blooming at the center of his chest.

"Don't tell me that. That ruins my street cred. I was really trying to be mean."

"No, the thing was, I just liked it," he said, taking a step closer to her. It was dark, and he wanted to give her this. A little bit of honesty. Because the truth was, they hadn't spoken with honesty about what had been happening between them at the time. She had called it a fling, and he'd let her do it, because he needed to put those parameters around it in order to deal with it. He needed that border so that he could allow himself to do it.

And he hadn't given her or himself any honesty about that.

"Why did you like it?"

"Because you didn't act charmed by me. And I found that fascinating. You were not my type."

"I wasn't your type?"

"No. I didn't like squeaky-clean, fresh-faced virgins. I liked women who knew what they're doing."

"That is actually really insulting. I'm not sure why you thought that you would come in here while I was crying and..."

"Because you got to me. You got to me and I couldn't explain why." The words were rough and tortured. His voice didn't even sound like his own. "And I kept telling myself that it wasn't anything. That I wasn't attracted to you, because I couldn't be. Because you weren't a rodeo queen, and you didn't have a single rhinestone on. Because you were too young for me. Because even before you told me that you were a virgin, I knew that you were more innocent than anyone that I should be... talking to at all."

He took a breath, and his chest hurt. "But yeah, I loved that attitude. From the beginning. It was why I couldn't stay away from you. And I couldn't stay away from you, you remember that, right?"

"I try not to. And actually, most of the time I remember my version of events. I remember the breakup. But I forget... I forget that I stood there and hid everything that I felt, and that I told you that I agreed. I mean, I know I did, but I forget...that you couldn't see inside me to how I hurt."

"I knew," he said. "I knew because I hated it too. You don't... You don't know, Tansey. I had feelings for you. In a way that I never had for anybody else."

He swore he could hear the snowflakes falling outside it went so quiet between them. It was like his heart barely dared beat.

He had never admitted that out loud. He had barely admitted it to himself in coherently formed sentences in his own mind. He had allowed himself to act on feeling only, and call it nothing.

Making excuses about what he couldn't feel and what he couldn't do. But the problem was—and he knew it— that his feelings were there; they were just erratic. Uncontrolled. And he couldn't handle them.

He'd never wanted to inflict them on another human

being. He had trained himself in that brutal art a long time ago. Built a wall up around himself. Toughened himself up. Because he had never ever wanted to feel…

"You know, I feel too much. And sometimes I feel nothing at all. And sometimes when I feel too much, it turns into anger. And it's bullshit no matter what scenario it is. Believe me when I tell you that. I didn't want to admit to myself that I had feelings for you. I didn't want to admit that you telling me you might be pregnant scared the hell out of me. Really, the hell."

"It scared me too. It scared me too and then it… I felt like I was dying. When I started bleeding. Because I wanted it. I *wanted* it. Even though I didn't want it. And it was such a mess. It was a horrible mess. And you were the only person that I wanted to talk to about it, and I texted you and you never texted me back." She was breathing hard now, crying again, and he felt like this was what he deserved. This conversation.

"I didn't know what to say," he said. "I didn't know what to say, because part of me wanted you to be pregnant. So that I could keep you anyway, even though I knew it was a bad idea. I'm… I'm toxic, Tansey, and I tried my best not to be toxic with you. I did. But I froze you out instead, and it wasn't better."

"So you know that about yourself and, what, you just sit in it?"

"Yes," he said.

"Why?"

"Because I don't want to fix it. I didn't want to care about you. I didn't want it. I wanted to *possess* you. I wanted to keep you. And hell, the contortions I would've gone through to do that if the whole pregnancy scare hadn't happened… I would still be torturing you. I can't even imagine. Not letting you go, not really, and not giving you what you wanted. Because I can't let myself care that deeply about someone. But it doesn't mean I don't want you. With absolutely every part of myself. It doesn't mean you're not the only woman I dream about."

"You…you do?"

"How many women do you think I've been with since you?"

She looked away from him. "I don't want to have this conversation."

"None," he said. "I haven't been with anybody. I haven't even wanted to. It's just you. You're the reason that I wake up at night hard. You're the reason I wake up in a cold sweat. You are what I want. You are everything that I want."

"Please don't," she said. "Please don't. Because if you can't give me one more piece of you, if you can't give me one more piece of who you are and why you're this way, then why are we having the conversation at all?"

"Do you want to know why? Do you want to know why I'm like this?" He swallowed hard. "My sister died. When I was fourteen. And I was…fucking destroyed. And it just… Everybody around me fell apart. They were so sad. And I was just so angry. So angry. At the universe, at God, at my parents, at the doctors. And at everybody for just crying all the time. Because it killed me."

"Flint," she whispered. "I didn't… I'm so sorry."

"I didn't want you to know. I didn't want to have the conversation with you, because I didn't want you to look at me like that. Like I was an object of pity that you could fix, because you can't fucking fix it, Tansey. Nobody can. That's what death is. It ends something, and you can't fix it. You can't get it back. It broke something in me. And I had to… I had to find a way to get rid of that anger…"

"What did you do?"

"I put a wall up…"

"No," she said softly. "What did you do? Because you are not acting this way because of a feeling you had. You must've done something."

"Yeah," he said, shame burning over his skin. "I did. You know my brother Boone? One time… We shared a room all the time when we were on the road. Right? When we were on the road with the rodeo. And one night he was crying. He was twelve. And he was crying and crying and he wouldn't stop. He just said how much he missed her. I told him to stop. I told him he had to stop. Because it was like… Every time he cried, it was like I was being stabbed in the damn chest. I couldn't handle it. I couldn't listen to it. Because everything that came out as sadness for him stoked the fire of rage inside of me. Because what was tragic to him was just so desperately unfair to me. I told him to stop crying and he didn't. He couldn't. So I punched him in his face. I punched him in his face and I told him he'd better not cry like a little girl anymore. Because it wouldn't bring her back. Because it didn't do anything. It didn't mean anything."

He watched her face, watched to see if she was shocked, because it still shocked him. He still hated it. And he still hated himself for it. "I still remember what that felt like. That anger. It was so pure. It was probably the most real thing I've ever felt in my life. I hated him. And I hated his feelings and what they did to me..."

"That was grief," she said. "That was grief. And I know that I've never experienced grief like that, but I know what it's like to feel angry. I know what it's like to feel like you would rather just be a toxic awful person than the bigger person. Because everything is terrible so why should you have to be anything but terrible."

"You know, my brother still loves me. A lot. He still loves me, because that's what younger brothers have to do. And we're still family. But you... You're not stuck with me. My brother needed me and I failed him. And that's all I know how to do."

"And you don't want a relationship because of what you'll..."

"Because if something happens, that's who I'm going to be. Because in sickness, that's who I would be. Because for poorer, that's who I would be. Because the dark side of those vows would show the dark side in me. And I have never wanted to submit anyone to that. Or a child. I can't imagine that. I would be such a bad father."

"Why do you think that? Because of a reaction you had when you were fourteen? To something hideously traumatizing. Flint, you can't live your entire life based on..."

She faltered. And anger ignited in his gut.

Didn't she understand? He was protecting her. From him. She'd seen a little bit of what he could be like when he was cornered, when someone got too close.

Didn't she understand this was for her?

"Isn't that what you've done? Lived your whole life

in response to a few things that hurt you? Turned them into the biggest thing about you?"

"That's not fair. That's not fair at all."

"Why? Anyway, who said I had to be fair. You wanted to know. You wanted to know why. And that is why. So now you know."

"I'm sorry," she said again. "I'm sorry I… But I want to fix it. I want…"

He didn't know why it hurt so much to talk about, still. It just did. And it probably always would. And it was the pain that he hated so much. That pain that wouldn't go away.

That pain that felt like it defined him.

"And that's why I didn't want to tell you. Because I don't want you to try to fix me. You need to understand that I'm broken, and I know that. I know it. The mistake was getting involved with you at all. And maybe not explaining it then. But I didn't want it to be… I was pretending. I was pretending that I could be something I wasn't. I was pretending that it wouldn't matter. That it could just be for a little while, and I wouldn't hurt you. I really didn't want to hurt you."

He moved toward her, and he put his hand on her cheek. But that was a mistake.

Because he felt it right then. All the anger and pain rising up inside of him, mixing with a desperation that twined around them both.

"Flint," she whispered.

And that was when he leaned in and tasted her lips for the first time in two years.

Chapter 10

She was living in a riot of pain. Of grief. And she knew that she should turn away from him. She knew that she should stop this. She knew that it was insane. He had just told her…everything. He had bared his soul to her. He had told her what he was, who he was. And it was… It was so painful. It was still spinning around inside of her, and she was trying to grapple with it, and failing.

He had lost his sister.

He and his brother…

And he felt like somehow that made him wrong. Made him beyond redemption.

Made him broken.

But it didn't. She knew that it didn't. And she knew she shouldn't kiss him. But his mouth was on hers, and she couldn't deny it, not any more now than she had been able to back then. Because he tasted like everything she wanted. Everything she had always wanted. And there was a reason it had been him. Only him.

And there hadn't been anyone else for him, not since her.

She had been so certain that he had broken her. But maybe they had broken each other a little bit.

"Flint," she whispered. "I haven't… There hasn't been anyone else."

He growled, his large hand cupping the back of her head as he deepened the kiss.

She knew that this was a mistake, for a variety of reasons. They should probably keep talking. They should probably keep talking instead of this. Because this was always there. And it was too easy. And it was maybe going to cut her open. But she couldn't stop. Because it was everything she wanted. Because it was maybe the language he spoke.

Or maybe it was just pure, unsquashed hope inside of her; no matter how much she wanted to believe she was immune, no matter how much she wanted to believe she knew better, she just didn't, never did, never would. Not when it came to him.

And so she kissed him. And kissed him. And there they were in an empty hotel, and there was nobody to walk in on them. Nobody to see.

"I need you," she said. "Please. Please."

Except, he didn't keep her on the couch; he lifted her up into his arms, and began to walk her through the lobby, up the stairs. He carried her away from the direction of her room, down the hall to where she hadn't been to before. He pushed a door open, and her eyes went wide.

It was amazing. A larger, much more masculine bed was in the center of the room, the large windows open. And she knew where they faced. The mountains. So even with them open, even with the lights on, and the darkness outside, nobody would be able to see them.

He set her down at the center of the bed, and pulled his T-shirt up over his head. His body...

It was so perfect. As perfect as it had ever been. His muscles well-defined and cut, every movement making them ripple and shift.

She began to desperately tear at her own clothes. She didn't have a bra on, thankfully, so it was just a sweatshirt, and the pants. And she wasn't embarrassed. Not to be with him. But she never had been. It was right. It felt right. It always did, and it made her want to weep. Because whatever happened, whatever happened when the sun rose, whatever happened when this was all said and done, she was going to be with him again now. And she wanted it. She needed it. Was desperate for it.

"I'm on the pill," she said, her lips feeling numb as she got up on her knees and went to the edge of the bed, putting her hand on his bare chest, her breath hissing through her teeth as she touched him. "I... After I..."

He put his hand over hers, pressed it more deeply against him. "I get it," he said. "Because...because I hurt you. Because I changed things for you. Because I... Fuck," he said. "I'm sorry I said that to you. About being defined by those things. I just hate that I did it. I hate that I did that to you."

"Well, don't hate it right now. Because you probably don't have any condoms, do you?"

He shook his head, a rusty laugh escaping his mouth.

"I sure as hell don't. Because there hasn't been anyone. Not even a temptation, and I definitely didn't plan on meeting anyone up here. Least of all you." He touched her face, skimming the edge of his thumb over her cheekbone. "Least of all you. But then… I never counted on you. Not ever."

She laughed, the sound almost a sob as she wrapped her arms around his neck and kissed him, pressing her naked body against his bare chest.

He growled, moving his hands down her back, to her hips, to her thighs. Then he lifted her up, wrapping her legs around his waist as he carried them both to the center of the bed. He was still wearing his jeans, and she arched against him, his erection, covered in denim, hard still against her body. Rough.

She moaned, rolling her hips against him.

She was so desperate for him. So filled with need, but it wasn't just physical. She felt like she had been alone for two years. While this person, the one person that had ever got to her in this way, was just out there, away from her. Gone from her. And it had been hell.

Singing about it… All the time. Hearing it over and over again, her own pain, unfiltered and raw, playing in her ears all the time…

It was hell, and this wasn't heaven. Because it had a time limit on it, like it always did. Like it always would. And it made her want to hide from truth, from reality, from the intensity of what was rioting through her, but she wanted it too much to hide from it. And that, in the end, was the hardest thing. To know that you were running square into the thing that had mortally wounded you before, and to accept that you were making the choice anyway.

That's what she was doing. She would never know better when it was him. Or maybe she did. Maybe she did, and it would never matter as much as being touched by him.

Maybe it would always be worth the burn to play with his brand of fire. She would despair of it in the morning. Maybe. She would despair of it for years. She knew that already, because she already had.

But now... Now she had him. Now she was with him. And it was everything, and so was he. She skimmed her hands over his chest, down his back. Up to his face again. And she cupped his cheek, and whispered against his mouth, "I want you. I want you so much."

"Tell me," he growled, flexing his hips against her again, her internal muscles pulsing as his hardness hit her right where she needed him most, unerringly.

"I'm wet for you," she said. "Only for you. Only ever for you. I can have anyone. I'm rich and famous. I basically have groupies. Men, women, I could have anyone I want, but I just want you. I just want you. You fucking broke my heart. And look at me, I'm desperate for you. You, Flint Carson."

He growled, and undid the buckle on his belt. Stripped his jeans off, and her breath caught when she saw him, totally naked. Glorious. Beautiful. She needed him. Needed this. More than anything.

"Take me," she said. "Make me yours again. Please. Please." And maybe she said other things, but they were incoherent. Other things, but she didn't understand them. She didn't understand anything except him. He was like a map to herself. This desire a guiding star, bringing her home.

And maybe it would never, ever make sense to anyone else, but she didn't need it to.

She only needed him. Only ever him.

"Take me," she whispered, and he thrust home.

She gasped, tears forming in her eyes, because it felt so right. To have him in her. So deep, she couldn't tell where he ended and she began. And she didn't want to. She wanted this. This feeling of being one. This feeling of being his.

And he began to move, and it was like an ignited spark within her soul. She clung to his shoulders, and she kept her eyes open, because she didn't want to look away.

His name was her every heartbeat.

Flint.

Because whatever happened after this, he was here now. Whatever happened after this, he was hers now.

Whatever happened after this, she would be okay. She had to be okay. Because this had to be worth the risk. This had to be more than a sad country song about being drunk and lonely and missing the one you shouldn't.

Because they had to be more than that. More than a country song. More than a few verses, a chorus and a bridge.

More than her anger. More than her hurt. More than his grief.

Right then, she felt like it might be true. Like they weren't just Tansey and Flint, but all the stars and everything else. Like they weren't just the bad things, but a whole universe of possibility.

She didn't want the moment to pass, because once it did, there would be reality to contend with.

And she didn't want it.

She just wanted him.

That was the scariest thing. After all this time, after all of this.

Knowing better. Knowing he was the cowboy her mother had warned her about...

She just wanted him.

As orgasm crashed over her like a wave, she let herself get taken under.

His heart was still beating so hard he could barely breathe.

He was back in bed with her. With Tansey. And he could pretend that sex was all the same. That he had been the one with experience, so he was the one who was armed against this kind of thing. The one who knew what it was. Whatever that meant. Because there was no defining what this was. Not easily. It wasn't that simple, and it never could be.

It was something different, though. It was something he'd never experienced before, and it was why he hadn't been able to touch anyone since.

She shifted beside him, and he rolled onto his side and looked at her.

And there was something still about it. Something peaceful.

A feeling that he hadn't let himself feel in more years than he could count.

"I'm not really sad that I'm stuck up here anymore."

"Good to know."

"You haven't been with anybody... Why?" She frowned.

"Why haven't you?"

"Well. I could go into a whole monologue about broken trust. And another one about being famous. And how it affects the way that people see you. How it affects the way that you interact with people in all of that. But the simple truth is... I didn't want to be."

He shook his head. "Me either." He wasn't good with feelings; he wasn't good with words. And it wasn't just that he didn't like sharing his feelings; at this point, it was like a language that he had lost. He had feelings— he could acknowledge that. But he had done such a good job of pushing them behind a wall, of suppressing them, that the truth was, he didn't quite know how to translate them. Within his own self, to his own self.

"There was something different about being with you. The idea of letting somebody else put their hands where you'd put them... It was like cursing in a church. Walking on top of sacred ground, when you're supposed to leave it be. I don't know."

She rolled onto her back and looked up at the ceiling. "I don't think I can claim to have felt like it was sacred ground. I just couldn't imagine... I just couldn't imagine. And maybe we needed this. Maybe we needed something more finished. Something not quite so painful." She turned to her side again and put her hand on his chest. He closed his eyes. There was a goodbye in those words. He knew that. Goodbye had always been the only option. Because he couldn't do forever. Which meant goodbye was inevitable, which meant he couldn't rail against what she was saying. Not without changing everything, the entire landscape that he had built up inside of his chest.

The map to who he was.

He remembered vaguely thinking that she was a map to somewhere else, but… He wasn't sure he could follow it.

He wasn't sure he wanted to.

And that meant accepting the silent goodbye.

But for now, they were here. For now, there was no leaving here.

"You changed me," he said finally. "Everything that I'm doing… It's because of you."

"Well, because you were angry at me," she said.

"Does it matter? It was still a change."

"I guess not. Because I guess the same could be said for me."

"What are your plans for Christmas?" he asked. His own family would have their big rowdy get-together, and he would pretend he didn't hate it.

"I'm going to visit my mother. In Palm Springs. That's where her house is. She wanted to be warm. She wanted palm trees." He saw a tear slide down her cheek. "I'm always so afraid that I might lose this. You know, the money is a big deal. My mother raised me in a trailer, never knowing if we were going to have enough to make rent, to keep the lights from being shut off. I found that in the end, revenge wasn't the important piece so much as love. Giving back for the love my mother showed me. She's a tough woman. But she loves me. I know that having me made her life harder, but she never acted like I was a burden. She always said that I was a gift. I like giving her things. I like paying her back… I like…"

"You bought your mother a house," he said. "And on top of all of that, you're her daughter. I don't think you'd lose her if something happened with your career."

"Maybe not. But she's the only person that stayed in my life always. The only person who was there at every step, and I finally got to give back to her, and what if someday it isn't enough?"

Unspoken was the idea that she clearly felt like she hadn't been enough for her father.

"Do you think you weren't enough for me?"

The words scraping his throat raw, it was dancing close to things that he didn't want to talk about. Things that he didn't want to admit.

"What else is a woman supposed to think? If I had been enough…"

He reached out and put his hand on her cheek. "No. If you learn one thing from what I told you, if you take one thing away from it, then take this. If there was anything that could fix me, it would've been you. It was never fair for me to touch you. Because when I tell you my problems are mine, and when I tell you they are built into the deepest part of who I am, I need you to believe that."

She didn't say anything. "Like I said. I think we needed this. I think this is important."

He nodded slowly. Except he didn't really like that conclusion for some reason. He'd always been like this with her. He wanted it both ways. To have her. To stay safe. He already knew he couln't do both.

"I might not be able to fix all the things inside of me, but maybe I can fix what I did to you," he said.

"I don't need you to fix me, Flint. That's actually been part of the conclusion that I've come to. Yeah, I was angry at you. I was. But I was afraid too, because if I hadn't been, I wouldn't have saved all of that for a song. I would have said it to you. Yes, I was hurt by what happened. You know that. I was devastated. I let myself believe that what you said about yourself was wrong. I let myself believe that because things changed for me they would change for you too. But I wasn't trying to spare you by holding back, I was trying to spare myself."

"That's all any of us are trying to do," he said, the words coming from somewhere deep inside of him, and he hadn't realized how true they were until he'd said them.

But he made a concerted effort to shut off any realizations that might come as a result.

"My family always does a big Christmas thing," he said finally. "And I pretend that I like it. But I don't. I pretend that I like it, because you have to do that with your family. You have to do that for your family. Especially when… You know, I feel like they've all moved on without me. Like they've all reached some kind of healing that I just can't find. Some of my brothers have lagged behind a little bit. But now three of them are getting married." He laughed. "Well. Not all of them. My brother Buck… Something happened a long time ago, and he left. There was an accident and he… He wasn't the same after. I know that eats at my parents. Because even though he didn't die, they lost another child. He was never himself, and then he went away. He's the only one that didn't stay. The only one that didn't stay on the ranch, the only one that didn't stay in the rodeo. I'm angry at him, you know. I'm angry at him for leaving. For not doing what I do."

"And what's that?"

"I don't feel any of it either. I don't feel healed. I don't feel happy to be there. I can't handle the emotions of it. I can't handle the way my mom wants to talk about my sister and share memories. I can't handle sitting around and telling stories, like there could ever be happy memories of somebody that you'll just miss for the rest of your life. But I do it. And if I want to rage, I do it on the inside. Because I did what I had to do to deal with myself so that I could be there for my family. So honestly, fuck him."

He watched a series of complicated emotions flit across Tansey's face. And of course, he saw pity among them.

"I never wanted you to feel sorry for me," he said.

"Only a jerk wouldn't feel sorry for you. Are you sorry for me that my dad left?"

"Well, yeah…"

"I'm sorry for you. Because this is hard, and terrible. Because it's more than anyone should have had to deal with. Because it's difficult and sad. Because…"

"What?"

"Because it's not fair. All the things that happened to us that break our hearts before we can ever make choices. You don't choose your family. And I had a terrible father. You have a great family, but it still came with tragedy, and I… I just don't think it's fair."

"No. It's not." An idea turned over in his head. "But

you know, I was going to take the opportunity to decorate the hotel while it was empty."

"You were going to decorate."

He shrugged. "I told you. That's the thing I'm good at doing. And I figured I would do it myself. Get the Christmas decorations up before the guests start coming to spend their holidays here. There's a lot of people planning to spend Christmas Day right here. We got a big Christmas dinner and…there's a big tree out on the back porch that I haven't brought in yet, and decorations ready to go in one of the back offices."

"Let's do it," she said. "Let's decorate."

"You want to decorate?"

She nodded. "We had a tiny tinsel tree in the mobile home, and then… We don't really do Christmas every year. Because sometimes I'm busy, and we're not always in the same place. We always call. But if I'm by myself, there's no reason to put up decorations and…"

"Well. If you're interested."

And he didn't say what he knew. That they were both maybe trying to make the night last longer. Because who knew what would happen come morning. When trees could be moved and roads could be plowed, and the temperatures would get above freezing and everything would start melting.

Yeah, he didn't know what would happen after that.

Chapter 11

She waited, wrapped in just the robe again, while Flint went and got boxes of ornaments from where they'd been stored back in the manager's office.

He was shirtless, and in her mind, she knew this would always be Christmas. This man, wearing nothing but jeans low riding on his lean hips, carrying big boxes of decorations.

And it made her a little bit sad, because it was another thing that would belong to Flint Carson forever.

You have to figure that out.

She did. Because she hadn't slept with him again to break her own heart again. She had wanted to say goodbye.

Not because anything he'd told her about himself horrified her. No. He wasn't the monster that he thought he was, and she knew that. It was simply that she also knew who she was.

And they had tried this before.

And now she needed to listen when he told her who he was.

And what he wanted.

She pushed off the sadness, and watched as he went toward the back of the major lobby area, throwing open the doors at the back.

They had the whole place lit up, and she wondered if anyone could see that, at 2:00 a.m., this giant building was a beacon of light on the hill. If anyone could see the outline of his body as he stood there, backlit in the doorway. Snowflakes whipped in around him, and she just sat and stared.

"What are you doing?"

"Christmas tree," he said. "It is a huge ass tree."

He had already placed a stand at the center of the room, and he disappeared a moment later, and then came back. The tree was huge. It must weigh hundreds of pounds, and he had it hefted over his shoulders, like one of those guys at the gym that did all the major weight lifting like it was just a fun thing people did on a Saturday morning.

"You need help?"

"Oh come on," he said, a grin curving his lips.

So she just sat there, and watched as he positioned the tree in the stand. It was massive.

But she didn't really care about the tree. Mostly, she was watching him. How beautiful he was. How perfect.

There was just no other man that made her feel this way. No other man that captured every facet of her attention. But she didn't think there was a more beautiful man in the entire world. How could there be? And she sat there, living in the feeling she'd had when they had walked up from her truck. When she had let those broad shoulders—so perfectly defined and glorious, revealed to her now—shield her from the wind.

And she realized, it was the man he was.

Not the man he could be.

Because she listened to him talk about his family.

It wasn't that he didn't do that, all the time. Shoulder other people's burdens, protect them.

He used his strength all the time, every family gathering, every Christmas. He denied himself, and his own comfort, for the people he cared for.

The issue was, he just didn't have the capacity to extend it to her too.

It was a painful realization, but one she could accept. How could she not accept the fact that he gave everything to a family that loved him so much?

Family was supposed to be who you did that for.

Her father had never done it for her, and look at the way it had broken things.

His older brother was gone, and that, she knew, put more pressure on him. It was why he was angry.

Because he was already at capacity.

She couldn't ask him to do any more.

It would make her love a burden.

It wasn't a flaw in him. It was actually because he was just so...

"All right," he said. "Let's get some decorations on this thing. Well, let's start with a fire, because now I'm freezing."

"That's the hazard of going outside half naked in this weather." She grinned. "Not that I'm complaining." She didn't want to slide into morose thinking. She didn't want to think about when the sun would rise. She didn't want to think about anything but this moment.

Because this would be the moment that sustained her. The moment that moved her on. That moved her into a place of acceptance about what they'd had, and what was possible. Because that was the issue; that was why she was so hurt. It was believing they could have had more if only... If only he could change. And she realized that he couldn't. That he needed to be who he was to survive, and to be there for his family.

It wasn't a deficiency in him.

It was almost sadder than if he just wasn't good at all.

But only almost.

And this was their moment. So she was going to take it.

He built a fire, big and warm, almost enough to take her robe off. But she felt like maybe decorating the Christmas tree naked was a bridge too far.

They took strings of sparkling white lights out of boxes, and he put up a ladder so that the lights could get wrapped all the way around, all the way to the top.

There were large sparkling red globes, and gold stars, and when they were finished, she had never seen anything more beautiful.

A Christmas tree that was theirs. That had nothing to do with her mother's stress with the season, or her childhood guilt over making her mother put any extra effort into anything, because she already worked so hard, and she definitely didn't deserve to feel guilty over the presents that she couldn't buy Tansey.

Just something that belonged to them. And even in this moment it was absent the sadness that had been inside of her ever since...

Ever since she had met this man, and then had to figure out how to live a life that didn't have him anymore.

Ever since they'd lived one summer that had defined so much of who they were. Because even he had admitted that it had changed him.

And maybe that was the real thing that she needed to understand. That it had been fate, even if it had been a bruised and bloody fate, one that they'd had to fight to find the meaning of.

Maybe she had to accept that sometimes she had to go through hard things, terrible things, to become who she was supposed to be.

Wasn't that every highbrow Hollywood movie? The complicated happy ending, rather than the traditional one.

She had certainly never seen that sort of happy ending in real life.

In real life, her mother was having a happy ending by herself, in Palm Springs with other people her age, laughing and drinking and enjoying life by the pool. Reaping the benefits of having been a good mother, a hard worker, and not having to do it anymore.

She didn't have a man. She didn't need a man. The lesson of her heartbreak had been that she didn't need one to be happy.

Tansey had needed her heartbreak for her fame, and she needed this bittersweet moment to find the next phase.

Flint was important to her. But that didn't mean he was her forever, not in a way that meant he would be in her life always.

He was forever in terms of how he'd changed her, though.

And maybe that was the most real way for a relationship to last.

"Hang on just a second."

He went behind the reception desk, and bent down for a moment, and then music filled the room. Old-fashioned Christmas carols. And she looked around the glittering space, looked at the way his body was in the firelight and the way the tree sparkled.

It was the sweetest, sexiest moment of her whole life. And she didn't know how those two things combined to become one thing, but they had. Did.

He reached his hand out. "Want to dance?"

"I don't know how," she said.

"Me either. But I want to."

She took his hand, and he lifted her up off the couch, and twirled her in time with the music, her robe spinning out around her, exposing her legs, and maybe more, but there was no embarrassment with him. She laughed, and he brought her back to him, and they swayed back and forth, and whether or not it could be called dancing was up for debate.

But it was perfect. This moment, was perfect. Even if she couldn't see past it.

And with the music swirling around them, and the firelight glowing, she stretched up on her toes, and she kissed him.

* * *

His heart was pounding so hard he thought it might burst through his chest.

He had never liked Christmas. He had never liked any of the symbolism associated with it. But for him, he knew that this would always be Christmas. Every time he had to sit through an endless family present-opening session, every time they went down to the fanciest restaurant in Lone Rock for their annual Christmas Eve dinner, he would think of this. He would think of her.

The only person he'd ever wanted to do a romantic thing for. The only person who had ever made him wish that he was someone else.

He didn't waste time regretting the things that had happened. He didn't waste time railing against the universe anymore for taking his sister away from them. Because it didn't do any good. It only reopened old wounds.

But this made him want to do that. She had always made him want to do that, and maybe that was the biggest reason he had let her go. Because she made him wish that things could be different. And he knew that that was an endless trap that you could fall into and never get out of.

But right now, he just wanted the moment. He wanted to surrender to it. To her.

And so he did. He kissed her, with every ounce of desire in his soul. He held her against him, relishing the feel of her curves against his body as he did.

He kissed her. Kissed her like he might die if he didn't, and he wondered if part of him had. All these years when he'd been without her. All these years when he'd told himself that he didn't need her. That he had done the right thing. *How can anything but this be right?*

He cradled her face in his hands, kissed her deep, kissed down the elegant column of her throat, sliding his tongue over the line of her collarbone. At the same time, his hands found the belt on her robe, and undid it slowly, pushing it away from her body. Letting it fall to the ground. She was beautiful. And it was like unwrapping a Christmas present. The only one he'd ever cared about. The only one he could remember ever wanting.

She was famous now. A woman the whole world wanted a piece of.

But she was a woman that he had. A woman whose body he knew better than his own, even though before tonight it had been two years since he'd seen her. Two years since he'd touched her.

Mine.

The word welled up inside of him. He couldn't remember the last time he'd wanted anyone or anything this badly.

Maybe he never had. Because he hadn't let himself.

Because wanting… Wanting like this, it was almost a curse. But he couldn't turn away from it. Not now. Not when it was like this. So desperate. Her hands went to his belt buckle, undid it slowly, then to his jeans.

And he let himself feel what he hadn't that first time. The all of it. That she had never let anyone else inside of her, except for him. And he had done what with that?

Why had he taken it if he had known that he couldn't honor it? Why had he taken her if he had known he couldn't give her what she deserved?

Maybe because he wasn't as strong as he liked to

think. He was weak. For her. It had always been that way. From moment one.

And right now he just needed her. He hadn't needed sex in two years. It wasn't just about that. Wasn't just about a simple dry spell, because if so, he would have done something about it. If so, he would have found someone else. That was just sex. For him, it was about her.

And he wanted to show that to her.

He laid her down slowly on the thick rug in front of the fireplace, kissed her mouth, kissed her breasts.

Her body was a brilliant gift, something rich and lovely in the firelight. Something that nothing and no one would ever be able to overshadow.

She was his summer. And now she was his winter too.

Or maybe he'd made his own winter these past two years, but she was the reason why. The reason why it felt so dark. The reason why everything in him had changed.

Because it had been an eclipse on anything good when he let her walk out of his life.

He wanted to show her that.

He wanted to give her everything.

He kissed his way down the softness of her body, kissed her inner thigh, then licked a line to her center. She gasped. And he fed off of her. Off of her pleasure. Off of her arousal. Her need.

He let himself disappear into the moment. Into the glory of pleasuring her. The responsibility of it. The honor of it.

To be allowed to taste her like this. To be allowed to touch her like this. Who was he? He was just some dumbass. And she had always been special. Always been singular. And the men in her life, him included, had made her feel like she was second. Had made her feel like she wasn't good enough. Made her feel like she was a burden. How dare they? And how dare he?

He didn't deserve this moment. He didn't deserve her.

But he was taking her. Because he needed it. Because he needed her to know.

He licked her, took her essence as an offering, a gift. Even as it fed his soul.

The taste of her. The sound of her cries. Her desperate arousal, the way that she clawed at his shoulders, the way that she cried out her need when he pushed two fingers inside of her and took her to the heights.

He waited for her to come down, and then he kissed her hip bone, her stomach, back up to her mouth, where he let her taste the evidence of her own desire on his lips.

"You," he said, "are like no one else. You are like nothing else. You are air. And I hadn't realized that I'd been suffocating all this time."

"Flint…"

The way that she said his name, all sweet and tender and questioning, it did something to him.

The way that she looked at him, like he might be something amazing. Something great.

He wanted to be.

He wanted to be more than he'd been. He wanted to be something better. Something right for her.

He wanted that.

He kissed her, deep and long, lost himself in her.

But it was what she did next that he couldn't handle. It was what she did next that broke him.

She pushed against his chest, reversing their positions, and once he was stripped naked, she knelt down before him, and took him into her mouth. She looked up at him, her beautiful green eyes piercing him through the soul while she racked his body with torturous pleasure.

Fuck.

He pushed his hands into her hair, held her there, bucking his hips, desperate for release and desperate for it to go on forever.

He could remember when a blowjob had been entertainment. When it had meant nothing to him. When it had touched nothing but his cock. And now... It was like it was all of him. He couldn't take pleasure anymore unless it was her. He couldn't take pleasure with her without involving everything. His whole body. All that he was. His soul.

She sucked him deep, and he growled. "No. I need to be in you."

It was her turn to kiss him. Her turn to let him taste what she'd done to him.

And then she straddled his hips, angling herself so that the head of him was pressed against the slick entrance to her body. He gritted his teeth as she lowered herself onto him, allowing him in, inch by torturous inch.

She was so tight, so perfect.

And he had never done this before her. Taking a woman without a latex barrier. That was the kind of thing reserved for trust.

Trust.

She had trusted him so much back then and he had broken it.

He didn't deserve it now. But he needed it.

Needed her.

Needed all these things that he had no call to want. Dammit all, he did.

With his whole soul.

His heart was raging, as she began to move. She began to ride him like she was made for it. And hell, she had to be. Had to be made for this, for him. Because God knew he thought he might be made for her.

In another life maybe. One where he hadn't lost so much. One where he hadn't hurt so damn much.

That realization almost stopped him, but then, he was overcome, seeing her body as she rose over him like that, feeling the clasp of her around him, watching the pleasure on her face as she began to chase her own climax.

He wasn't a man who had the ability to do what she did. To take feelings and turn them into song lyrics. Hell, he couldn't even take feelings and turn them into words.

He couldn't take feelings and turn them into much of anything.

But he wanted to. For her.

He wanted to do more, to be more. To be better. For her.

He wished that he could erase his past. His loss. His pain. Because it had broken him.

And he never wished that. He never wished it because there was no point. Just like there was no point in tears. No point in regret.

But she had come to him untouched, and not without pain, and he had come to her broken beyond repair.

He wished he could be different.

And he gave himself up to that. To the need to be more than he ever had been for her.

Because who had been there for her?

Here she was, worrying about what she could give her mother… Who worried about what they could give to her?

She thought she wasn't enough.

And he had been part of that.

"You're beautiful," he said, gripping her hips and guiding her up and down on his cock. "The most beautiful woman I've ever seen. You deserve everything. You deserve the world."

Hands braced on his chest, he could see her eyes begin to glitter. See tears welling there, and it just made him want to give her even more.

"You deserve everything you've got. You deserve all the money from that song. You are absolutely perfect. In every way."

She closed her eyes, and began to shake, and he could feel the tenuous grip he had on his control beginning to slip. "You're a star," he said. "And you're more than enough."

And then she dissolved, and he went right along with it, his climax like a vicious beast, grabbing him around the throat and shaking him hard.

"I love you," she said. "I love you."

And just like that, very deep inside of her, with her words echoing inside of him, it was like a sledgehammer had been taken to the walls all around his soul. The gates that held back his emotions demolished with three simple words.

And he felt like he had been dragged out into the middle of an open field, naked. Exposed and vulnerable to every attack.

It was as if blinders he had put up intentionally had dissolved. As if everything that he had put up between them had vanished.

Everything.

I love you.

And it was too much. Too much. It reminded him of the moment when he had hit Boone. Because it was like something sharp and vicious was cutting open his insides. Like his heart was going to explode. It wasn't that he felt nothing. It was that he felt everything, and he had no idea how to combat that. No idea what to do about it. There was nothing, he realized. Because the problem was knowing it was the truth. Knowing that what he had been protecting himself all along from was the intensity of it.

The desperation of it.

And he couldn't un-know it now.

He felt terrified. Utterly terrified. Because she loved him, and he felt more than any one person should. Because she loved him, and he felt like he might break apart. Because she loved him, and it truly felt like hell. Because she loved him, and he was faced with the realization that she was so fragile. So beautiful. And life had come along and taken that from him. It had already taken so much.

The more you cared, the more you could lose.

And he realized…

That was all this was. It was all it had ever been. All he had ever been truly afraid of. It was losing someone he loved again. It was caring so much he could be in that position where he felt too much. Where he wanted too much.

He had punched Boone, because Boone had felt all of the things that lived inside of him. All of the things he wanted to turn away from. All of the things he wanted to deny.

But he was still holding her, and he was still in her, and he couldn't help himself. "I love you too."

He lay back on the floor, feeling like he had just lost a war.

One he had been fighting for the better part of his life. One he hadn't even realized he'd been on the slow path to losing from the minute he had first seen her.

Every bit of his resolve. Every bit of everything, it was broken. Demolished. And so was he.

He knew why he had been fighting it all this time. Knew why he had been fighting her.

He damn well did.

Because this was terrifying. He was happy to throw himself on the back of an angry bull; he was happy to work until his body ached and his hands bled.

It was the feeling. That was what he didn't want to do. Not what he couldn't do. It was the thing that scared him. Believing so much in something, hoping so much. Loving someone so much, and losing them anyway. Losing everything anyway.

"You love me?"

He sat up, staring straight at the Christmas tree that they had just decorated together.

Staring straight at the Christmas that could be his if…

"Shit," he said.

"What?"

"I…"

He was suddenly choked. By the memories. The memories of that night that they had broken up. The memory of the night that he had lost her.

That he had let her walk away.

She had thought that she might be pregnant with his baby and he'd said he didn't want it. Of course he wanted it. He wanted everything with her. He wanted a whole life. A baby and everything, but facing down that possibility, that little bit of hope… It had been too much for him. He hadn't been able to claim it. He hadn't been able to admit it.

And now… He felt swamped with it. With the loss of it. The loss of that potential future. The baby, her.

All the things that he hadn't been able to say then. And he wanted to say them now.

So he looked up at her, and he tried. "I don't know if I'll be a good dad," he said. "I don't know if I'll be able to be a good husband. I have lived in absolute fear for so long, Tansey. For so long. Because when I was a kid, I knew my sister was sick. Of course I did. We spent all that time in hospitals, all that time around doctors, and it wasn't like my parents didn't try to prepare us. But you don't understand *dead* when you're fourteen years old. And you can't. It's just the most absurd thing. I had a sister. And she was wonderful. The cutest kid. The sweetest… And why? *Why?* It never made any sense. That I could never… I couldn't live with what it made me feel. I had to figure out some way to stop it. I couldn't help Boone with what he felt because it was killing me. As if my own pain wasn't enough, I had to

watch it torture him too. I had to watch it torture everybody, and that was what broke me. It absolutely broke
me into pieces. And that was the man that met you."

He sat there, his words so heavy. Everything so
heavy. "I have told myself that I did not have it in me
to give anybody the support they needed if they were
going through a hard time. That I didn't have it in me,
because of the way I reacted to Boone. But when you
said that… When you said you loved me just now… It
was like you shone a light on all those dark places inside
of me, and I can't pretend I don't know what it really is."

"What is it?" she asked.

"Fear. I'm afraid. I'm a coward. Because you're a
gift. A beautiful, lovely gift. Too perfect to be real almost. And more what I want than I ever wanted to
admit. More than I ever wanted to want. And suddenly
it terrifies me. Like the sky might cave in and take you
away from me." He cleared his throat. "When you told
me that you thought you might be pregnant… It was
the ferocity of what I felt that shut me down. Because
it was like…hope, with teeth. It's the best way I can
describe it."

"I know all about that. About hope with teeth. Every
time I've ever looked at you, Flint. And wanted to believe that we could be something that we were never
meant to be. Because you were that cowboy, the one
that I was supposed to stay away from. The one that
I was never supposed to love. You were that cowboy.
And I knew better. But something in me didn't want to
know better. Because it just wanted you. What I really
wanted was you."

"I don't know what to do with this. I don't know.

But I know that I can't walk away from you. Not again. Not ever again."

"I can't walk away from you either. I need you too much. I need us."

"I… I don't know if I can. I don't know… But I want it. I want to do whatever I have to do to figure this out. To fix myself. So that I can be what you need."

"Flint…"

"But you were always enough," he said. "It was me. It was always me. I was the one who couldn't cope. I was the one who flinched. You were always enough. What your father couldn't do was fix himself. I want to. For you. For us. For the future. I'm glad you wrote that song. I'm glad you told the truth about what I did to you. Because I needed to know. I needed to really know."

"But what about you?"

"It ruined me. Broke me. And now… You put me back together. I'm still not quite in perfect condition. But I'm trying. I want… I want forever. Please."

"Are you serious?"

"I am dead serious. I know that I don't deserve that level of trust. I know that I don't deserve for you to give that to me… But damn, I want you. More than I've ever wanted anyone or anything. And I want you more than I want to be the kind of safe I've been all these years. Because it was too late. The minute I caught you outside that gate, the minute that happened, it was too late. Too late for me to keep doing what I was doing. Too late for me to hang on to all the ugly stuff. All the broken stuff. I tried. And I nearly broke us both. So now I just want to surrender to it."

"I had accepted… I had accepted the idea that there

was no way for us to have a happy ending. That I was going to have to accept that it was going to be another kind of happy. You know, the kind when you walk away, but at least you learned something."

"It's the easy way," he said. "This… What I want with you… It's going to be the hard way. Because I'm not perfect. And I am certainly not perfectly healed all of a sudden just because I want to be. This might be hard. Deciding to be together instead of just deciding to walk away wounded. I know that. I get that. But I think it's worth it. You and me. I think it damn well will be. Those endings… Those endings where people are apart, it's not better. It's not deeper. It's just easier. Because it's easier to walk around with your own shit and never have to deal with it. It is so much harder to have to take someone else's on, and I got to ask you to take on mine."

Her face went soft. "Well, you're gonna have to take on mine too. I'm not exactly in perfect working order myself. I couldn't tell you what I wanted then."

"Tell me what you want now. I will do my damnedest to give it to you, because I love you. Because you are worth it to me. Because you are everything. You are everything and none of it matters. Because there is no protection worth having, there is no piece of my soul worth preserving, if you are out there in the world and I'm not with you."

Tears started to fall down her cheeks. "I want to spend the rest of my life with you. I don't want this to end. I want you to be the father of my children. I want you to be everything. I fell in love with you, Flint, even knowing that I shouldn't. I fell in love with you even though it wasn't what I wanted. I was afraid, but I knew that loving you was worth the risk. I just did somehow. These last two years I questioned it, and I tried so hard to call it something important. To call it something worthy. I tried to tell myself that I didn't need that fairy-tale happy ending. But I wanted it with you. It was never enough to not have you. When you sent me away, I was devastated." She wiped tears away from her cheek. "I waited until I got to a motel six hours down the road, and then I cried. For days. And then…"

"Do you think you were pregnant?"

She nodded slowly. "Probably. Even if we would've stayed together, I think I would have lost it."

"But I could've been there for you," he said. Everything in him felt wrong. Sad. Angry at himself for the choices that he'd made. For the ways in which he hadn't protected her. The ways in which he had protected himself instead. "I wish that I would've been there for you. Because if there's one thing I know, it's that I cannot promise you a life without pain. It's something I'm coming to accept. The fact that I can't escape it no matter how much I might want to. But I can promise to be there for you. And I can promise to help try to carry the burden if it's too heavy. And to carry you if I have to."

"Yes," she whispered, closing her eyes. "But I need you to do something." She put her hand on his chest. "I need you to forgive yourself. Because our relationship shouldn't be a penance that you're paying. Our love isn't you making up for the past. You did the best you could then. I just want you to do the best you can do now."

"I promise you that," he said, his heart about ready to pound through his chest. "I promise."

He felt raw, and exposed. He felt fundamentally changed. His whole world felt like it had been tilted a bit. Or maybe like it had been put right. It was a lot, to recognize that he was afraid, and had been all this time.

And he was going to take a long time to sort through it; he knew that. But he knew one thing now. And he knew it well.

"I love you."

Chapter 12

Of all the things Tansey had thought she would hear from him as the sun was just beginning to rise over the tops of the mountains…that was not it. The night had not turned out the way she had expected. Because she had been certain they would be parting from each other in the morning, again.

She had even been ready for it.

But she kept thinking about what he said. About how redemption, change, was the hardest thing.

She knew it was true.

Forgiveness, and the choice. The choice to just love.

To believe that it wasn't her that was broken, but her father. To believe that she was enough all on her own.

But that she really wanted to be with Flint all the same.

She had accepted that she might say she loved him, and not have a life with him.

She had never imagined this. The chance to have a life with him.

And suddenly, none of it mattered. If she ever wrote another song—but she was pretty sure she would. It just all felt like…there was more now. More than striving. More than trying to show people that she was worth something.

More than trying to be the best. It was the strangest thing, but loving him, being in this moment, it made her feel like she might be able to live for herself for the first time.

And living that way with him…

It was a happy ending that was somehow beyond anything she had ever fantasized about.

"I love you too," she said.

"Marry me. The whole thing. Everything. The forever thing."

"Just like that? Just like that you aren't scared anymore?"

"I'm terrified. Fucking shaking in my boots. It's just that now I know it doesn't matter. I would rather love you, and live every day with some kind of fear that I might lose you, than not have you in my life. I would rather feel everything. Be damn near overflowing with it, than live comfortable and empty without you."

"You make it sound awful."

"No." He smiled. "It's wonderful."

And she thought what she had concluded earlier. That they were some kind of fate. Even if it was a bloody, hard-won fate. And she knew that it was even more than that. Because they had the chance to be the kind of fate that she had imagined briefly earlier tonight. The kind that was bittersweet and sad.

But they were choosing to be more. The kind of fate that was more. The kind of fate that was everything. She realized that this kind of fate involved a whole lot of choosing. Because you could fall right into a man's arms, but unless you chose each other, you might not end up together. Unless you decided to let go, of all kinds of things, of hurt, of fear, and embrace hope…

Hope with teeth.

She knew exactly what he meant by that. And she would risk getting savaged by hope every time, if it meant getting to be with him.

But as she looked at him, as she went willingly into his arms, she realized, it wasn't hope with teeth. Not anymore.

This was hope with strong arms, with a steady smile and the truest heart she knew.

"This is a song," she said.

"I can't wait to hear it," he said.

She grinned at him. "I can't wait to live it."

Chapter 13

He decided to go home for Christmas with Tansey. She called her mother and invited her to come from Palm Springs, and she had agreed to make the trek, which had surprised Tansey, since her mom was pretty wedded to her warm weather and palm trees.

But it also pleased her.

He would've done whatever he had to do to make sure they could do Christmas in both places, or maybe he would've had to disappoint his family.

He was willing to do that.

Because he was done performing. Done trying to do things to make up for what he thought he lacked.

But there was one thing he needed to do. And it was the thing that made Christmas so special this year.

Not just because he was going to be introducing Tansey as his fiancée, but he was pretty excited about that.

First, he had to give her the ring.

Which he intended to do at midnight on Christmas Eve. Then on Christmas morning she could wear it and show his family.

Yeah. He was looking forward to that.

But first, during a family board game, he sneaked into the kitchen to find his mother. "Hi, Mom," he said.

She turned to him, smiling. "What is it, honey?"

He reached out and pulled her into his arms, hugging her. "I just wanted to tell you that I love you. And that I'm sorry. It's been hard for me to say things like this. But… Things are changing for me. I'm going to try to change. I'm going to try to be different."

His mother put her hand on his forearm, and patted it. "Flint, honey. You never needed to change."

"I did. I think… I think in time you'll see the difference."

"Well, I love you all the same."

He nodded, and walked out of the kitchen. The next person he needed to talk to was Boone. When he walked out into the hall, Tansey was there. "Are you okay?" she asked.

"Yeah. I'm just… You know. I'm doing what we talked about."

"Yeah. It's going to be fine."

"I know it will be. Because I have you."

"Good luck." She squeezed him, and he went outside, where he knew his brother was, down at the barn.

Boone was facing away from him, on the phone. "Yeah, well, if you're going to go on a bender on Christmas Eve, you might want to fucking call your wife and let her know where you're at…No idea…She texted me, because she was looking for you. And I think you should be ashamed that your wife has an easier time getting a hold of me than she does you…Yeah. Well. Get over yourself. You're drunk. And it's not even 5:00 p.m., and your wife and your two kids are…Seriously. Whatever. I'm not going to lie for you. I'm going to tell her that you're drunk. It's your problem to sort out, Daniel." He hung the phone up and turned around. "Oh. How long have you been standing there?"

"That Daniel Stevens?"

"Yeah. Fucker." He rubbed his hand over his face. "It's… You know, it's Christmas Eve and he's not home and Wendy texted me looking for him and… I can't lie for him. And I'm not going to. She's way too good for him. He's such a dick."

The ferocity on Boone's face told a whole story. But Flint had a feeling his brother wasn't in the space to tell it. Daniel was another rodeo rider, and a friend of Boone's, and he'd gotten married ten years ago. Flint had met his wife on a few occasions. She was very pretty. He had to wonder if his brother thought so too.

"Well. Sounds like you should do the opposite of lying for him. You should probably tell on him."

"Yeah. I have half a mind to."

"Boone…" He cleared his throat. "This is going to seem like it's coming out of the blue for you. But… You know I brought Tansey home."

"Yeah. And the song was about you."

"The song was about me. And she and I had a lot to work out. In regard to that. We had to address why I broke up with her in the first place. And I told her about…about the thing I am most ashamed of."

"What's that?"

He looked at his brother, and he could see that Boone genuinely didn't know.

"When you were crying about Sophia. And I hit you. And I told you not to cry anymore."

Boone looked away. "Hey. That's not a big deal. We were kids. You were a kid."

"Yeah. I was. But there was still… I was afraid. I was afraid of everything, and most of all, I was afraid of that pain never going away. Never ending. And your pain made mine worse. So I lashed out. And then… I have carried the guilt for that, and I use that guilt as an excuse. I used it to tell myself that I didn't deserve to have relationships because I wouldn't be able to be there for someone, because look at what I did to you when you needed me most." He shook his head. "But that wasn't it. I was just afraid of how much I felt. And I took it out on you. And I used it as an excuse my whole life."

"There's no guidebook on how to handle stuff like that," said Boone. "And I'm not gonna claim I'm any less messed up than you."

"Yeah. But some of the messed up you are might be my fault."

"No," said Boone. "Hell no. You were always there for me. And yeah, you're kind of a stoic bastard. But you're a good man, Flint, and you have been the whole time. Not saying you haven't made mistakes. I've heard the song."

"Well. She forgives me. I'm going to marry her."

"Good," said Boone. "You should. And hell, if she can forgive you, I certainly can. Even if I don't feel like there's much to forgive."

"Thank you," he said, and he meant it. Because whether Boone was willing to admit it or not, Flint knew that he needed that forgiveness.

And then he did something he knew his brother would be allergic to. He reached out and hugged him. Clapped him on the back. "I'm going to ask her to marry me," he said. "Well. I already did. But I'm going to get down on one knee and give her a ring and everything."

Boone looked at him long and hard. "Good for you."

"Do you think you're ever going to do that?"

He chuckled. And it sounded kind of bitter. "I have a barrier to that. It isn't the same thing you have. But it's…an issue."

And yet again, he wondered about the phone call he just overheard.

"Well. If you want to talk about it, I'm here. And newly in touch with my feelings."

"Wow. I'm going to pass on that."

"Okay. Love you."

And he'd said it. And he meant it. Boone flipped him off, and that felt about perfect.

At midnight, he and Tansey were in his room, and that was when he did it.

"I have something for you." He got down on one knee in front of her. "Tansey Martin…will you marry me? For real. Forever?"

Tears sparkled in her eyes as she nodded, and he took the ring out of the box and slid it onto her finger. "I know you can buy yourself any piece of jewelry that you want."

"But I want this one. Because it's from you." She smiled. "I have a song that I want to play for you."

"Well. Then I want to hear it."

She sat down on the edge of the bed, holding her guitar, and this one was different. A little more upbeat than the songs she usually played.

And this song was about love. Choosing it, hanging on to it.

Love is cactuses
Good-luck charms and bad-luck nights
Sunny days and colder weather
Letting go and holding on
And I've heard the best revenge is living well
But the best is letting go
So you can just love
In the end, it's all that matters
In the end, it's the greatest

And he knew it was true. The real story of them. Good and bad and the two years in between, when they didn't have each other at all. And he was grateful. So grateful, that she had decided to let go of all the anger she had every right to have, so that they could love each other instead.

She had apologized to him recently, for the song. For the fact that some people would never accept they were back together, because they were still holding on to that story she'd told so well.

"It's part of our story," he'd said. "And I wouldn't trade it. Because it had to happen for us to end up here."

It was true. He'd had to break again to know that he wanted to be whole.

"You know," he said. "I was wrong, about winning. I

said that you couldn't love anything. That you couldn't care about anything more. But loving you, that is winning. And everything else… Everything else is just noise."

She kissed him. "I love you. And it's winning for me too."

"It was the cactus."

She laughed. "You can't prove that."

And he smiled against her mouth. "You can't prove that it wasn't."

* * * * *

Don't miss any of The Carsons of Lone Rock series from New York Times *bestselling author Maisey Yates!*

Rancher's Forgotten Rival
Best Man Rancher
One Night Rancher

CLAIMING THE RANCHER'S HEIR

Chapter 1

Creed Cooper was a cowboy. A rich, successful cowboy from one of the most well-regarded families in Logan County. He also happened to be tall, muscular and in possession of the kind of good looks a lot of women liked.

As a result, nearly nothing—or no one—was off-limits to him.

No one except Wren Maxfield.

Maybe that was why every time he looked at her his hands itched.

To unwind that tight bun from her hair. To make that mouth, which was always flattened in disapproval—at least around him—get soft and sexy and get all over his body.

And he had that itch a lot, considering he and Wren were the representatives for their respective families' vineyards. Rivals, in fact.

And she hated him.

She hated him so much that when she saw him her eyes flared with a particular kind of fire.

Fair enough, since he couldn't really stand her either.

But somehow, years ago, a piece of that dislike inside him had twisted and caught hard in his gut and turned into an intensity of another kind entirely.

He was obsessed.

Obsessed with the idea he might be able to use that fire in her eyes to burn up the sheets between them.

Instead, he had to listen to her heels clicking on the floor as she paced around the showroom of Cowboy Wines, looking like a smug cat, making him wait to hear whatever plan it was she'd come to tell him about.

"Are you listening to me?" she asked suddenly, her green cat eyes getting sharp.

She was dressed in a tight-fitting red dress that fell to the top of her knees. It had a high, wide neck, and while it didn't show a lot of skin, it hugged her full breasts so tight it didn't leave a lot to the imagination.

Even if it had, his imagination was damn good. And it was willing to work for Wren. Overtime.

She had on those ridiculous spiked heels, too. Red, like the dress. He wanted to see her in only those heels.

He wasn't into prissy women. Not generally. He liked a more practical girl. A cowgirl who would be at home on his ranch.

Wren looked like she never left her family showroom, all glass walls and wrought iron furniture. Maxfield Vineyards was the premier wine brand for people who were up their own asses.

And still, he wanted her.

That might be her greatest sin.

That she tested control he'd had firmly leashed for the last eighteen years and made him want to send it right to hell as he burned in her body.

Of all the reasons to hate Wren Maxfield, wanting her and not being able to do a damn thing to make himself stop was number one on the list.

He looked around the Cowboy Wines showroom, the barrels with glass tabletops on them, the heavy, distressed beams that ran the length of the room.

And then there was him: battered jeans and cowboy boots, a hat for good measure.

Everything a woman like Wren would hate.

A testament to just why there was no reason to carry a burning torch for her fine little body.

Too bad his own body was a dumbass.

"I wasn't listening at all," he said, making sure to drawl it. As slow as possible. He was rewarded with a subtle flare of heat in those eyes. "Make it more interesting next time, Wren. Maybe do a dance."

"The only dancing I'll ever do is on your grave, Creed."

The sparring sent a kick of lust through him. They did this every time they were in a room together. Every damn time. No matter that he knew he shouldn't indulge it.

But hell, he was afraid the alternative was stripping her naked and screwing her against the nearest wall, and that wasn't a real option.

So verbal sparring it was.

"What did I die of?" he asked. "Boredom?"

Those eyes shot sparks at him. "It was tragic. You

were found with a high heel protruding out of your chest."
Her magic lips curved upward and he felt it like she'd
pressed them against his neck.

"Any suspects so far?"

"Your own smart mouth. Are you going to listen to
me or not?"

"You're already here. So am I. Might as well."

He leaned back in his chair and, for effect, put his
boots up on the table.

Her top lip curled up into a sneer, and that thrilled
him just as much as if she'd crossed the room to strad-
dle his lap. Okay, maybe not just as much, but he loved
that he got to her.

"Fantastic. As you know, things at Maxfield Vineyards are changing. My father is no longer the owner.
Instead, my sister Emerson, her husband, Holden, and
our sister Cricket and I now have ownership.

"This plan is Emerson's idea. To be clear. As she is
the person who oversees our broader brand." She waved
a hand in the air as if to distance herself yet further from
whatever she was about to say. "I had to defer to her on
the subject. She doesn't think a rivalry is beneficial for
any of us. She thinks we should join forces. A large-
scale event where both of our wines are represented.
As you know, wine tours and the whole wine trail in
general have become increasingly popular."

"A rising tide lifts all boats and gets more people
drunk?"

"Basically," she said.

"I'm not really sure I see the benefit to me," he said.
"Seeing as everything is going well here."

"Everyone wants to expand," she said, looking at him as if he had grown a second head.

"Do they?"

"Yes," she responded. "Everyone."

"Well, the way I see it, our business is running well. We have just the right amount of staff, every family member has a position in the company, and it supports us very well. At a certain point, Wren, more is more. And that's it."

She looked at him, clearly dumbfounded. There were very definite and obvious differences between the Cooper and Maxfield families. The Coopers might be wealthy, but they liked their winery to reflect their roots. Down-home. A Western flare.

In the early days, his father had been told that there was no way he would ever be successful unless he did something to class up his image. He had refused. Digging in deeper to the cowboy theme was ultimately why they had become so successful. There was no point in competing with fancy-pants places like the Maxfields'. It wasn't the Coopers' way.

Joining up with the Maxfields made even less sense than trying to emulate them, in his opinion.

"Come on," she said. "You're ambitious, Creed, don't pretend otherwise."

And that was where she might have him. Because he didn't like to back down from a challenge. In fact, he quite liked a challenge in general. That she was issuing one now made him wonder if she was just baiting him. Taunting him.

He wasn't even sure he cared. All he knew was that he instantly wanted to take her up on it.

There was something incredibly sexy about her commitment to knowing her enemy.

"What exactly are you proposing?"

"I want to have a large event featuring all of the wineries in the area. A wine festival. For Christmas."

"That's ambitious. And it's too early to talk about Christmas."

"All the stores would disagree, Creed. Twinkle lights are out and about."

"Ask me if I care."

"I'd like to do a soft launch, a large party at Maxfield in the next month," she continued as if he hadn't spoken. "We'll invite our best clients. Can you imagine? The buzz we'll make joining forces?"

"Oh, you mean because everybody knows how profoundly our families dislike each other?" He paused for a moment. "How profoundly *we* dislike each other?"

It wasn't a secret. They were never civil to each other. They never tried to be.

"Yes," she said. "That."

"And how exactly do you think we're going to get through this without killing each other?"

She looked all cheerful and innocent. "Look on the bright side. If I do kill you, you'll get that dance you wanted so badly."

"Well. A silver lining to every cloud, I guess."

"I like to think so. Are you in?"

The only thing worse than giving in to the attraction he had for her would be hurting a business opportunity for it. He didn't let other people control him. Not in any way.

Least of all Wren Maxfield.

And that meant he'd do it. No matter how much he'd rather roll in a pit of honey and lie down on an anthill.

"How is this going to work? Logistically. I'm not going to roll up to your event in a suit."

"I didn't think you would. I thought you might be able to bring your rather…rustic charm." The way she said *rustic* and *charm* implied that she felt the former did not go with the latter.

He smiled. "It goes with me wherever I go."

"Do you have to wear a hat?" She wrinkled her nose.

"That is nonnegotiable," he said, reaching up and flicking the cowboy hat's brim with his forefinger.

"I figured as much." She sniffed. "Well. I can accept that."

"You have no choice. We'll provide the food. Barbecue."

"You really don't have to do that."

"I am not standing at a fancy party with nothing but raw fish on a cracker to eat. And anyway, if you want my clients, you better have meat."

"With wine."

"Hey. We work hard to break the stereotype that cowboys only like beer. I myself enjoy a nice red with my burger."

"Unacceptable."

His gaze flickered over her curves. That body. *Damn* what he'd like to do to that body. "Too repressed to handle a little change, Wren?"

Color flooded her cheeks. Rage. "I am not. I just don't like terrible ideas."

"It's not a terrible idea. It's *on brand*." He said the

last bit with no small amount of self-deprecation, and a smirk.

"Whatever. I don't care what you like with what. Really. I just want to know if I can count on you to help me put this together."

"You got it."

"I look forward to this new venture," she said. She smiled, which was strange, and then she extended her hand. He only looked at it for a moment. Then he reached his own out, clasped hers and shook it.

Her skin was soft, like he had known it would be. Wren was the kind of woman who had never done a day's worth of manual labor in her whole life. Not that she didn't work hard, she did. And he knew enough about the inner workings of a job like theirs to be well aware that it took a hell of a lot of mental energy. It was just that he also worked on his own ranch when he wasn't working on the wine part of things, and he knew that his own hands were rough as hell.

She was too soft. Too cosseted. Snobby. Uppity. Repressed—unless she was giving him a dressing-down with that evil tongue of hers.

And damn he liked it all, as much as he hated it.

The thing was, even if he'd been a different man, a man who had the heart it took to be with someone forever, to do the whole marriage-and-kids thing, if he'd been a man who hadn't been destroyed a long time ago, it wouldn't be her.

Couldn't be her.

A kick of lust shot through him, igniting at the point where their hands still touched. Wren dropped her hold on him quickly. "Well. Good. I guess we'll be seeing a lot more of each other, then."

"I guess we will. Looking forward to it."

"Dear reader," Wren muttered as she walked back into the family winery showroom. "She was not looking forward to seeing more of his arrogant, annoying, infuriating, ridiculous…"

"I'm sorry, what?"

Wren stopped muttering when her sister Emerson popped up from where she was sitting.

"I was muttering," Wren replied.

"I know. What exactly were you muttering about?"

"I was muttering," she restated. "Which means it wasn't exactly meant to be understood."

"Well. I'm nosy."

"I just had my meeting with Creed."

"Oh," Emerson said, looking her over. "Huh."

"What?"

"I'm checking you for burn marks."

"Why? Because he's *Satan*?"

"No. Because the two of you generate enough heat to leave scorched earth."

She narrowed her eyes at her sister. "You'd better be talking about anger."

Regrettably, anger was not the only thing that Creed Cooper made her feel.

Oh, Creed Cooper *enraged* her. She typically found herself wanting to punch him in the face within the first thirty seconds of his company.

He was an asshole. He was insufferable.

He was…without a doubt the sexiest man she had

ever encountered in her entire life and when she woke up at night in a cold sweat with her pulse pounding between her thighs, it was always because she had been dreaming of him.

"Yeah," Emerson said. "Anger."

"What?" Wren snapped.

"It's just… I don't know. The two of you seem to be building up to some kind of hate-sex situation."

Wren shifted, hating that she felt so seen in the moment. "No."

"Why not?" Emerson asked.

"Several reasons. The first being that he disgusts me." Her cheeks turned pink when the bold-faced lie slipped out of her mouth.

"Is that what the kids are calling it these days?"

"You would know. You're…*on fleek* on the internet. Or whatever."

"That is an incredibly passé bit of pop culture there, Wren. And I think we both know disgust is not what he makes you feel."

She pulled a face. "Can we talk about business?"

"Sure, sure. So, what was your conclusion?"

"He's a dick."

"Yeah. I know. But what about the initiative?"

"Oh. He's on board. So I guess we'll be having a party. But he's insisting on barbecuing."

"Barbecuing?" Emerson asked, her sister's hand rising upward, bent at the wrist, her fingers curled.

"Yes." Wren lifted her nose. "Beef."

"I guess that's what we get for joining forces with cowboys."

"Says the woman who's married to one."

Emerson shrugged. "Sure. But I don't let him plan my parties. He has many uses, the primary one being that he allows me to do good work and save horses."

"Save horses?"

She batted her lashes. "Ride a cowboy?"

"For the love of God, Emerson."

"What? He's hot."

She was not here for her sister's smug married-frequent-sex glow. Emerson had very narrowly escaped an arranged marriage with a man their father had chosen for her. The whole thing with her husband, Holden, had been dramatic, had involved no small amount of blackmail and subterfuge, and had somehow ended in true love.

Wren still didn't quite understand it.

Wren also didn't understand why she felt so beset by her Creed fantasies. Or why she was so jealous of Emerson's glow.

Wren herself wasn't overly sexual.

It wasn't her thing. She'd had a few boyfriends, and she enjoyed the physical closeness that came with sex. That much was true. It had been a while since she'd dated anybody though, because she had been so consumed with her job at Maxfield Vineyards. She enjoyed what she did for work quite a lot more than she enjoyed sex, in point of fact.

Her dreams about illicit sex with Creed were better than any sex she'd ever had, and she found that completely disturbing.

Also, proof that her subconscious didn't know anything. Nothing at all.

"Great," Wren said. "Good for you and your libido.

But I'm talking about wine, which is far more important than how hot your husband is."

"To you," Emerson said. "The hotness of my husband is an entirely consuming situation for me."

"Anyway," Wren said, her voice firm. "We get our joint party."

"But with beef."

"Yes," Emerson said. "And then hopefully in a few months we'll have the larger event, which we can presell tickets to. Hopefully we can bring a lot of people into town if we plan it right."

"I do like the way you're thinking," Wren said. "It's going to be great," she added, trying to affirm it for herself.

"It will be," Emerson agreed. "Have you talked to Cricket about it at all?"

Cricket was their youngest sister. She had been… She had been incredibly wounded about the entire scandal with their father.

The situation with their parents had gone from bad to worse. Or maybe it was just that they were all now aware of *how* bad it had always been.

The reason Holden had come to Maxfield Vineyards in the first place had been to get revenge on their father for seducing Holden's younger sister and leaving her emotionally broken after a miscarriage.

After that, Wren and her sisters found out their father had carried on multiple affairs over the years, all with young women who were vulnerable, with so much less power than he had. It was a despicable situation. Holden had blackmailed Emerson into marriage in order to gain a piece of Maxfield Vineyards, but he and Emerson had ultimately fallen in love. They'd ousted their father, who was currently living out of the country. Their mother remained at the estate. Technically, the two of them were still married.

Wren hoped that wouldn't be the case for much longer. Her poor mother had put up with so much. She deserved better.

They all did.

But while most of the changes that had occurred around the winery really were good things, their sister Cricket had taken the new situation hard. She had a different relationship with the place than the rest of them did. Cricket had been a late-in-life baby for their parents. An accident, Wren thought. And it had seemed like no one had the energy to deal with her. She'd been left to her own devices in a way that Emerson and Wren had not been.

As a result, Cricket was ever so slightly feral.

Wren found her mostly charming, but in the current situation, she didn't know how to talk to her. Didn't know what Cricket wanted or needed from them.

"She's been… You know," Emerson said. "Cricket. In that she's not really talking about anything substantial, and she's been quite scarce. She doesn't seem to be interested in any of the winery's new ventures."

"It's a lot of change."

"True," Emerson said. "But she's not a child. She's twenty-one."

"No," Wren said. "She's not a child. But can you imagine how much more difficult this would have been for you ten years ago?"

"I know," Emerson said softly. "It is different for us.

It's different to have a little bit more perspective on the world and on yourself. I think she feels very betrayed."

"Hopefully she'll eventually embrace the winery. She can have a role here. I know she's smart. And I know she would do a good job, whatever Dad thought about her."

Emerson shook her head. "I don't think that Dad thought about her at all."

"Well, we will," Wren said.

The Maxfields had never been a close family in the way people might think of a close family. It wasn't like there had been intimate family dinners and game nights and things like that. But they had been in each other's pockets for their entire lives. Working together, deciding which direction to take their business. Their father was a difficult bastard, that was true. But he had entrusted his daughters with an extreme amount of responsibility when it came to the winery. It was weird now, to have the shape of things be so different. To have everything be up to them.

"Everything will be fine," Wren said. "It's already better, even if it is a little difficult."

Emerson nodded. "You're right. It's better. And things will only get even better from here."

"You agreed to do *what*?"

Creed looked at his older brother, Jackson, who had an expression on his face that suggested Creed might've said he planned to get out of the wine business and start raising corgis, rather than just coordinating an event with the Maxfield family.

"You heard me the first time," Creed said.

"What's the point of that? They're a bunch of ass-holes."

Normally, Creed would not have argued. Or even felt the inclination to argue. But for some reason, he thought back to Wren's determined face, and the way her body had looked in that dress, and he felt a bit defensive.

"You know the girls are running it now," he said. "James Maxfield absolutely was an asshole. I agree with you. But things are different now, and they're running things differently."

"Right. So you suddenly kissed and made up with Wren Maxfield?"

The idea of kissing Wren sent a lightning bolt of pleasure straight down to his cock. And the idea of… making up with her made his gut turn.

"Not a damn chance," Creed responded.

"So, the two of you are going to do this, while at each other's throats the entire time?"

"The logistics aren't exactly your concern. The logistics are my concern, as always. You just…be a silent partner." Creed narrowed his eyes. "You're awfully loud for a silent partner."

"I'm not technically a *full-on* silent partner," Jackson said. "It's just that I would rather invest money than make decisions."

"So then I'm letting you know what the plan is." Creed thought back to the moment he had told Wren that he was going to barbecue. Now he had to barbecue. "We have to bring some grills."

"I'm not even going to ask."

"Fine with me."

"I'm sorry, what are we planning?" Their younger

sister, Honey, walked into the room. She was named by their mother, who had been so thrilled to have a daughter after having two sons that she had decided her daughter was sweet and needed a name that suggested so.

Honey had retaliated by growing into a snarky tomboy who had never seen the use for a dress and didn't know which end of a tube of lipstick to use. He had always been particularly fond of his sister.

"An event. With the Maxfields," Jackson said.

Her mouth dropped open. "Are you out of your mind?"

"I asked him that already," Jackson grunted.

"Well, ask again. Then check him for brain damage."

"No more brain damage than I had already," Creed said.

"Then why are we doing this?" Honey asked.

"Because," he said, taking a long moment to chew on the words that were about to come out next, because they hurt. "Wren had a point. She thinks we should join the wineries together. Make this area more of a tourist destination for wine. Wine trails, and things like that. There's no point in being competitive when we can advertise for each other. People like to try all different kinds of wines, and experience all different atmospheres when they're on vacation."

"You sound like a brochure," Jackson said.

He probably did. Mostly because Wren had sounded like one and he was basically repeating her. "Well. That's a good thing," Creed said. "Since we need some new brochures. And somebody has to write them. It isn't going to be either of you."

"True," Honey said cheerfully.

"You do have to help me barbecue. And you have

to help set up this party. I need you two there. If for no other reason than to be witnesses."

"Witnesses to what?" Jackson asked.

"Just in case Wren decides to murder me."

"You could take her," Honey said.

Yeah. He could take her. That was for damn sure. But not in the way his sister meant. "You know I would never hurt a lady."

"That's far too gallant if the lady is willing to murder you," Honey said pragmatically.

"You could try to be less annoying," Jackson said.

"Look," Creed said. "She came to me. So, it's up to her to behave herself. I didn't go to her, and I wouldn't have."

Though, truth be told, he would have to behave himself, too. The prospect of spending extra time with Wren Maxfield was definitely problematic. But he'd spent the last five years *not* touching her. A few weeks of working in close proximity shouldn't be an issue.

Hell. They *wouldn't* be.

Because when Creed Cooper decided something, he stuck to it. Control was what he was all about. He might be a rich cowboy who could have everything he wanted, but that didn't mean he *did* have everything he wanted. Not anymore. Not after he had experienced the disastrous consequences of that kind of behavior.

He had learned his lesson.

And he would never again make the mistakes he'd made as a kid.

That was for damn sure.

Chapter 2

Sometimes it still felt strange and disorienting to walk through the large Italian villa-style home, knowing their father would likely never return. That everything here had been previously certain but now...wasn't.

For as long as Wren could remember, her life had been on a steady course. Everything had been the same. From the time she was a child she had known she would work for Maxfield Vineyards. And the only real question had been in what capacity. Emerson's contribution had been based on her strengths. She was a social media wizard, but that was not something anyone could have anticipated, considering the medium hadn't existed in the same form when they were younger.

But Wren... Wren had always had a talent for hospitality. She had always been able to make people feel at ease. Even when everything had been going well in her parents' marriage, from the outside looking in, there had been an invisible band of tension in the house. The tension had only ever been worse when they were dealing with the Coopers. Whatever the reason, her father hated that family. And he had instilled a hefty dose of that dislike in her. Though, Creed had taken that dislike to a personal level.

Even so, Wren was an expert at managing tension. And making everything seem like it was okay. Delightful, even when it was decidedly less so.

Even when she and Creed wanted to dismember each other, they could both do their jobs. She imagined that was why he was in his position in his family company. The same as she was in hers.

Event planning and liaising with other companies in a personal way to create heightened brand recognition was something she excelled at. But, it had also been the only real surprise in her entire life. Apart from when James Maxfield had been utterly and completely disgraced.

Yes. That was really the first time her life had taken an unexpected turn.

She still wasn't sure how she felt about it. On the one hand, her father was clearly a monster. And, having never been…*emotionally* close with him—not in the way Emerson had been—it didn't devastate Wren. But it did leave her feeling adrift.

Now she was drifting into uncharted territory with this Cowboy Wines partnership, and she truly did not know how she felt about that either. But it was happening. So, there wasn't much to be done about it.

In fact, she was meeting with Creed this morning. The two of them were going to be talking logistics and deciding which wines to feature. They wanted to showcase the broad spectrum of what each wine label did best, while not stepping on each other's toes. Unusual, since generally they were deliberately going head-to-head.

But now they weren't. Another unusual thing in a slew of unusual things.

She got into her shiny little sports car and pulled out of the grand circular drive that led to the top of the mountain where the family home sat. She took the drive all the way down to the road, and as she put distance between herself and the villa, she was surprised to realize the pressure she hadn't noticed building in her chest began to get lighter and lighter.

And that shouldn't be what was happening. She should be feeling more and more stressed the closer she got to Creed. It didn't track with what she knew to be true about herself.

That she loved her family and her life and *hated* him.

She mused about that as she maneuvered her car down the winding two-lane road, through the picturesque main street of Gold Valley, Oregon.

Her family had been based here all her life, but she had always felt somewhat separate from it. She and her sisters had gone to boarding school on the East Coast, coming back to Oregon for summers.

All the men she'd dated had been from back east. Long-distance relationships that had become inconvenient and annoying over time.

But those men had been like her. Educated in the

same kinds of institutions, from families like her own. In fact, in those groups, often she was among the poorest. Hilarious, all things considered. But that made her feel…somewhat out of place here. She didn't go out drinking at the Gold Valley Saloon, a favorite watering hole of most people who lived here.

She didn't have occasion to eat at any of the local restaurants, because they had a chef at home. They threw lavish parties at the villa, and ultimately… She just didn't often venture out of the estate. She had never considered herself sheltered. Not in the least. Instead, she had considered herself worldly by comparison with most of the people who lived in Gold Valley.

She had traveled extensively. Been to some of the most lavish resorts in the world. But suddenly it seemed obvious to her that she existed in a very particular kind of bubble—by choice—and there was something about having to face who her father really was that had…well, *disturbed* the bubble she lived in. It hadn't popped it altogether. She remained in it. But as she passed through town, the thoughts about her father passed through her mind, and she focused on getting her armor in place so she could deal with Creed.

Creed's family vineyard was beautiful. The winery facilities themselves were not her style at all, but they were pretty, and she could appreciate them. Rustic barns that had been fashioned into showrooms and event spaces, along with picnic tables that were set up down by the river, live bands often playing during the summer. She knew that food trucks came in during those events and added to the down-home atmosphere.

She could see why it appealed.

Now she really was worried that she had a headache. Wondering about the local bar and appreciating the aesthetic of this place. She snorted, pulling her car into the showroom lot and getting out, immediately scuffing her high heel on the gravel.

Oh, *there it was*.

All the ready irritation that she possessed for this place, and the man she was about to meet.

Her beautiful yellow leather pumps all scuffed…

And then, she nearly fell off her beautiful yellow leather pumps, because suddenly he was standing in the doorway, his arms crossed over his broad chest and his expression as unreadable as ever. He looked cool. His lips flattened into a grim line, his square jaw locked tight. His green eyes were assessing her. And that was the thing she hated the most. He was always doing that. Looking at her as if he could see straight through her dress. As if he could see through her chest. As if he could see things she wasn't sure she had ever examined inside herself.

She didn't like it.

Added to the *long* list of things she didn't like about him. That one went right below his being way too handsome for his—or her—own good.

"Howdy, ma'am."

"Sup, asshole." She crossed her arms, mirroring his own posture.

"I thought you were supposed to be a lady."

"That's the thing. I know how to behave like a lady in the right venue. I also know how to go toe to toe with anyone. A by-product of my private school education. Rich people are mean."

"Well. *You're* certainly mean."

She shifted uncomfortably. "Not always."

She didn't know why she felt compelled to strike at him. Constantly. Why had they slipped into the space of open hostility with such ease?

You don't know?

Okay. Maybe she had a fair enough idea. But she didn't want to marinate on it. Not at all.

"Just to me?" he asked. "Aren't I special."

He moved away from the door and allowed her entry into the tasting room. There, he had several bottles of wine out on the table. They were already uncorked, glasses sitting next to them.

"Isn't this nice?" she asked.

"You didn't answer my question."

"You're certainly something," she responded. The answer seemed to settle between them, rather than striking immediate sparks. But that left an odd note lingering in the air. They just stared at each other for a long moment. And it was like everything in the air around them went elastic, stretched, then held tight.

"Nice to know."

She had hoped that his voice, his words, might banish that strange threat of tension. But it didn't. No. If anything, it felt worse. Because there was something about that voice that seemed to shiver over her skin, leaving goose bumps behind.

"Don't let it go to your…head." His eyes dipped down, to her lips, then lower.

"Let's drink wine," she said, far too bright and crisp and obviously trying to move them along from whatever was happening now.

"Did you bring some for me to try?"

"Yes. I have a crate in the car…"

"I've got it." He extended his hand.

"What?"

"Keys?"

"Oh." She dug in her purse for her key fob, and clicked it twice. "It's open."

He went outside and returned a moment later with a crate full of wine bottles slung up over his shoulder.

And it was… Well, it was impossible for her not to admire all that raw male beauty. His strength.

He had big hands. The muscles on his forearms shifted as he slung the crate down with ease onto the table, beginning to take the wine bottles out. They looked small in those hands. For some reason, she had an immediate image of those hands on her hips. All that strength, all that…largeness…

That was another thing.

She felt outside a lot of experiences here. And she had never… Well. Not with a man like him.

All of her past relationships had been based on having things in common. Liking each other. Being able to see a potential future, where she served as the appropriate ornament, and they served as the appropriate accessory.

The kinds of people who fit into each other's lives with ease, and because of that decided to make a go at fitting into bed with each other.

As a result, she hadn't had the most exciting sex life. It had been fine.

But she never had a wild…well, a wild anything.

She hadn't gone out to bars and hooked up.

Creed Cooper was a bar-hookup kind of guy. She just had that feeling.

That he was the kind of man women saw from across the room, all warm with whiskey and the promise of bad decisions, and thought… *He looks like a terrible choice.*

Before gleefully climbing on.

She had never done anything like that and there was something about him that made her think of those things. If she was honest, made her yearn for those things. A rough, bad decision like the kind she'd never made before.

"Let's get to pouring," he said.

And so they did. Portioning out samples for each other to try.

Infinitely safer and better than her standing there pondering the potential badness of climbing on top of Creed.

"Should we start here?" He picked up a glass of Maxfield Chardonnay.

"It's as good as any as far as I'm concerned," she said. Though, now she was feeling fragile and like maybe she shouldn't be drinking around the man. Her thoughts were doing weird things. But she'd been in a weird space since she had driven away from the house today. Or maybe, since even before then.

She was familiar with this wine, and it was one of her favorites. Citrusy, with notes of white peach and apricot. It was a decent wine for her mood because of the tartness.

"Nice," he said. "Very nice."

"I thought it might pain you to admit that," she said.

"Not at all. Actually, I would be disappointed if I

didn't like your wine. Because I would hate to be in competition with somebody who was terrible."

"I suppose that's a fair call," she said.

"Us next."

He offered her Cabernet Sauvignon, and the notes were completely different from the Chardonnay. Smoky oak and rich espresso. It reminded her of him. Full-bodied and rich. Tempting, but a very bad idea to overindulge in.

"Nice," she said.

"A compliment from you," he said dryly. "What an achievement."

"Not one I would think you'd care about."

"I didn't say I *cared*. I was just remarking."

"You're irritating," she said, taking another sip of the wine. They moved through the wines, and she felt a looseness in her limbs. Relaxation pouring through her. She knew how to taste wine without getting drunk. So she had to assume the feeling had something to do with him. Which was honestly more disturbing than thinking she might have overindulged.

"Why shouldn't I be irritating? You're no better."

The smug male arrogance in those words rankled. He tipped his too handsome face backward and took another sip of wine. "You know, this event might also need a bouncy castle."

"No," she said.

He wasn't serious. She knew that. That was ridiculous. This was not going to be some family Sunday picnic. He knew her well enough to know that, whether he agreed or not.

"A dunk tank."

"Absolutely not," she responded. "It's happening in October."

"This is your problem, Wren. You can't think outside the box. You want to bring two labels together that historically have never had anything to do with each other. You want to bring together two very different types of people."

"The kinds of people that are at my winery do not want bouncy castles. Or children running around anywhere."

"Oh, they want perfect little Stepford children just like all of you were?"

Irritation twisted in her stomach. "You don't know me. You don't know us."

"Don't I? You're proving that I do. You're all worried about appearances here, like you always have been, when this whole thing with your daddy should have taught you appearances don't mean much of anything."

"How dare you?" She was trembling now, irritation turning to total outrage. "How dare you bring my father into this?"

"It was too easy."

"I've been through enough. We've been through enough. I don't need you flinging things at me about my family that I can't control. You want to talk about living in a box… You've never even left here, have you?"

"We both know that's not true. A fair amount of travel is required to do this job."

"Did you even go to college?" she asked.

"No," he responded. "I was too busy working to build the family label. I guess you think attending college makes you smarter than me, but all it means is you were from a different sort of family. You see, we are not from money. Not like you. You think that makes you better, but it doesn't. Because you know what else? My dad never sexually harassed a woman either. Unlike yours."

Raged poured through her and she fought to keep from showing just how mad he'd made her. He was doing it on purpose. He didn't deserve the satisfaction of knowing he'd succeeded in getting to her.

"Where is your damn wine cellar?" she asked. "I want to go look at what else you have."

"You don't want to keep having this conversation?"

"I never wanted to start having it," she said, each word coming out in a monotone. Because if she allowed her voice to amp up, she was going to say something she would regret.

Not that there was much she could say in anger that she would regret having spat out at Creed. It wasn't the anger that scared her. It was everything that hummed underneath it. That it could still hum underneath when she was so infuriated with him. When he was being such a…such an unrepentant asshole.

"Wine cellar's this way," he said.

He led the way to the back of the barn, where there was a staircase that led straight down.

She was reluctantly charmed by it. By the uneven rock walls that gave it the vague feel of a French country home. The thick, uneven slabs of wood that made up the staircase, making it feel old-world and resonant.

She was irritated she didn't hate it. She was irritated that he had homed in on the exact thing about herself that was bothering her at the moment.

That he had managed to poke at her exact point of insecurity. All the things she had been thinking of when she had driven into town. About how there was this whole other life here—a whole other life in general—that she had never even considered living because she was a...a *Stepford child*. It was exactly what she had been.

Going where her father had chosen for her to go, growing into exactly what he had wanted her to grow into. Taking the job he had given her. And she was still doing it all. All of the exact same things she had done before her father had gone away. Before he had stepped down from the company in disgrace.

And it did make her wonder... What creature had she been fashioned into?

And for whom?

She didn't think there was an alternative reality where she would be in favor of a bouncy castle at her event, but she truly didn't know. She could only speculate.

Everyone is a product of their circumstances. Don't be so hard on yourself.

She nearly nodded at the affirmation she gave herself. The problem was, she couldn't agree. Because she wasn't actually ever all that hard on herself.

She never made any mistakes. Not in the way that she thought of mistakes. Because she had always, without fail, done exactly what she had been charged with.

By your father.

And still, her father had never been effusive about his pride in her. But she had lived for that praise. Because who didn't? Who didn't want to make their father happy? And her father was... He was a monster.

All these thoughts had her feeling absolutely and completely off-kilter. And that was only serving to make her even angrier at Creed. How could she handle all of this stuff *and* him? And how dare he cut her so close to the bone?

He didn't know her. He didn't have the right to say the things he'd said. To say things that made her feel more seen than anything anyone in her family had ever said. That was for sure.

"So, the Cooper family is just all rainbows and butterflies?" she asked as they made their way through the aisles of wine.

"And horseshit," he said. "Which wine were you thinking?"

"I don't know. Pick something good."

"The array of wine upstairs is good," he said. "That's why I picked them."

"Something different." She felt difficult and she didn't care.

"Rainbows and butterflies," he reiterated. "And my dad's not a criminal."

"And all of you work here at the family winery because you just love each other so much."

"Is that difficult for you to believe?"

It wasn't. Not really. There was a reason she was choosing to stay at the Maxfield winery, after all.

A reason that went beyond just being afraid to start over, or not knowing what else she would do.

Emerson was her rock, and Cricket needed her.

"I'm close with my sisters," Wren said. "I love them."

"And I love *my* family. You ought to love your family."

"I'm just saying. I'm not in a box. I just know who I

am." Those words had never felt less true. Not that she loved her family. She did love her family. It was just that right now she felt like she was wearing a Wren suit and somewhere inside was a different creature. She felt like she was inhabiting the wrong body. The wrong space.

"Honestly, Wren, if you believed that, you wouldn't be so bound and determined to try to convince me."

"You don't know me," she said. "You're not my friend."

"Something we can agree on."

"You don't get to say what I know or don't know. You just don't."

"Too late. I did."

"You're such a… You're ridiculous."

"Just take a bottle of wine so we can get on with this. I will feel a lot better dealing with you if I'm drunker."

"This isn't exactly a picnic for me either," she said. "You are without a doubt the most insufferable man I've ever known."

"You don't like me, Wren?" he asked, taking a step toward her. "However will I survive?"

"The same as you always do, I imagine," she said. "High on an unearned sense of self-confidence and a little testosterone poisoning."

He huffed. "You like it," he said.

"I'm sorry, what?"

"You like it. My testosterone. You'd like to be poisoned by it, admit it."

"There's that sense of unearned self-confidence," she said, her heart hammering steadily against her chest. "Right on time."

"It's not unearned. I watch you. When we fight. Your face gets all flushed."

"That's called anger."

"Why? What is it about me that makes you so damned angry?"

"You... You are just...a useless, base ape."

"Base?" He asked the question with a dangerous sort of softness to his voice, and it made her tremble. "That's what you think? That I'm like an animal who can't control himself?"

"Yes," she spat. "I know all about you and your reputation. You get drunk at the bar, you pick up women every night of the week."

"I don't get drunk," he said. "That's not me."

"Maybe that's how you see yourself, but it's not what I hear. I hear that you're just a big, dumb, blunt instrument. You might go on and on about how you pulled yourself up by your bootstraps, but your daddy made all this happen. You might wear a cowboy hat, but there's a silver spoon in your mouth the same as mine. So don't you dare go acting like you're better than me just because you can't be bothered to put on an ounce of refinement. Because you don't have the manners to leave my dad out of a conversation. Just because you can't be bothered to try to be a...a civilized human being."

"You think I'm an animal, Wren?" he asked again, his voice low and rough. "You think I don't control my baser instincts? I have, Princess. You don't even know. Maybe it's time you saw what it looks like when I don't."

And that was how she found herself being backed up against one of the stone walls in the wine cellar, six-foot-plus of angry man staring down at her, his green eyes blazing. "You want an animal?" He put his hand on her hip, and she nearly combusted. "I've half a mind to give you one."

Her heart was thundering so hard she felt like it might rattle the buttons clean off the front of her blouse. And if it did, it would leave her top open. And then he would be able to…

She was throbbing between her thighs, her throat utterly and completely dry. This couldn't be happening. This had to be some kind of fever dream. The kind of dream she had every other night when she had to deal with Creed.

When anger turned into something much hotter, and much more *naked*.

But it couldn't be real. Anger couldn't really turn into this seething, hot well of need, could it? This couldn't really be what was beneath all of their fighting. That was… That was her being confused.

Her having some kind of fantasy that allowed her to take control of him.

That was just what she told herself whenever she had sex dreams about him.

That sure, he might be hot, but she didn't actually want to *have sex with him*. It was just that the idea of manipulating him with her body appealed to her subconscious, because it was always such a sparring contest in real life.

And the idea that maybe her breasts could reduce him slightly was tempting.

But that wasn't real. People didn't really do this.

She didn't really do this.

You're just trapped in a box…

And suddenly, she wondered what it might be like

if she did really do this. If she dared. If she returned his volley right now.

If she let herself be the animal she'd accused him of being.

She'd gotten to him. Really and truly. Something about her accusing him of lacking civility and control clearly irritated him. And she wanted to keep on doing it. She wanted to push him.

She arched her hips forward, and her pelvis came into contact with the evidence of just what he was feeling, there in the front of his jeans. He was hard. He might be mad, but he was hard. For her.

"Oh, I see," she said. "So that's your real problem. Pulling my pigtails on the playground because you like me?" She rolled her hips forward, and she nearly gasped at the sensation. She might be taunting him, but she was on the verge of overheating. Spontaneously combusting. "If you want me to lift up my skirt so you can see my panties, you should've just asked."

"You're infuriating," he bit out.

"No more so than you."

"You know what, I'm tired of that smart mouth of yours. Maybe it's time you found something else to occupy it with."

And before she could say anything else, those lips had crashed down on hers. He was kissing her, hard and deep. And he was so… Hot and strong and male. So far and beyond any man she had ever touched before. She was used to civilized men. And he might be angry that she'd called him uncivilized, but the fact remained that he was. Dangerously so.

She was panting, writhing against him as he cupped

the back of her head so he could take the kiss deeper. His tongue was hot and slick against hers, and the friction made a well of need open up between her thighs. She felt hollow, she felt… Like she might die if she didn't have him. Thrusting hard and deep inside her.

"You talk big," she said against his mouth. "I hope you've got the equipment to back that up."

"I've never had any complaints, Princess."

"I'm sure I could find a few."

"No, baby. You're not going to have any. Not after this."

"Are you just going to talk? Or are you going to fuck me?"

She had never spoken to a man like that in her life. Had never even dreamed of saying something so raw and carnal. Because she'd never been this desperate before. And it didn't matter. Because it was Creed Cooper, and he didn't even like her. So it didn't matter what he thought of her. Didn't matter if he thought she was dirty or bad or wrong for talking to him that way. For demanding that he take her up against a wall. For fighting with him with one breath, and demanding he do something about the heat between them with the next.

There were no boxes here. That was the beautiful thing. There was nothing but this.

"My pleasure."

Then her shirt was torn open. Buttons scattered all over the floor, and she didn't care. He pulled her bra down, exposing her breasts, and then those big, rough hands were cupping her tender flesh, his thumbs skimming over her nipples.

She gasped, arching toward him, reveling in the way she filled his palms. She had never been like this.

And suddenly, as he stripped layers of clothes off her skin, she felt like that suit had been removed along with it. That layer that had felt so foreign. So wrong. And even though she had never in all her life behaved like this, the situation suddenly felt more real. Suddenly felt more like who she was. Like the Wren beneath all that she had been created to be.

It was her turn next. She pushed his shirt, shrugged it over his shoulders, and revealed a body that put her wildest fantasies to shame.

She hadn't known. Not really.

She hadn't even begun to guess how beautiful the man was. How much all those muscles would appeal to her. His chest hair, the scar on his side. Everything that made him a rough, uncultured-looking man, the likes of which she had never had before.

And everything after that became a blur.

A fumble born out of desperation.

She worked at his jeans while he pushed her skirt up over her hips, hooking his finger around the elastic on her underwear and shoving it to the side while she freed his cock. It was big and thick, gorgeous. And she had never particularly thought that part of the male anatomy was *gorgeous* before, but that was the only word for it. A thing of actual beauty. She was far too happy for herself to be annoyed with him that his outrageous ego was not in fact misplaced. He had earned the right to be full of himself.

And all she wanted was to be full of him, too.

"Please," she whispered against his mouth.

"That's the first time you've ever asked me nicely for anything," he growled, pressing the head of his arousal to the entrance of her body, teasing her, teasing them both.

She'd never been so wet so fast in her life. So ready. She had never craved penetration like this before. She had never craved another person like this before.

She had never thought much about her sex drive, because it had never really felt like a drive. She had thought of it as something like a sweet tooth. Something people had to varying degrees, and sure, sometimes a piece of cake would be nice. But she just wasn't one of those people who obsessively craved sugar, or sex.

This felt like a drive. An urge. Something that came from deep inside her that she couldn't control or minimize. This was something like insanity.

"Did you still want that fuck, sweetheart?" His voice was a growl, feral and compelling.

"Yes," she said. "Please yes."

And then he was inside her.

He was so big that it stretched at first. Hurt a little bit. But in the best way.

Every time he drew away and then thrust back into her body, he did so with a growl. And she clung to him, the hard drive of him deep inside her everything she had fantasized about and more. She had not truly known that it could be like this. She had thought that people made up stories. She had thought for sure that...

Well, when her sister had lost her mind over Holden, Wren had judged her.

But she hadn't known it could be like this.

Raw and terrifying. Wonderful. Electric.

There had been no more denying this than there was denying herself air.

It seemed to make perfect sense now. This thing that had mystified her only a moment before. This anger turned need that rocked everything she was.

Of course, this was right next to the anger that was always threatening to combust between them. Of course, this was the other side of all that need. Of course.

How had she ever thought it was anything else?

He whispered things in her ear. Dirty things. Shocking things. But he called her beautiful. And he kissed the side of her neck, and it made her feel like she might break apart. She didn't know why.

And then suddenly, everything came to a head, and she couldn't breathe. All she could do was cling to him, to keep herself from collapsing onto the ground, to keep herself from flying into a million pieces. She dug her fingernails into his shoulder and cried out as pleasure took over. He wasn't far behind. On a growl, he found his own release, his body pulsing inside her. And when it was over, they both collapsed there against the wall, sweaty and breathing hard.

"This wine," he said, reaching around her. "This will do." He grabbed the bottle, then bent and picked his shirt up from off the floor. He righted his clothes disturbingly fast, and then left her standing there.

She tucked her blouse as firmly into her skirt as she could, crossing the bottom ends and getting the thing to more or less cover her breasts. And then she just stood there for a moment, shell-shocked.

She'd just had sex with Creed Cooper against the wall. And he had walked away like they hadn't missed a beat between talking about wine and screwing each other senseless.

She pushed the skirt down over her hips. If it wasn't for the intense throbbing between her legs... If it wasn't for that, she would have thought she had hallucinated it all. Because how... How had that just happened?

She grabbed another bottle of wine, not even reading the label, and walked back upstairs. He was in position, his face like absolute granite.

"Want to finish tasting?"

"Are you... Did you hit your head down there?" she asked.

"Where?"

"Why are you acting like we didn't just have sex?"

"It's done," he said.

There was something bleak in his green eyes, and it disturbed her. She was a woman. Wasn't she the one who was supposed to freak out about this kind of thing? She wasn't particularly worried about how many partners she'd had, but it was one of those things other women often seemed to worry about. But he was the one who looked...well, vaguely ashamed.

"It's just that..."

Those green eyes were hard as emeralds now. "I don't really want to talk about it."

"Why not?"

"It's not going to happen again."

Well, on that they could agree. Because there was no way—absolutely no way—that she would ever do anything like that with him again. It had been stupid to do it the first time.

Even though it had felt amazing. She wanted to tell

him that. She wanted to cling to him, for just a little while longer. To make him hold her up, because her knees still felt weak. To tell him it was the best sex she'd ever had, and she didn't know what to do with the knowledge that the man who could make her body do things she hadn't known it could do was the one man she had decided she hated more than any other.

She wanted to ask him why that was, because he had taken pleasure with her, too, so maybe he could understand it. He'd certainly had more partners than she had. Had more experience overall. So surely he should be able to…

And she realized she was being a ridiculous stereotype. A woman who was putting emotions into something that had been purely physical.

She had been caught up in that moment. In being outside herself. Well, she had done something out of character. And that was that. There was no going back. But there was also no need to continue on with it now.

He was still Creed. She was still Wren.

She didn't like him any more now that she'd seen him naked than she had before.

Well. That wasn't true.

The man had given her the most insane orgasm of her life. It would be impossible not to like him slightly more now than she had before.

"I trust you to make your selections," she said. She felt numb and shaky. And maybe he had a point that the two of them should act like nothing had happened, but she couldn't do it while in the same room as him.

"I'll just leave you to it."

"You're leaving?"

"Yes," she said. "We'll be in touch."

It wasn't until she got back in her car, and was safely back on the road, that she started shaking. She had lived out some kind of fantasy she hadn't even fully realized she'd had. She'd had sex with her enemy up against the wall. She didn't intend to have a relationship with him. They couldn't. They couldn't even be in the same room without biting each other's head off.

She didn't like him. He didn't like her.

It had been just… Just to feel good.

And then, in spite of the shaking, in spite of the nerves riding through her body, she felt a smile curve her lips. Maybe what she'd done had been out of character. But it had been her choice. And she had liked it. She had liked it a lot. And what was wrong with that? What was wrong with doing something wild? She hadn't hurt anybody, not like her dad. And she hadn't done it for anyone else. She had done it for her. She had done it because she hadn't been able to make any other choice. Because she had wanted it so damn much.

That was a Wren choice. The real Wren. The Wren who lived somewhere deep inside her. Who didn't just do things for approval, or because it was easy. Because it was the next step on the path.

She couldn't help but be proud of herself for that.

And she couldn't be ashamed of it either.

For the first time in her life, Wren Maxfield had done something truly spontaneous. And she was just going to enjoy it.

Chapter 3

Eighteen years of flawless self-control had been completely destroyed in under an hour. He could throw a whole parade fueled by his guilt and regret. The trouble with guilt and regret, for him, was that it was such a tiresome old standby that his body immediately converted it to anger.

He was currently outside on his ranch trying to burn off the rage that was firing through his veins. She had done this to him. She had made him into something he didn't recognize. Or worse, something he did recognize. Someone he knew from a long time ago. Someone who had made mistakes others had to pay for.

Damn Wren Maxfield.

And damn his libido.

He was thirty-four years old. He was better than that.

Better than a quick screw against a wall. Better than ig-
noring her and what had happened right after.

Dammit. He had not handled that well.

He picked up a large boulder, hefted it upward, then
walked about five feet before dropping it down in the
spot where he was building a retaining wall near his
house.

The ground was soft and slick here, made of clay,
and when it rained, it had a bad habit of turning into a
flood, and quickly. So he was building a wall to make
sure that the water funneled where he wanted it to fun-
nel. He'd already dug a trench, which had helped with
a little of his frustration. Lifting boulders would hopefully be the antidote for the rest of it.

"I thought I might find you here."

He turned and saw his brother, Jackson, standing
there, leaning against the stone post at the bottom of
the driveway.

"What are you doing here?"

"Thought I might ask you the same thing. Since you
didn't show up to the winery this morning."

"I had work to do here." He gestured to the stones.

"Looks like it. Except… Normally you let us know
when you're not coming in."

"Since when are you so up in all the winery stuff?"

"I always have been. It's just that I don't usually have
to come looking for you. So maybe you don't notice."

"Did Dad send you?"

"No. But he did ask after you."

"Well, Dad needs to keep himself busy."

In the two years since their mother had died, their
dad had become something of a hermit. The work at the

winery had shifted more to Creed, Jackson and Honey. It was difficult for Law Cooper to deal with the loss of his wife. In fact, it could be argued that he hadn't dealt with it at all. He'd simply buried his head in the sand, doing things on the ranch that didn't require him to interact much with people.

"You know, I'm not sure I believe Dad asked after me."

"He did," Jackson said, a strange blankness in his expression. "He worries about you. He worries about all of us. Hell, I think he worries about everything these days."

"Maybe he should start doing winery work again. It might take his mind off things."

"Might."

"Anyway. Now you know where I am. You could have called like a normal person."

"You wouldn't have answered. Because you're avoiding me."

"What makes you think I'm avoiding you? I don't come into work one morning and you immediately think it's about you? Nice ego on you, Jackson."

"All right, not me specifically," Jackson said. "But something."

"It's just this whole thing planning the party." Creed figured he would get close enough to the truth without actually giving his brother all of it, and that would probably be more believable. "That woman is giving me hell."

"Scared of a girl?" Jackson took a swing at him, verbally. He was his older brother, and Creed knew he lived for that.

Creed wasn't in the mood.

He shot his brother a dead-eyed look. "I live for the day a woman gives you hell."

"Not going to happen," Jackson said. "I'm not going to let myself get tangled up in knots over a woman. Especially not a Maxfield."

"The only other Maxfield is Cricket. And she'd kick your ass if you came near her."

Jackson snorted. "I'd kick my own ass ten ways till Sunday if I ever did anything that stupid. She's... young." He grimaced. "Wren, on the other hand, is perfectly age appropriate. If you want her, just have sex with her and get it over with."

Creed gritted his teeth. "That's not always the answer, Jackson."

"Look," he said. "I know you had a bad experience. But it's not like you're a monk."

"No," Creed responded. "I'm not. It isn't that I quit having sex, but I don't let my body tell me what to do."

Too bad he had. Too bad he had one hundred percent followed his libido and nothing else.

And he knew that he should talk to Wren about the fact that they hadn't used protection. But she was a grown woman. She was probably on birth control, and if she wasn't, she would handle anything she needed to on her own.

"The problem is that you banged her already," Jackson said, his expression suddenly going sly. "And you're pissed about it."

Creed about ground his teeth into powder. "Go away."

"You did. Well, what the hell are you going to do about it now? Is there any point beating yourself up over it?"

His brother's question gave him pause. "I mean, I think there's always a point in beating yourself up about something."

"Yeah, but you're a martyr. So, let that go for a second. You're a grown person, she's a grown person. You don't like her, who cares? You've been with plenty of women you don't even know."

"Sure. But then the *possibility* for liking them exists."

"What does it matter? You're not going to be in a relationship with her."

"No, but it seems…like the wrong thing to do."

"Sometimes the wrong thing to do feels pretty damn good. Maybe you should try it."

"You forget. I did."

"You're not sixteen anymore. Neither is she. You're not going to have your life gutted by some girl and her family intent on keeping her to the straight-and-narrow path they put her on."

And that was the bottom line of it all. Creed had to keep control, because he knew what happened when he didn't. And more to the point, he knew the way that other people could then take control of your life.

"I know that."

"Yeah, but you act like you don't sometimes."

"If I didn't learn from a mistake like that what kind of fool would I be?" Creed asked.

"The normal kind."

"Well, whatever is going on with that now, you don't know what it's like to disappoint him quite in the way that I did."

Jackson only chuckled. "You don't know everything about my life, little brother. And I don't claim to know everything about yours. But quit moping. We have things to do."

"Since when do you care about any of it?"

"I don't. But honestly, talking about this joint venture with the Maxfields is about the only thing that's gotten a reaction out of Dad in way too long. He was interested in it. And… I care about that."

Well, so did Creed. Anything to get their dad out of his depression. They'd already lost their mother. They didn't need to watch him slowly slip away, too, because of his sadness.

"Then it'll get done. Don't worry about it."

And maybe Jackson even had a point about himself and Wren. They were adults. And as long as everything proceeded with a bit more planning and caution than they had yesterday, what was the harm?

Maybe it was possible for Creed to drink his wine and have his beef, too. Or something like that.

"I'll be down at the winery in a couple of hours," he said. "I really do need to finish this wall."

"All right. See you back at the ranch." His brother tipped his hat, and turned and walked back toward his truck. And he took with him Creed's excuses.

Creed supposed he should write his brother a thank-you note for that. He was right. Creed was good at self-flagellation when it came to losing control. But sex with Wren had been incredible.

What was the harm in going back for more?

That was, if she wasn't too angry at him.

A slow smile spread across his face. Of course… Anger, with them, didn't seem to prevent the sex from happening.

Quite the opposite.

He might never have experienced anything like this before, but he was eager to experience it again.

Wren had managed to keep her interactions with Creed confined to text messages for the last couple of weeks. His responses had all been short and on-topic, and that weirded her out more than anything else. There was no teasing. No goading. Of course, she hadn't teased or goaded him either.

It was weird and unsettling. To not be engaged in some kind of sparring match with him. She would have said that she wanted this distant professionalism that didn't leave her feeling hot, bothered or angry. Anyway, it got all of the planning done for the event. And today it was all ready to go. An open house, of sorts, set out on the front lawn of Maxfield Vineyards.

Thankfully the late October weather was playing nicely, and it was sunny and warm. Oregon Octobers were a gamble. They could be infused with all the warmth of spring, with deeper golds infusing the air. Or they could be gray, damp and snarling, with a harsh bite in the wind.

Today was golden, and so was the event.

There was no dunk tank. Neither was there a bouncy castle. But there were barbecues and smokers, coupled with lovely covered seating areas, and some places that had quilts set out like an old-fashioned picnic. She had to admit, the barbecue was a nice touch. It did make everything seem welcoming.

And people from Gold Valley, along with folks from

the neighboring town of Copper Ridge, seemed to be pouring in to engage in the event.

It was a success. And she was… Well, she was thrilled.

But she felt like she should be something more.

Maybe that was the problem. She was mentally pleased. But she wasn't as happy as she might have been. Because she knew that Creed was going to be here soon. If he wasn't already.

She had spent a few hours early this morning making sure everything was ready to go, so she could go off and get herself dressed and also maybe so she could avoid him.

Anyway, they had a very good team hired to take care of all the logistics, so it wasn't as if she needed to micromanage anything.

Her stomach twisted, butterflies jittering there. She told herself it was because the event was about to begin, and that always made her feel a little bit nervous.

But she could no longer pretend that was the case when it felt like the crowd parted and the sun shined down upon those who had just arrived. Law Cooper, Jackson Cooper, the family's friend and surrogate son, Jericho Smith, and petite, feisty Honey Cooper.

But it was Creed Wren couldn't look away from.

Creed, with a black cowboy hat on his head, a black suit jacket, white shirt opened at the collar, showing a wedge of chest that she now knew full well was as spectacular as advertised.

He had not shown up in jeans and a T-shirt.

Often, even at formal events, he did wear them, as if he was very intentionally flouting convention. He somehow never looked unprofessional. And she knew that had to do with the fact that his choices were just so damned intentional. He wasn't rolling into places that way on accident. No, he was wearing his country roots like a second skin, and it was provocative in their sorts of circles.

But for this, he had dressed up. For this, he had worn a suit. She wanted to...

Well, there was no use marinating on what she wanted to do.

The things she had wanted to do every day since the last time he had touched her.

She had tried to simply appreciate the triumph of a good rebellion. But it wasn't that easy. Because her body was so greedy and desperate for more of what he had given her. For more sex as it existed for others, more of this realm that had been completely unknown to her prior to Creed's touch.

She was *so* messed up.

She probably did need to see a therapist. What had happened with her dad was no small thing, and now she was climbing on top of men who were mean to her. That had to say something about her mental state.

But her physical state had enjoyed it quite a lot, and it was difficult for her to accept it as a one-off. Especially when she kept having sweaty dreams about it.

"Well," she said, looking him up and down. "Don't you clean up nice."

"You, too," he said.

She was very aware that the eyes of every member of his family were on her.

In fact, she was so certain, it took her a while to absorb it since the fact was vaguely embarrassing. But when she did catch his father's eyes, she did not see the speculation she had expected. Instead, he had a strange, wistful look on his face.

"Wren," he said. "Right?"

"Yes," she said.

"You look very much like your mother."

She blinked, feeling a strange sensation at the comment. Her mother was beautiful. But Wren didn't have a lot in common with her. At least, she'd never felt like she had.

Over the years her mother had become more and more quiet. More withdrawn.

And Wren could understand why now. Because clearly not all had been well in her parents' marriage. Her mother must've had a sense that her husband was unfaithful at the very least. A predator at worst.

"Do you know my mother?" she asked.

"A long time ago," he said.

"Let's go find you a place to sit," Honey said, grabbing hold of her father's arm. "Nice to see you."

The youngest Cooper clearly didn't think it was all that nice to see Wren. Jericho and Jackson, on the other hand, were perfectly pleasant. They were both stunningly handsome men, Jackson as tall as his brother, and a bit broader, his eyes the same green. Jericho was even taller, with darker skin and brown eyes, and wide shoulders that looked capable of carrying any number of burdens upon them.

She found them both aesthetically pleasing. But her reaction wasn't the same as what Creed made her feel.

Which was a shame, really, because Jericho and Jackson were so much more pleasant.

"Good to officially meet you," Jericho said, extending his hand. She shook it, then Jackson's.

"It's a great event," Jackson said. "A great idea."

"Well, it's my sister Emerson's doing. Actually, a whole lot of this new direction is."

"I hear her marriage started the tidal wave."

Wren laughed. "The blackmail did."

"Was the blackmail related to the marriage?" Jericho asked.

"Oh, yes," Wren said. "Well, not now. I mean, in the sense that Emerson and Holden are totally fine and no one is being blackmailed to stay in the marriage. It's complicated."

At least, it had been. But now Holden and Emerson just loved each other.

Jackson and Jericho left, which put Wren and Creed far too close to each other.

"Nice to see you. In fact, I was beginning to think you had vaporized."

"No," he said. "Just getting my head on straight. Figured it would be best to focus on the planning of all of this."

"I suppose so," she said.

"Looks amazing."

"You were right about the barbecue. People love it."

"Now, I'm surprised you didn't burst into flame."

"You know, I might have, but recent events left me somewhat inoculated."

"Good to know. I thought they might have left you…"

"Oh, now you're concerned? You certainly didn't

show any concern when you decided to pretend nothing happened."

"Is that what you want to fight about now?"

"I don't know. I haven't decided yet. There's such a huge array of things we could fight about. Considering we haven't seen each other in a couple of weeks and a whole lot has happened. Though, I do think the obvious thing to fight about would be the sex that we had, which you're still trying to pretend didn't happen."

She had not intended to open with that. She hadn't intended to be talking about this with him with guests all around them, and members of their family in close proximity. But it just kind of poured out of her. Maybe it was him. But maybe it was her, too. Maybe it was everything that she was.

Everything that she had become in the last couple of months.

This creature she was trying to remake herself into, in her own image, and not that of her father.

And really... What was the point of watching what she said around Creed? Everything was already as horrifying as it could ever be. Everything was already ruined. There was no dignity left to be had.

She had climbed him like a tree and had an earth-shattering orgasm seconds after he had thrust into her. She was sure she'd left him bleeding from digging her nails into his back. She'd probably caused hearing damage with how loud she'd screamed when she'd come.

There was pretty much no coming back from that.

Her dignity was toast.

He knew how much she wanted him. But the flipside was she knew how much he wanted her. And she suspected the fact that he had pretended that nothing had transpired between them was only evidence of just how much he wanted her.

Something about wanting her bothered him.

But then, he had come to this event all dressed up.

She couldn't figure the man out.

And as much as it pained her to admit it, she sort of liked that about him. That he wasn't easy. That she didn't intimidate him. That he didn't want her money or her influence. Everything about him that was so annoying was simultaneously also compelling, and that was just the whole thing.

"Come here," he said, his voice suddenly hard. "I want to show you something."

There was a big white tent that was still closed, reserved for an evening hors d'oeuvre session for people who had bought premium tickets, and he compelled her inside. It was already set up with tables and tablecloths, everything elegant and dainty, and exceedingly Maxfield. Though there were bottles of Cowboy Wines on each table, along with bottles of Maxfield select.

But they were not apparently here to look at the wine, or indeed anything else that was set up. Which she discovered when he cupped her chin with firm fingers and looked directly into her eyes.

"I've done nothing but think about you for two weeks. I want you. Not just something hot and quick against a wall. I need you in a bed, Wren. We need some time to explore this. To explore each other."

She blinked. She had not expected that.

He'd been avoiding her and she'd been so sure it was because he didn't want this.

But he was here in a suit.

And he had a look of intent gleaming in those green eyes.

She realized then she'd gotten it all wrong.

"I… I agree."

She also hadn't expected to agree.

But her heart was about to fly out of her chest, and she was achy and wet between her legs already. She sort of wanted to ask him if they could try it up against the wall of the tent. But she had a feeling that would only culminate in the two of them falling through the filmy fabric and embarrassing themselves.

She just didn't have the willpower to resist him.

"I want you now," she whispered, and before she could stop herself, she was up on her tiptoes and kissing that infuriating mouth.

She wanted to sigh with relief. She had been so angry at him. So angry at the way he had ignored this. Because how dare he? He had never ignored the anger between them. No. He had taken every opportunity to goad and prod her in anger. So why, *why* had he ignored this?

But he hadn't.

They were devouring each other, and neither of them cared that there were people outside. His large hands palmed her ass, pulling her up against his body so she could feel just how hard he was for her. She arched against him, gasping when the center of her need came into contact with his rampant masculinity.

She didn't understand the feelings she had for this man. Where everything about him that she found so disturbing was also the very thing that drove her into his arms.

Too big. Too rough. Crass. Untamable. He was everything she detested, everything she desired.

All that, and he was distracting her from an event that she had planned. Which was a cardinal sin in her book. And she didn't even care.

He set her away from him suddenly, breaking their kiss. "Not now," he said, his voice rough. "Tonight. All night. You. In my bed."

"But can't we just…"

"We are in a tent."

"I don't really care," she said, amazed.

"You don't?"

"Maybe I'm having a nervous breakdown," she said. "It's entirely possible. It has been a very weird few months. And I just… I don't know. I don't know who I am anymore. I'm not sure I want to know who I am. You're right. I've been in a box. And I didn't want to admit it. I just wanted to be mad at you. I just wanted to yell at you. But then we kissed, and then we did other things, and I've spent the last two weeks being incredibly confused about it. But you know what confuses me most? That I'm not ashamed. But I'm not sorry. I think it was good. Because even if it was the biggest mistake of my life, at least it was my mistake. I've done everything that's ever been asked of me. I've dated only men that were expected. I've never had sex outside of a relationship."

"It's fun," he commented.

"Apparently. I know that now. And…it was just for me."

"I don't know about that. I got something out of it, too."

"Well, good for you." She sighed heavily. "Okay. I'm not baring my soul to you or anything like that. But… Look, it's been weird. The whole thing with my dad. I swear to you, I didn't know how awful he was."

"I'm sorry that I brought your dad up the other day."

"No. It's okay. I mean… It's not. It was painful. But I'm working through things. And, I think I'm getting there. Better. This is part of it."

The left side of his mouth lifted. "Sexual healing?"

"Why not?" she asked. "Nothing else has worked." She took a breath, and then everything just poured out. "I worry about Cricket. Because she's not really talking to anyone. My mom is just kind of… Well, she's doing what she does. She's hiding. Emerson has Holden, and she seems to be coming out of it just fine. I feel like I'm in a weird space. I can't exactly live in denial. I'm too involved in this business. I feel the loss of my father too much. But I don't really feel okay about any of it. Or over it. I'm not sure that I feel okay about me. I need to figure out what I want."

"You're not thinking about leaving the industry, are you?"

"No," she said. "I think I feel like *this*—" she gestured to the interior of the very Maxfield tent "—is mine. But… What I'm saying is a little rebellion is what I need right now."

"Happy to be a part of it."

"Yeah, well." It was unexpected just how easy it was to tell him all of this. Somehow, she couldn't really be embarrassed around this man.

She had yelled all kinds of unflattering things at him over the years. She was not the best version of herself when he was around. It was like he tapped into some unfettered part of her that she didn't normally have access to. And when he was in the room, she just let fly.

It now extended to sex, apparently, and again, she wasn't even embarrassed about it. She had a total and complete lack of inhibition with him.

And right now, that felt like a gift.

Because she'd had nearly thirty years of being inhibited. Of following a very specific path. And Creed represented something wild and free that she'd never thought she could be.

Maybe that was the real reason he made her so angry. That he had been free in about a thousand ways she was sure she never would be.

"Then let's go do our jobs," he said. "The sooner we get finished with all of this…"

The last part was left unspoken, but the promise in his tone was clear. And her whole body responded to that. Effortlessly. Deeply.

And she knew she had made the right choice. To continue down this path with him.

It might end badly… But there was something in her that didn't fear the consequences. Not really.

She had gone down the expected path before. She had done it all of her life. And look how that ended. With her father…

There were no guarantees.

There were no guarantees. And she would rather live free.

Chapter 4

His body was on fire.

He was burning for her, and he'd decided to jump into the flames. That was control. He'd made a choice and he was resolved in it.

Or he'd just decided to take his hands off the wheel and let the car steer itself. One or the other.

He had to admit that the event was going well. His father even looked like he was enjoying himself. Though, his entire countenance had taken on an odd tone after he had met Wren.

Creed didn't really understand it.

He knew that there was…weird blood between the Maxfield and Cooper families, but he didn't fully know why. He had always assumed it was because they were business rivals, but effectively… They weren't anymore. Maybe it was just old habits dying hard. Except there had been no animosity in his father's bearing. None at all. He'd shown a strange kind of wistfulness. A sadness. But then, everything his father did these days was wistful and sad.

The old man missed his wife, and there wasn't much anyone could do to fix that.

They all missed their mother. It didn't matter that it was the natural order of things to lose a parent. You knew that you would. If everything went according to plan... You did.

But you were never ready for it. It was never time.

It would always feel too soon.

But it *really* had been too soon.

And they'd been suffering the aftereffects of grief, as a family incomplete, ever since.

Incomplete and different. Jackson had been distant. But Jackson had always been closest to their mother. Still, it was just another thing.

Creed hadn't had a drink or a bite to eat all day, mostly because he felt like he was being fueled by desire for Wren, but he was about ready to go and get himself some brisket when everything inside him went still.

He'd experienced this a couple of times in his life. But not for a long while. And it was never for a *good* reason. It was only ever for one reason. He closed his eyes, steeling himself.

Why the hell would she come to this?

He turned slowly, and that was when he saw her.

Louisa Johnson. Her accomplished doctor husband, Calvin Johnson. And as far as all the world was concerned, their four children. Including their oldest son, who was taller and broader than his father.

As a matter of fact, the boy looked a hell of a lot like Creed.

His stomach went acid.

He hadn't seen the kid in… Maybe going on four years.

The boy was eighteen now. Creed knew his birthday. Every year marked itself on his heart. A deep groove. A line in a particular chart that spoke of the hours, weeks, months, years that he'd been father to a son he could never acknowledge.

It was a small town. He couldn't always avoid Louisa. But her actually coming to one of his events was a study in sadism. Even he didn't think she could be quite that evil.

Just self-centered and hell-bent on creating the life she wanted. Never willing to admit she had given her virginity up to somebody other than her longtime boyfriend. And that when she'd gotten pregnant at sixteen it had not been with Cal Johnson's baby. But she'd gone and fixed that uncomfortable fact really quickly, slept with Cal right away and claimed the kid was his.

Creed knew the truth.

Creed had thought they were in love.

A virgin himself, he'd believed that having sex with her meant something. That her climbing into the bed of his truck with him had mattered. And he'd been so overwhelmed by desire that he hadn't stopped to think about anything.

He was sure… He had been so sure that it meant she was going to break up with that college-bound boy for him. Even though he wasn't from a fancy family, wasn't a future doctor. He'd been sure she'd fallen for him all the same.

But no.

And even when she had found out she was pregnant...

He wondered, to this day, if Calvin knew who fathered the kid. Wondered if he didn't especially care, not given the life they had built on the back of that lie.

Creed realized he had been standing there frozen for a full minute, and Louisa hadn't even looked his way.

The kid was harassing a younger sibling, laughing.

And then Calvin reached over and playfully punched his oldest son in the arm, gently telling him to knock it off.

They were a family. Built by years and birthday parties, Christmases and good-night kisses. By fights and celebrations and soccer games and barbecues in the backyard. In the face of all that, genetics didn't matter.

Except they mattered to Creed.

Because he'd had eighteen years of never getting to know that kid, and all the regret that went with it.

But what was he supposed to do? She hadn't put his name on the birth certificate, refused to admit they'd ever had sex. Creed's father had tried, he had damn well tried to get a court-ordered paternity test, but the judge refused to do it. To subject an underage girl to scrutiny, to call her a liar when she said staunchly that the only boy she'd ever slept with was her longtime boyfriend.

There had been nothing Creed could do, and everyone had said that he was just mounting a smear campaign against a girl who had rejected him. A girl who'd already found herself in a *delicate situation*.

They were happy. Clearly. She had Calvin. Their four kids.

What was he?

He didn't even know.

Suddenly, he felt a soft hand on his shoulder. "Is everything all right?"

He turned and saw Wren. Louisa wasn't looking at him, not even with the full force of his anger turned in her direction. But Wren had seen him.

"Fine," he responded.

"You look like you're about to start a fight."

"No," he said, turning away. "I'm not."

"Good."

Suddenly, the feeling inside him went from hungry to ravenous. And he needed this damn thing to be over so he could lose himself in Wren's body.

He lived with the mistakes of his past every day. But having to stare them down was a particular kind of torture he was never quite prepared for.

And he needed something, anything, to find a little oblivion. If it wasn't Wren, it would be the liquor on the table, but he would rather have her.

It was strange, the exchange they'd had back in the tent, and this one. Because it wasn't as sharp and hardedged as most of their interactions.

But it was still tinged with that same kind of raw grit. Which he recognized now as just desire. Only not desire like he'd ever known it before.

The closest thing that came to it was that sixteen-year-old lust haze he'd found himself in with Louisa. But that had been born out of inexperience. Out of desperation to know what it felt like to be inside a woman.

Well, he knew what it felt like now. That wasn't why Wren created this wildness in him.

It wasn't about knowing what it was like to be inside a woman, but what it was like to be inside *Wren*.

He knew the answer to that now, but a simple answer wasn't enough. He wanted more. He wanted her.

And that want began to eclipse the pain in his chest.

He was desperate for it. Because the promise of it—of her—was so big, so intense, with the capacity to take away this hurt. And he wanted that. He damn well did.

Needed it. Especially now.

He bent down slightly, careful to make it look like they were just having a business exchange, and not like they had shared any kind of intimacy.

If you could call sex against a wall *intimacy*.

"I can't wait until you're naked beneath me," he said.

She arched a brow. "Who says I'll be beneath you? I was kind of thinking I might like to be on top."

"There's time for that," he said. "There's time for a whole hell of a lot."

"So many promises."

"I promise you one thing—you're going to be screaming my name all night."

She looked up at him, her eyes glittering a challenge. "You'll be screaming mine."

"I plan on it."

They parted then, the tension between them so intense it would combust if they didn't release their hold.

So they did, because they both knew they were in a public setting, and a professional one. And whatever the hell he thought of Wren, whatever she thought of him, they were both damn good at their jobs.

He turned away then. From the direction that Wren walked. From the place where Louisa stood with her family.

A piece of his family. A piece of his heart.

He would focus on getting through all of this. And then he would focus on getting Wren into bed.

That was his life.

Work. Sex.

What the hell else did he need?

Everything was done, everything was cleaned up, and Wren was sitting in the driveway of Creed Cooper's house. She had made her excuses to her family about being tired, having a headache and a few other things she couldn't readily remember, and scampered off almost immediately after the last guest left.

She knew Emerson thought she was acting strange, but Wren didn't much care.

Wren was obsessed with Creed.

And if she were honest with herself, she could admit she had been obsessed with him for quite some time.

She might have couched that obsession in irritation, but the fact of the matter was, it had been deeper than that.

He hadn't annoyed her at all today.

No. Quite the opposite. He had been wonderful at his role during the event, and more than that, she had seen humanity in him that she didn't particularly want to see.

She had no idea what had been going through his mind when he had been standing there staring into the crowded party right before she had come up to him. But she had seen that it was something. The intensity that had come off him in waves had been palpable, at least to her.

She wasn't entirely sure whom he had been looking at, but she thought it might have been Louisa Johnson, a woman Wren knew because she and her husband frequented the winery and often had birthday parties and events there. It was common for wealthy families to come to Maxfield for special events. It was a status symbol. And Louisa had always seemed like the kind of woman who enjoyed her status.

Wren quite liked her. Louisa was nice, and she was funny, and a generous tipper to the waitstaff.

If it was Louisa that Creed was staring at, though, Wren had the feeling that he *hated* her.

And there was really only one reason for people to hate each other like that.

Love gone wrong.

Wren screwed up her face.

Well, there were actually a lot of reasons for people to hate each other. She and Creed hated each other, for no real reason.

Except, as she got out of her car and walked toward his front door, she couldn't find any of the hatred that she normally felt. She only felt giddy. Excited to have his hands on her, to have him make good on all those promises he had issued earlier at the event today.

She liked it when their verbal sparring had a bit of an edge, even if it wasn't a fight.

There was something electric and exciting about their exchanges.

She liked the danger that came with talking to him.

She just did.

She walked up to the door, prepared to knock, when it opened, and she found herself being dragged inside and pressed against that door, six-foot-plus of muscular man pinning her there as he kissed her. Kissed her with all the pent-up longing she knew had been building in both of them for the entire day.

She kissed him like he might hold all the answers she was so desperately seeking.

"Please let's make it to a bed," she whispered against his mouth. "I like the desperate stuff, but I really just want to see you naked."

"I can oblige," he growled.

He picked her up off the ground and carried her straight to a staircase, taking them two at a time. There was an edge of darkness to all of this that was so different from how it had been before. That first time had been charged by anger, the kind of anger they commonly felt toward each other, reasonable or not.

But this was different.

He seemed fractured, broken in some way, and like he thought perhaps this might put him back together. She was used to him looking at her and being irritated. And that one day down in the wine cellar he had found pleasure. But today, he seemed to be after something altogether deeper, and she wasn't entirely sure she could help him find it.

But she wanted to.

And that was perhaps even more surprising than his looking to her for something deeper in the first place.

He pushed open the door, revealing a large bed made of heavy wooden beams. The bed was the largest thing in the room, a clear indicator of exactly where his priorities were.

His house was Spartan. Everything about it was serviceable, practical. And she knew full well he didn't need that much mattress for sleeping.

No, he was a man who clearly used his bed for more athletic pursuits. And she knew already he was a man who did those pursuits well.

"You said you wanted to see me naked." He set her down lightly on her feet. Then he moved away from her, unbuttoning the crisp white shirt she'd been looking at all day. Exposing that gorgeous chest, those impressive abs. He shrugged the shirt and jacket off, his body a thing of outright beauty the likes of which she had never seen before she'd seen him.

"Trading," he said, gesturing to her.

She reached behind her back and grabbed hold of the zipper tab on her dress, pulling it down slowly, letting her dress pool at her feet. She was wearing only heels and a matching red lace bra and panties.

She wasn't insecure about her body. Men, in her experience, were quite simple about things like that.

But the hunger in his eyes surpassed anything she had ever experienced before from other men. This passion, which seemed to simmer so intensely it was bound to bubble over, was something foreign to her. Something entirely different from all her previous experiences. Sure, she had found sex pleasurable before. But she had not found it to be fire and hunger. She hadn't found it to be the air she needed to breathe. She had never felt like the urge to be touched was so intense it was a physical agony.

And she could see all that she was feeling mirrored in his face as he looked at her.

She hadn't known. Hadn't known that having him, this man—this man who didn't even like her--look at her like she was… Like she was a wonder. Like she was perhaps the most beautiful thing he had ever seen…

Like she was seen.

Her.

Wren Maxfield.

This new version of herself that she was finding, inventing and creating as she went along…

He was captivated by her.

He wanted her.

It was a revelation.

Because she wasn't insecure about her body, but she felt new and fragile in her skin. In all that she was, in all that she was going to be.

Didn't even know what that might be in the end.

But when Creed looked at her, she thought she might be closer to finding it.

And it didn't make sense, how it was somehow more affirming to have it be him who made her feel that way, but it was.

Maybe because her sister Emerson would be supportive of her no matter what. Her mother would say that she loved Wren regardless of what she did.

Creed wouldn't. Creed found her intolerable.

He would never tell her anything just for the hell of it. He wouldn't pretend that he wanted to touch her, kiss her, be inside her. He would only do what he wanted to do.

It was freeing.

And with all the freedom it gave her, she reached

behind her back and undid her bra, throwing it to the ground, glorying in the look of absolute need on his face.

She wiggled out of her panties, leaving herself standing there in nothing but her high heels. And then, she leaned backward on the bed, arching her breasts upward, letting her thighs fall slightly apart. She knew she looked like a wanton. And she had never been one, not particularly.

But she wanted to be.

Here. Now. For him.

She wanted to take this thing between them and test it to the breaking point. Wanted to test *herself* to the breaking point.

And whatever dark emotion was rolling beneath the surface of his skin… She wanted to unleash it.

Because she wanted to go as far as she could. She wanted to take them both to the edge.

This felt safe, with him, because it wouldn't be forever.

Because they didn't have a relationship, and they wouldn't. Because it was only this. Only her trying to figure out who she was, and only him trying to contend with whatever demons were clawing at him right now.

She could take it. For now.

And he could take her. Imperfect and new and unsteady.

They could both please themselves.

It was a miracle.

And she badly needed a miracle.

Creed didn't disappoint.

Because then he dropped to his knees, a position of submission she had never expected from him. He was beautiful from this angle, too. The planes of muscle on his shoulders and chest intoxicating. His strength, bowed before her...

Oh, she shivered with it.

Of course, immediately following that submissive posture he revealed that it was not submissive at all. Because he grabbed hold of her ass and pulled her forward, burying his face between her legs and licking her until she screamed.

Until she couldn't breathe.

He had all the control. There was no restraint. No quarter given.

He tortured her with pleasure, and if that wasn't the most Creed Cooper thing on the planet, she didn't know what was.

That he sank to his knees and yet managed to still have all the control.

And she didn't want to fight it. Didn't want to stop it. No. She surrendered to it. To just taking. Everything that he wanted to give. To the slow glide of his fingers inside her, and the wicked friction of his tongue against her. She surrendered to all of it. To the absolute glory of knowing this man needed to taste her.

Because that's what this was.

He *needed* to taste her.

He had no control. His movements didn't have finesse. It was a devouring. He had fallen upon her like a beast, like a man possessed.

Because of her.

Tension coiled inside her, and she just let go. When her orgasm broke over her like a wave, she cried out with her pleasure, completely unembarrassed by the sound that came from her body.

She felt remade, and she wanted him to feel the same. She scooted herself back farther on the bed, her thighs open even wider, an invitation.

"Take what you need," she said.

A shudder wracked his big frame, and he undid his belt buckle, sliding it slowly through the loops and letting the belt fall to the floor. He undid the closure on his pants, and took his shoes, socks, pants and underwear down to the ground. And then she could see him. Fully naked, fully erect.

Hands down the biggest guy she'd ever seen.

He was stunning.

She'd thought so the first time, too. But now she had a moment to really look. And…

Truly, he was beautiful. She couldn't wait to feel him inside her again.

He reached over to the nightstand and grabbed a condom. And something, a small alarm bell, went off in the back of her mind. She dismissed it. Pushed it to the side.

He tore it open, rolling it onto his length before positioning himself at the entrance of her body. Those green eyes, her adversary's eyes, meeting her as he slid inside her, inch by agonizing inch. She felt full, of him, of desire. Of need. She had been so ready for him that she let her head fall back, a deep sigh of pleasure on her lips.

And then he began to move, slow and languid at first, letting her feel each delicious inch of him on his slow glide out, and back in.

And then it all became harder, more frantic, a desperate race to completion. She wrapped her legs around his hips, letting him thrust deeper, harder. And she arched against him each time, meeting his every thrust, chasing a second climax, which before, for her, had been unheard of.

But it was Creed.

It was Creed making her feel these things.

And when their eyes met again, and she saw the hollow bleakness there, she felt him all the way down in her soul.

She kissed him.

She kissed him deep and long and hard, and she tried to…to give him some of the wonder and pleasure inside her. Because if he could feel her pain, then maybe he could feel her pleasure, too.

She didn't want him to be hurt. And he was. She could see it.

And even if it was over another woman… Well, Wren wasn't his woman. Not really. This was just sex. And she would make it the best ever. She would make sure she took away some of his loneliness. Some of his bleakness.

She got a perverse kind of pleasure out of that. That she, a woman he didn't even like, might give him something that the woman he had once loved denied him.

Wren was making assumptions. But she was pretty sure she was assuming right.

He thrust into her, hitting the spot deep inside that sent sparks shooting off behind her eyes, made her come so hard she could scarcely breathe. And then he followed right along with her, shaking and shuddering his pleasure as he came deep inside her.

And she just held him for a while. Pressed his head against her breasts as they both lay there breathing heavily.

She didn't want it to be over.

"We're just getting started," he mumbled, and she wondered if she had said the words out loud.

She was afraid she might have.

"You wanted to be on top, remember?" he mumbled.

"Yes, but I think you killed me. I'm too weak."

"I have food," he said. "I have cake."

She lifted her head. "How do you have cake?"

"My sister. She makes excellent cakes."

"Well, I could have some cake."

"If you eat my cake, I'm going to expect you to put out."

"I will put out for cake."

"Will you ride me?"

"Only if you promise that later you'll tie me to that headboard."

She was shocked by the words as they came out of her mouth. Because she'd never wanted anything quite like that before. And at first it had just been to dare him, but now she found she really wanted it.

"I think that's a deal I can stick to."

And some of the bleakness from his eyes did seem to be gone, so she supposed she had accomplished her goal.

She wouldn't think about what would happen after tonight.

She didn't want to.

Tonight, she just wanted to be the Wren she was becoming with him. Tonight, she wanted to be new.

Tonight, she wanted to be with Creed.

Chapter 5

It had been two weeks since he'd last had Wren Maxfield in his bed. Two weeks, and she was all he could think about.

It was starting to impact…well, everything. His work, his sleep, his ability to be a halfway decent person and not be an absolute dick anytime someone in his family wanted to talk to him.

He wanted her again, but he didn't know how to justify it. Sure, they were going to be working together on that big cross-winery event, but it wouldn't just be the two of them working on it.

He didn't know if that night after the party had been transformative because he'd been in a really dark place, or if… He just didn't know. All he knew was that he wanted more. And Wren didn't seem to be coming back for it. Which was a damn shame.

And then, as if his thoughts had conjured her up, he looked through the windows of the tasting room and saw her standing outside. She was staring at the door, not moving.

He watched her, without changing his position, until she turned and her eye caught his. There was something bleak and strange in her expression, and he didn't know how to read it. So they just stared at each other through the window.

If she was waiting for him to make the first move, she was out of luck. She was the one who had come here to knock on his door. She was the one who was going to have to close the gap.

Finally, she did.

Finally, she walked through the door, but then she stood there in the entry, her hands clasped in front of her. "We need to talk."

"We do?"

"Yes. We do."

"I've been waiting to see you," he said, "and I have to tell you, it's not talking I want to do."

"Well, it's talking we need to do. Creed…" She closed her eyes and swallowed hard. "Creed, I'm pregnant."

Suddenly, he felt like he was falling into a chasm. A chasm that led to some moment eighteen years ago. A moment he didn't want to relive.

But you knew this might happen. You did. He pushed the thought to the side. *You tried not to think about the fact that you screwed her without a condom, but you know you did.*

No. Wren was the same age as he was. It didn't seem possible that the woman wasn't on birth control. Or that she wouldn't have said something about the condom if she wasn't taking something.

You didn't say anything about it either.

"I didn't even think," she said. "After the time in the wine cellar. I didn't think. It didn't occur to me until we were at your house and you took a condom out of your bedside drawer that I realized…that we didn't."

"You're not on…the Pill or anything?"

"I haven't been in a relationship in like a year and a half. And I… I didn't really like the way I felt on it. It made me gain weight, so I quit taking it after I broke up with my last boyfriend." She grimaced. "I'm not really somebody who hooks up."

"Well," he said, his voice rough, "I am. I am, so I sure as hell should've thought of a condom. Because I use them all the damn time. I… I'm sorry. I should have thought of it. I should've done better."

"No," she said. "That's stupid. I should have, too. I… Creed, I want to keep the baby."

Cold fear infused itself into his veins. "You want to keep the baby?"

"Yes. I understand that it might surprise you. But I… I'm thirty-two years old. I would like to have a baby. And I'm at a point in my life where I don't really know what's coming next, what I want to do. And this pregnancy feels like… Well, it feels like a pretty clear sign of something that I could do to change my life. Because it's happening. And I… I want it. When I found out a couple of days ago, I cried. I spent the entire day crying. I've been avoiding my family. Because I knew that I needed to tell you first. But I also knew… I knew immediately that I wanted the baby. I… I just *do*. And I don't need anything from you. I'm completely fine and taken care of. I have a house, I have a business, and I don't need you to be involved at all."

"I will be fucking involved," he said, his voice hard.

"I didn't mean you *couldn't* be," she said. "I just didn't want you to think I was making demands of you, or your money…"

"This baby is mine," he said.

"Of course it is," she said.

"No," he said. "You misunderstand me. That wasn't a question. It was a statement. This baby is mine, and that means I will be involved. I am this baby's father."

Echoes of everything that he had lost were shouting inside him. Because he knew how easy it was for a woman to take a child from a man.

A *girl* to take a baby from a *boy*.

That was the thing. They'd been kids. And everything about it had been messed up. All of it.

But he was not a child anymore, and he would be damned if anybody took anything from him.

His child.

For his son, it was too late. He couldn't have his son. Not now.

He had just seen that boy with his…with the man he thought was his father, with his siblings. They were a family. Creed never could be. He was just a man who had donated the material that had created the boy.

That wasn't being a *father*. He could never have that back. That boy was grown.

Even if he found out about Creed someday… He could never be the boy's dad.

No, he had lost that chance. But he would never lose that again. Never again.

"You're going to marry me," he said.

"I… I most certainly am not," she said. "That is… It is not a good reason for people to get married."

"It is the only damn reason for people to get married. It's legal protection, Wren. For both parties involved."

"That's not how the world works anymore."

"It is damn well how the world works. What's to keep you from taking my name off the birth certificate?"

"I won't."

"What's to keep you from preventing me from seeing my baby?"

"I won't," she repeated. "I won't do that. We were both involved in this and…"

"You say that, but you don't know. You don't know how it will go. You're marrying me. You're marrying me, and we're going to live in the same house. I am not missing a moment of my child's life."

"Creed, I didn't say that you would. But we are not in a relationship. We don't even like each other, let alone love each other."

"That doesn't have anything to do with this. This isn't about us."

"Be reasonable. I didn't even think you would want this baby."

"Because you don't know me," he said. "Not at all. We were naked together, that's it. But you don't know me well enough to think that you know whether or not I want this child. I do."

He did. With every breath in his body.

And the resoluteness he felt over what needed to be done was as intense as it was real.

"I am not letting you take this baby from me."

"Creed, I won't. But I don't have to marry you to…"

"We are getting married."

"Or what?"

Everything in him turned to ice. If she wanted an ultimatum, he would give it to her.

"Or I'll do what I have to do to make sure that most of the custody is with me."

"What?"

"Do you think it's fair? For one parent to only be with the child on weekends? Do you think it's fair for one of us to miss that much of the child's life? Because I don't. But if you think it's fair, then you won't mind if it gets flipped on you. Do you think it'll be fair to miss a week of the baby's life?"

"I'm the mother," she said.

"And I am the father," he said, the conviction in his voice shocking even him. "I'm the father," he repeated. "I'm not missing this."

"Creed…"

"You listen to me," he said, speaking with all the firmness he could when his life had just been turned completely upside down. "You listen to me, Wren Maxfield. Either you become my wife, or I'm going to have to make this difficult."

"You listen to me," she said. "You might be used to issuing edicts, but you don't get to tell me what to do. Because I've lived my entire life walking on another path that was set out for me by someone else. By a man. I will not be dictated to. If you want to fight, I will give you a fight, Creed. You can bet on it."

And then, she turned on her heel, walking out of the room.

And he could see that she was certain that she could get her way.

All he could see was another woman walking off with his child.

It wouldn't happen. It wouldn't.

It wasn't for another hour that the shock wore off.

And that was when he clutched his chest like he might be having a heart attack and leaned against the wall of the tasting room.

He was going to be a father again.

And Wren Maxfield was the mother.

And he had no idea how in hell they were going to survive this.

Chapter 6

She was a coward. She had run away from him, and she could see that whatever was driving him to be unreasonable, and make actual threats, came from a place she didn't understand.

She could see that, and still, she had run away from him rather than sticking out the conversation to see where it might go. And wasn't that basically what he was saying? That he assumed she would be a coward when push came to shove? That she would keep their child from him because it was easier or less challenging, because she didn't want to deal with him?

And maybe… Just maybe it had been easier for her to assume he wouldn't want anything to do with the baby. Maybe that's why she'd been able to come here and tell him about the pregnancy.

Before that, she had spent two days in agony.

She hadn't been lying to him when she'd said she cried. She cried enough to make a flood. It just wasn't good timing. At least, that was what she told herself in the beginning.

Wrong time.

Wrong man.

And then she thought… Maybe he was the right man. Because he wouldn't want anything from her. Because he was not a paternal type, and there was no way he was secretly yearning for a wife and family.

She had never considered herself particularly maternal, either, but when she looked at the situation objectively, she could see that, well, this was an opportunity.

Because she had everything she needed to raise a child, including the assumed support of her family. She had job security. Money. A place to live. A great many things that people took for granted. From that standpoint, she was in a spectacularly great place to raise a child. And the more she thought about it, the more she had wanted to grab hold of this major life change and see where it took her. The more she thought about it, the more she had felt…a sense of excitement, rather than one of despair.

But her revelation had been selfish. Utterly and completely.

It had never included him.

She didn't know how to include him in that.

And then he demanded that she did.

Honestly, he'd demanded it in the most extreme way she could have imagined. Even if she had let herself truly think about a scenario in which he wanted the baby, wanted to be in the baby's life, she had not imagined that he would…demand marriage and issue threats.

But that's what he'd done. And it became clear that she really didn't know all that much about him, and that lack of knowledge actually mattered.

Having sex didn't mean they knew each other.

Oh, they knew things *about* each other. Creed knew things about her that no one else did. She had done things with him she hadn't done with any other man.

Including that moment of absolute loss of control. The lack of protection.

But that didn't mean they knew each other.

And so she was now looking for the person she should have gone to in the first place.

Emerson was at the house she shared with Holden, working from home today, which was something Wren could never have imagined Emerson doing before. Given that Emerson had been wholly and completely tied to the family home.

But not only had she moved away from the estate, she seemed to prize the separate life she and Holden had built.

Wren would be fascinated by it if she didn't find it so annoying.

She parked her car and got out, walking to the door. It took a couple of minutes, but her sister opened it, wearing a large, elaborate-looking robe, her hair piled on her head, her fingernails manicured to perfection, a giant wedding ring that she'd gotten from Holden glittering on her finger.

"Well," Wren said. "Good afternoon to you, too."

"I was taking pictures," she said.

She swung the door open wider, and Wren saw that the couch and coffee table were set just so, a glass of rosé in her sister's glass, and a book sitting next to it.

"Are you reading?"

"I was taking pictures," Emerson said dryly. "It's a great afternoon to indulge in a little Maxfield luxury and *hashtag self-care*, don't you think?"

"I think that I'm glad you run the internet properties and not me. Since I don't understand any of this."

"Luckily, you don't have to. Because I'm a savant."

"An influencer savant." But Wren smiled, because she really did find her sister to be a wondrous magical creature.

Emerson should be annoying. She wasn't.

"Where's Holden today?"

"He's gone to visit his sister. She's getting settled in her new house after getting out of the rehab facility. We are hopeful that she's going to keep doing better and better."

"I'm glad to hear it."

Holden loved his sister, and Wren and Emerson's father had caused her immense distress. Wren was rooting for her.

"So what brings you by? Because you look like an absolute disaster."

Wren stepped into her sister's house and craned her neck so she could see her reflection in the mirror on the wall. Emerson wasn't kidding. Her makeup was smeared, in spite of the fact that she hadn't been crying. She assumed that maybe she had wiped her fingers firmly across her eyes to try to keep the tears back. But she hadn't even been conscious of doing it.

Her hair was in disarray, and there was just something…shocked looking about her expression. Her skin was pale, and her cheeks seemed especially hollow.

"Well, I feel terrible," she said. "So that's fair." She sighed heavily. "I have to tell you something."

Emerson looked bemused. "Am I hiding a body? Should I get a shovel? Because you know I will."

"I do know you will." Wren sighed heavily again. "I don't think I'll need your help with that. Though, I guess we'll see how all this goes. I'm pregnant."

Her sister's schooled expression became very serene. Wren could tell that Emerson was covering shock, because there was no way she was that serene about such an announcement.

"Congratulations," she said. "I didn't expect that."

"Well. Just wait until you hear the next part. Creed Cooper is the father."

A bubble of sound escaped Emerson that was almost a laugh, but not quite. "That doesn't surprise me at all. I actually figured you were here to tell me that you slept with him. But obviously that ship sailed a while ago."

"Multiple times," she muttered.

"I mean, I can't exactly lecture you."

"Why not?"

"Well, I jumped into bed with our father's enemy while I was still engaged to somebody else. So, when it comes to making good sex choices… I mean look, luckily, I married him. It all worked out in the end. But, I get how men can make you really stupid. And I didn't get that before Holden."

"Well, Creed doesn't make any sense to me. I don't like him," Wren said helplessly. "I don't like him and yet… I want him. I want him so much. And the sex is so good. It's the best sex I've ever had. I mean, that's weak. It seems like just the thing you say. But sex with him is like a whole other thing."

"I get it," Emerson said. "I mean, I profoundly get it."

"I guess you managed to use condoms, though."

"Yeah," Emerson said. "That we did."

"We forgot. And…"

"What are you going to do?"

"Well, I was all resolute. I'm not a kid. I'm in a great place to raise a child, and everything has been so out of whack I just… I kind of *want* to. I mean, I really want to. I was shocked by the realization, but it's true. I want to have a baby. I want to have *his* baby. It'll be… so cute. But I didn't think he would want me to have a baby. And I didn't think he would care. I thought this would be just my decision, but he told me today that I have to marry him."

That successfully shook Emerson's composure. *"He what?"*

"He demanded that I marry him. Like, demanded. *With threats.*"

"I mean…" Emerson blinked. "Okay, that's shocking."

"I know."

Emerson's expression turned thoughtful. "Well, obviously something happened to him."

"You think?"

"If I know one thing about hardheaded, alpha cowboys, it's that usually demands like that spring from an emotional wound."

"With all the experience you have with them?"

"I may not have experience across a vast section of

them, but the one I married was basically a giant walking open wound."

"Gross."

"I know. But everything he did, seducing me, forcing me into marriage, tearing my dress off…tying me to the bed… What was the point I was making?"

Wren narrowed her eyes. "This isn't helping me, Emerson."

"Right. My point. *My point* is everything he did that was awful came from a place of being so angry on behalf of his sister. And a lot of things got twisted up inside him, but he couldn't quite deal with all that anger. It took time for him to sort it out. But ultimately he did. Ultimately, *we* did. But he wasn't being an asshole just to be an asshole. My experience is they're all just lions with big thorns in their paws."

Wren's mouth flattened into a line. "And you want me to… What?"

"I mean, find the thorn. Identify it. Pull it out."

"I'm not going to end up like you," Wren said. "I… I can't say that I hate him anymore, but I also don't really want to marry him."

She imagined the bleakness that had been on his face that last time they were together. She had cared about that. About the pain he was experiencing.

"He *is* hurting," Wren said. "I just don't really know why."

"That's what you have to find out."

"I don't know how to talk to him. Every time we do talk, it… Well, it's exactly what just happened—we fight. Or we have sex. Fighting or sex. Those are the two options."

"Would either one be so bad in this situation?"

"I probably shouldn't have sex with him again."

"Honey, the horse has bolted from the barn, and is in the pasture with the stallion, and is already knocked up."

"I meant emotionally, for *emotional reasons*."

"Right, right," Emerson said, waving her hand.

"You still think I should have sex with him?"

"You seem to want to. And it sure makes men act nicer," Emerson said. "Anyway. As established, I make bad decisions on that score." An impish grin crossed her face. "But I don't regret them."

"I don't know if I regret this. I don't know what I regret."

Wren wanted the baby. She was sure of that. It was all the other things she couldn't quite figure out, including how she felt about Creed. *That* she couldn't quite navigate.

But if Emerson was right, if there was a thorn in Creed's paw, so to speak, then Wren was going to have to approach him differently.

She might not know all she needed to know about him, but she knew him well enough to know she was going to have to come in with a plan. A counteroffer. He wasn't simply going to accept her *no*. She was going to have to come up with an arrangement that would make him happy.

And in order to do that, she was going to have to identify that thorn.

And she couldn't identify the thorn without talking to him.

That was the problem.

She didn't especially know how to talk to Creed.

She knew how to fight with him. She knew how to fuck him.

She wasn't sure she knew how to do anything else.

But they were going to have to figure it out.

For the sake of the baby, if for nothing else.

She realized that for the first time in a very long time, her thoughts weren't consumed with the winery. The winery was something she loved, but not something she had built with her own hands.

She found herself suddenly much more concerned with her life, her future.

And even in the midst of all the turmoil, that was an interesting development indeed.

Chapter 7

Creed knew he had basically lost his mind earlier, but he didn't regret it.

In fact, he was making plans to call his lawyer. He was going to do whatever he had to do to get his way. That was when Wren showed up on his doorstep.

She looked strange. Because she was wearing jeans and a T-shirt, and she looked smaller somehow, and yet resolute.

It was the resoluteness that concerned him.

"I'm sorry I left things the way they were earlier," she said, breezing into his house without an invitation.

She wandered into his living room, sat on his couch.

When she had come before, she had been in his bedroom, his bathroom and his kitchen for a cup of coffee before she had run out in the early hours of the morning.

Not his living room. But there she was, sitting on

the couch like a satisfied, domesticated feline. Except he had the feeling that nothing about Wren was particularly domestic.

"What exactly are you here for?"

"Not to agree to your demands. Sorry. But it's ridiculous to think that we have to get married just because we're having a baby."

"Is it?"

"It is to me. I'm pretty much one hundred percent *not here for it.*"

"That's a shame. Because I'm one hundred percent…" He frowned. "Here for it? What the hell does that even mean?"

"Why?"

She was glaring at him with jewel-bright eyes, and it was the determination there that worried him.

"What do you mean 'why'? I told you earlier. It's because I'm not going to take a back seat to raising my child."

"Why? I mean, you don't even know the kid."

"Neither do you, and you're sure that you want it."

"Sure. But I'm…you know, carrying it. I sense the miracle of life and whatever," she said, some of the wind taken out of her sails.

"No, if you can be certain then *I* can be certain."

"You have to be honest with me," she said. "Because when I left here earlier what I realized was that I don't actually know anything about you. We have worked in proximity to each other for the last five years. And we fight. We… We create some kind of insane electrical surge when we are together, and I can't explain it. And somehow in all of that, I convinced myself that I knew you. But that night that we were here together after the party, there was something wrong. I knew it, even though I didn't know what it was. And when I told you I was pregnant… Look, I didn't expect you to be thrilled about it. But I didn't expect you to demand that I marry you. And I think the problem is, we just don't know each other."

"We know each other well enough. I'd be good to you. I wouldn't cheat."

She didn't look convinced. Not by his offer, not at all. And she should be. What the hell more could she possibly want? Love, he supposed. But here they both were in their thirties, not anywhere near close to settling down, and they were having a kid. Neither of them was young enough or starry-eyed enough to think there was some mystical connection out there waiting for them.

He'd lost his belief in that a long time ago.

Maybe Wren hadn't.

But he didn't see Wren as a romantic. Particularly not after the way things had worked out in her parents' marriage.

"What?" he asked.

"There are other reasons to get married. I just… You would really be faithful to me?"

"Wren, I can't even think about other women when I'm with you. I can't imagine taking vows to be true to you and then betraying them."

"That's nice," she said. "But a lot of men can. You know, my father, for one."

"So that would matter to you," he said.

"Yes," she said. "If I was going to do it… I don't share."

"So now you're considering it."

"I need to know *why*."

"It's not important."

"I have a feeling that it is."

Why not tell her? After all, his family knew. Well, Jackson did. And so did his father. Creed had never talked to Honey about it, but she had been a baby. A kid.

But anyway, it wasn't like no one knew. And he had never agreed to keep it quiet.

Wren looked at him directly. "Does it have something to do with Louisa Johnson?"

The name hit him square in the chest. "How do you…"

"I saw you looking at her. At the barbecue. And afterward…"

"It's not what you think," he said.

"Look. If you needed to be with me to deal with seeing an ex, it's fine. I knew what was happening."

"I wasn't thinking of her. I wasn't using you. Not in the way you mean." He was surprised how much it mattered to him for her to know that.

She looked at him, bemused. "Then what is it?"

"Do you know her at all?"

"They do birthday parties and things at the winery sometimes. That's it. I know her in a vaguely professional capacity."

"So you know her husband, then, and her kids."

"I've seen them. Yes."

He shook his head. "Her oldest son is mine."

For the second time in a couple of days, Wren felt like the ground had tilted beneath her feet.

Her thoughts were coming in too fast for her to grab hold of them.

He had a son.

Creed had a son.

"He… He…"

"You may not remember this, seeing as you didn't go to school here. But Louisa got pregnant in high school."

"I always got the impression that…"

"Yes. By design. That Cal is the father of all her children. She and Cal were dating at the time. She and I started… We were in a study group together, and I developed some pretty strong feelings for her. I knew she was with Cal, but you know how it is when you're young. And you think things will work out just because you want them to. That your feelings have to be good and true and right. Well, I thought mine were. I was a virgin, and what we got up to in the back of my truck sure felt like love to me. I thought it was the same for her. We made a mistake. So, now that you're pregnant… This isn't the first damn time I've made this mistake, Wren. I swore that I never would again. Twice is just… It's damn careless. Especially when you've got eighteen years between who you were and who you are now. I ought to know better."

"I mean… Yeah, I can't really argue with you there. I'd like to reassure you, but that does seem…"

"She didn't put my name on the birth certificate. She wouldn't even look at me at school. She acted like she didn't know me. And when I confronted her about it, she said we never slept together. She told everybody that the baby was Cal's. She was a virgin when we slept together. I knew the baby was mine. But she must have gone and slept with him right after to make sure he believed her. I doubted myself sometimes over the years.

I thought maybe… Maybe I was the crazy one. Maybe she hadn't been a virgin. Maybe the timing was all off."

"He looks like you, though, doesn't he?" She felt sick to her stomach. "I don't know him that well, but I remember seeing them all together, and I wouldn't have looked at him and thought he was your doppelgänger or anything, but now that I know…"

"I don't doubt it either," he said. "I haven't ever spoken a word to him. Never been close to him. And the fact of the matter is, he's not really my son now, is he? I didn't raise him. I'm not the one who taught him what he knows. I'm not the one who's been there for everything and paid for his upbringing and… I'm just a guy who had sex with a girl once a long time ago, and got left with a scar that's never going to heal. I can't do that again, Wren. I lost a child already. And I was never going to… I was never going to try to become a father again. I couldn't see any reason to. After all, I never had my first kid. But now it's happening. And I can't go through a loss like that. Not ever again."

"And you think I would do that to you?"

"I thought I was in love once, and I thought the woman loved me back. *We* don't even like each other."

Her heart felt bruised, sore.

He'd been so young to go through something like that. And she could see that it still affected him profoundly. How could it not? But she couldn't go paying for the sins of another person. It wasn't fair.

"We are going to have to get to know each other," she said, resolutely.

"No," he said. "I'm sorry. I'm not budging on it. You're going to marry me. One year. I want us to get married, I want legal acknowledgment of the kid, and I want us to try for one year. And then if you want to divorce, God bless you, but we're going to have to work out a real custody arrangement."

"Creed, it doesn't make any sense," she said. "We can't just get married."

"I won't accept anything less," he said. "I won't accept anything less than marriage."

She looked at him, and she could see that he was absolutely serious. More than that, she could see that what her sister had said was absolutely right. His demand was coming from a place of pain. Unimaginable pain. And it wasn't about simply pulling out a thorn. He wasn't even going to let her get close enough to touch it, never mind remove it.

It was going to require trust. A hell of a lot of trust, and she could see that he was fresh out.

This was his vulnerability. His weakness. The situation they were in, it was the man's worst nightmare. And she couldn't make it work with him if she was continually trying to hold her position, fighting him just for the sake of it.

She wanted her freedom. Her life. The chance to make a future for herself the way that she wanted it made. But not at the expense of their child having the best life he or she possibly could.

Creed might irritate her, but he was a good man. She knew it.

He could be the kind of father her own had never been.

Right now, they had the freedom to make whatever future they wanted. Whatever future they thought was best. She wasn't under the tyranny of her father, and she didn't have to pass any of her pain, any of her issues, on to her children.

Something her own parents hadn't managed.

But it all needed to start here. It had to start with this.

She took a breath, and then she sat down at one of the tables. "Okay. Get a notebook."

"What?"

"Get a notebook. We're going to write out what we both need. What we both expect. Creed, we are not going to make it through this if we don't trust each other. I can understand that you want marriage in a legal sense. If you need that, I can give it to you. But, during the pregnancy, that doesn't have to mean anything. It's not like we need to live with each other or be in any kind of relationship until the baby is born."

"You think that, huh?"

"I do," she said. "I think we need to focus on putting our child first. And we need to build some trust between each other. I would not take your baby from you, Creed. But I understand why you don't just take my words at face value. And, I'm not going to suffer for it either. I just found my life. I just found my purpose. Everything in my world got turned upside down when my dad... I've had to rethink everything. Everything I believe in. Everything I am. I'm not giving everything up to you. Sorry."

He looked hollow. Almost helpless, and that made her stomach drop into her feet.

"I can't bend on this," he said.

She looked at him. And she knew he was telling the

truth. His face was drawn and haggard, his tone was tortured.

"I know you can't. I'm going to bend as much as I can right now so we can find someplace where we can meet."

He stood, left the room for a moment, then returned with a pen and a notebook. He thrust it into her hand. "All right. Start listing your demands."

"First of all, if you want to be involved, you need to be involved. It's really important to me that you're either hands-on or hands-off with our child. All in, or all out." She looked at him, her jaw set, her posture determined.

"Why is that?"

"Because I won't have any of this lukewarm BS. That's how my dad was. He was there just enough to make us...try to perform for him. To make us try to do the very best we could to please him. But he never gave us anything back. Not really. I'm not going to put my kid through that. I want more for them."

"I want *everything*," he said, his voice rough. "I lost eighteen years with my son. I'm not losing any more time. I'm not losing that ever again."

"I won't ask you to. I promise. And that's why...my next thing. No more sex."

"Are you out of your damn mind?"

"No. I'm absolutely *in* my mind. We need to be able to deal with each other, and with this. I need to be able to have you at my house. You need to be able to be around for whatever you want, whenever you feel you need to have time with our child. If we have our own feelings in the way, our own situation, then this isn't going to work. We have to be able to be in the same room and not fight. And not… Well, you know that other *F* word that we seem to be so fond of."

He snorted. "If we had that kind of control, we wouldn't be in this situation."

"But you know as well as I do that getting out of control isn't going to work. It just wouldn't. It couldn't. We have to make this list and stick to it so we can give each other what we need. And I don't think we can do that if we get…all that emotion involved."

"Is that what you think?"

"Well, don't you? Don't you think it's too big a risk?"

His face went hard. Neutral. And then finally, "You're right. And really, it's all just a little control. Which, I had plenty of until you."

"Well, that's flattering. But, I don't doubt you can find it again."

"Sure. What else?"

"Holidays?" she asked.

"Together. Obviously. At my family place," he said.

Always with his family. Was he kidding? But the child was currently a zygote so as pressing matters went, that wasn't a huge one. "Okay, I think we can actually wait on that."

"Marriage," he said. "For the first year."

"Until the baby is born," she said. "I'll give you that. Marriage until the baby is born so you can be sure you have your legal protection. And then we can work out whatever custody agreement you want. We can cohabitate, whatever. But, if the primary concern is custody, and you making sure that you have all your parental rights… I'll go that far."

"I can deal with that. For now. Let's go get a marriage

license, then," Creed said, fully and completely matter-of-factly, as if they'd worked out everything.

"What, *right now*?"

"Do you have a better time frame?"

"I don't… I wasn't exactly thinking of a time frame. But… I'm like six weeks pregnant, Creed. We can chill out."

"Nope," he said. "It may have escaped your notice, Wren, but I don't have any chill."

"It didn't escape my notice at all. Nothing about you suggests that you have chill."

But he was already gathering his things, and he was ushering them both out the door and toward his truck.

"I can't… We're just going to go get a marriage license?"

"This isn't Vegas. We can't get married the same day. We need to figure out all the specifics."

She made an exasperated sound and got into the truck behind him. As they drove to town, she was completely and utterly overwhelmed by an out-of-body sensation.

Because *surely* this wasn't actually happening to *her*. She wasn't really going down to the courthouse to get a marriage license with the man who irritated her more than…

"You don't even like me," she said.

"I'm not pretending to *like* you."

That shut her up, because it was true.

He wasn't pretending to like her. He wasn't pretending that there was anything to this other than a legal practicality.

And that was how she found herself standing in front

of a clerk's desk in the old brick courthouse, filling out forms.

They could get married three days after the license was purchased.

"Then we'll get married in three days," Creed said.

She didn't reply, or say anything while they finished signing off on all the papers. But when they were back outside the courthouse, and walking on the sidewalk down Main Street, heading back to where they had parked the truck, she gave him the evil eye.

"You have to be joking," she said. "Three days?"

He lifted a shoulder. "Do you want a hamburger?"

"Do I look like I want a hamburger?" Her stomach growled. She frowned furiously at it. She did in fact want a hamburger.

"I think you do," he said. "Let's go to Mustard Seed."

"You don't know what I want more than I do, Creed Cooper," she groused, trailing along after him as he abruptly reversed course and headed to the small, unassuming diner that was just off the main drag.

"I believe I'm pretty good at anticipating what it is you want, Wren Maxfield."

"In bed," she muttered as he pushed open the door, holding it for her.

She stepped inside and looked around. She couldn't remember the last time she had been here. Maybe once. When she was a kid, and she had tried to hang out with some of the local teenagers during the summer. The floor was made of pennies, all glossed over with epoxy, making a coppery, shimmering surface. There was quirky local art everywhere. Little creatures made out of spoons and forks.

The tables were small, and there was a bucket of dry-erase markers on each one, everyone encouraged to create their own removable art on the surfaces.

"Do you come here often?" she asked him.

"Yes," he answered. "My favorite burger place."

"Oh."

A waitress who looked like she was probably the same age Wren had been the last time she had come into this place approached the table. "Chocolate milkshake," Creed said. "Cheeseburger, extra onions, French fries."

"I'll have a Diet Coke. And a cheeseburger. And sweet potato fries."

Then they sat staring at each other across the small table.

He was her fiancé.

A hysterical bubble of laughter welled up in her throat.

"What?" he asked.

"Well, of all the ways that I imagined getting engaged, it wasn't being dragged down to a courthouse to sign papers, then being taken out to a diner for a burger."

"Oh, right. I imagine you figured it would come with something fancy."

"And a diamond."

"Do you *want* a diamond?"

She had a sudden image of him getting down on one knee. Sliding a ring on her finger. And that felt…

That felt too close to real.

And the feeling in her chest was far too tender.

"No," she said. "A diamond won't be necessary."

"So what is it you think this is going to be?"

"In name only," she responded. "You want legal protection, and while I'm sure we could manage that without a marriage, I can appreciate the fact that this is maybe the simplest route. And… It's fine with me. We're having a baby together. I'm not going to act like this is somehow…going to bond us together in a way that it isn't." She sighed heavily. "It's weird, though. Because I certainly never expected to be starting a family without being *really* married. I never expected I'd do it with you."

"My brother seems to think it was inevitable."

"The baby?"

"No. The events leading up to the baby."

"My sister seemed to think that, as well."

"What do they know?" he asked, smiling ruefully.

A few moments later their food appeared, and Wren realized how hungry she was. The food was amazing, and she mentally castigated herself for any snobbery that had kept her away from a burger of this caliber.

"Okay, good suggestion," she said.

She tucked into the burger, and between bites, he looked at her. Hard. "So, you think this is going to be an in-name-only marriage. Does that mean you've changed your mind? You think it's all right if we sleep with other people?"

"Well, we can't sleep with each other," she pointed out.

"Right. Because you seem to think that's unreasonable."

"I do. It will only cause problems. I don't know what kind of marriage your parents had. My parents' marriage is a disaster, and it's only gotten worse as time has gone on. You know, for obvious reasons. I just… You and I don't have a great relationship. It's a weird relationship, but all the fighting… It's not personal. I think we can be okay. I think we can make something out of this and be good parents. And I have a lot more confidence in our ability to do that if we keep it simple."

"So, again, you now think it's all right for us to sleep with other people during this yearlong marriage?"

Discomfort rolled through her, and something like sadness. "Well, I'm not going to be sleeping with anyone."

"Why not?"

She stared at him. "I'm pregnant. Not exactly going to go out and find a new lover while I'm gestating a human being. I can't imagine anything less sexy."

He lifted a shoulder. "A lot of men like that sort of thing. I think you could find someone if you had a mind to."

"Do you *want* me to go find someone else to sleep with?"

"Just checking."

"For your information, I was celibate for eighteen months before we had sex." She dipped her French fry into the pink sauce so hard it bent. "I'll be fine for the next nine."

He leaned back in his chair and fixed her with a bold stare. "I don't do celibacy."

She was surprised at the zip of emotion that shot through her. Possession. Anger. She didn't like that. She didn't like the idea of him sleeping with other women. She stared at him. And she had to wonder if that reaction was what he was pushing for. If he was pushing to see if she was actually okay with all of this.

"Maybe I *will* find someone, then," she said. "How

about this, I'm probably not going to be actively looking for a lover, but if one presents himself... Who am I to say no?"

"Hey, you have needs, I'm sure."

Now he was just making fun of her.

"Do you have to be such a pain in the ass? What is it you want? Why can't you just say it?"

His gaze went sharp, intense. And everything inside her...shivered.

She wished she hadn't asked for honesty, because she was sure she was about to get it. Now she wasn't entirely certain she wanted it.

"Here's what I want," he said. "I want for no man but me to ever touch you again. How about that? But that's not reasonable, is it? Because this is just a temporary marriage and you want it to be in name only. And we need to have a *relationship* for the sake of our child, not based on *F* words that involve nudity—your words, not mine."

"Oh," she said.

She was equally surprised by how satisfying this was, that he was showing he was possessive. It went right along with the possession she had felt a moment before.

This was all very weird.

"That's it?" he asked.

"Well, what do you want me to say?" she asked. "You're right, it is unreasonable."

"And you're totally fine with other women touching me while we live together? While we have a marriage license?"

"No." She bit into her French fry fiercely and chewed

it with much more force than was necessary. "I hate the idea about as much as I hate you. Which is *a lot*."

"What are we going to do about that? Because it seems to me that it's going to be pretty difficult for the two of us to find neutral ground. We're never neutral. You want to prevent hard feelings by us not sleeping together, but we've got hard feelings already. If there's another lover in play neither of us are going to be nice, and you know it."

"We can't make it worse," she said, feeling desperate and a little bleak. "And we would. We could. It seems obvious to me. I mean, look at us now, after just a couple of… I don't know. Just after a few times. It's already an issue. We can't… We can't do that to our child."

"We could," he said, his tone horrendously pragmatic. She wanted to punch him. "Plenty of people do."

"I…"

"I know," he said. Something in his gaze shifted. "This is my only chance to do it right. I didn't intend to ever have the opportunity to do it again."

"I can't imagine," she said, her heart squeezing. "I can't really explain how it felt to find out I was pregnant. Because I was terrified. And it wasn't like I had completely positive emotions. I didn't. But I feel conviction. I know having this baby is what I want."

He shook his head. "I didn't know. When she told me she was pregnant I was terrified, too. I was sixteen. I wasn't ready to be a father. But I knew what I would do. I knew I'd be there for her. That I'd be there for the baby. Even if it felt scary. And then suddenly… The whole story changed. She acted like she didn't know me. She acted like we never slept together. It was losing the opportunity to be a father that made me realize how much I wanted it. But even then, I didn't really know. I was a kid. There was part of me that was relieved. Relieved that I didn't have to change my life at all. And damn, there's a lot of guilt that goes with that."

She nodded slowly. "I can imagine there is."

"But I've seen him, over the years. So there's never been an opportunity to really forget what I'm missing, what I don't have." His voice went rough. "I can't get over feeling like a piece of myself got stolen. It's just out there in the world, walking around. And sometimes I ask myself if it can't just be enough that he's happy. Because all the rest of it is selfish, I guess. He's got a dad. He's got a family. He's not missing anything because I'm not in his life."

"That's not true," Wren said. "He doesn't have you."

She was treated to a rueful, lopsided smile. "That's weird that you think not having me is a deficit, Wren."

"Well, what I mean is... Creed, if I didn't think that you would be a good father I wouldn't have bothered to try to include you in our baby's life."

"Maybe that's the thing," he said. "Maybe she just didn't think I would be a good father."

"She was sixteen. I imagine it's more that she didn't think. At least, not about anything much deeper than herself."

"Well, that probably is true."

"We'll do this right," Wren said.

He nodded. "So what do we do about the two of us?"

"We have nine months to figure it out. To figure out how we navigate sharing…a life. Because that's what we're doing. It's going to be complicated, and we don't need added complications. I'll tell you what… No relationships for either of us. For nine months."

He grimaced. "All right."

"Sorry. Get used to cozying up with your right hand."

He snorted. "In more ways than one, it's like being sixteen again."

"The fact of the matter is, we have got to find a better way to deal with each other than we have been. And I mean, we really do. So, we certainly don't have room for anyone else in this whole… situation."

"Fair enough."

"All right," she said. She extended her hand.

He looked at it. "I'm not shaking your hand."

"Why not?"

"Because it's not business, Wren. And it isn't going to be. You and me can't ever be business, sweetheart."

She lowered her hand, her heart fluttering. "I approach everything that way. Because of my dad."

"It's okay," he said. "We just… We are who we are. Can't do much about it."

"I want to do something about it, I guess. This whole figuring-myself-out thing is going to weave together with figuring out how we can be a family."

She would never have thought she would become family with Creed Cooper. But here she was.

"I guess so."

"Well." She looked down at her cleared plate. "I guess that's it. For now."

"For now. The wedding will be in three days."

"Are you going to invite your family?"

"Hell no," he said. "Just you and me."

"Don't we have to have a witness?"

"Bring your sister."

"Okay."

Then she stood up, and the two of them walked to the counter. Creed paid the bill.

"You didn't have to do that," she said.

"You're feeding my baby."

She looked around, feeling a little embarrassed. It wasn't like they would be able to hide it in the upcoming months. "I guess it can't really be a secret, can it?"

"Why does it have to be?"

"It doesn't," she said.

He had been treated like a secret before. And Wren wasn't about to do to him what Louisa had done.

Wren couldn't hate Louisa for it, though. She'd been sixteen. Who hadn't done a host of stupid things when they were sixteen? It was just that when Wren had done stupid things, they hadn't affected someone else for the rest of their life.

"It really doesn't," she affirmed.

Then the two of them walked out of the restaurant together, engaged.

It was so strange, because just a few weeks ago Wren had the sense of being on a different path from the one she had been on before. But she hadn't imagined that the path would lead here.

But this was one of those moments where she had to change.

It was actually a good thing. Because she needed a change anyway.

The only way to handle all of this change was to keep on going.

So that was what she would do.

The fact that she had to keep going with Creed…
Well, they would figure it out.

They had no other choice.

Chapter 8

It was his wedding day.

He hadn't ever imagined a wedding day. Hadn't figured he would ever get hitched. But then, what he'd said to Wren at the diner had been true. He had never planned to be in a situation where he got a do-over on the biggest regret of his life.

A slug of something hard hit him in the gut. It wasn't really a do-over. Because it wouldn't give him time back with his son. His son whose name he couldn't even think.

Because it wasn't a name he would've given to his kid. And it served as a reminder of the ways in which Creed wasn't part of his son's life.

But that didn't matter.

Today Creed was going to make sure he never missed out again. And the more he'd thought about it over the last few days, the firmer a conclusion he'd come to.

Sure. He could understand where Wren was coming from—she had the idea that they might be able to exist in a middle ground. And that the middle ground would be better than trying and failing at having a marriage.

But what she didn't understand about him was that he didn't do middle ground. He was all in. Or not in at all.

If he decided to make a marriage, then he was going to make it. And there would be no living separately. No other relationships.

No amicable divorce when the year was up.

He wanted to be in his child's life. He didn't want to have regrets. A real marriage was the simplest way to that path he could think of.

He would talk to her later.

After their wedding night.

As it was, he'd gone and dressed up for the occasion. Because she had liked it so much when he had dressed up for their winery event, so he was sure she would like it for this.

She'd said she would meet him at the courthouse. He assumed she was driving there with her sister.

And when he arrived, Wren was standing in front of the red brick building, wearing a simple white dress that fell just past her knees. On either side of her were her sisters. And her mother was there too, looking pale and drawn.

"Well, I didn't realize the whole family would be joining us," he said.

Wren grinned at him, then took hold of his arm, leading them ahead of her sisters and mother. "I had to bring them all," she said. "And they don't know the whole situation."

"Meaning?"

"They don't know that it's temporary."

He nearly said right then that she didn't seem to realize that temporary was off the table. But he decided to save that for after the vows. Instead, he bent down and brushed a kiss across her cheek. The action sent a slug of lust straight down to his gut.

She turned to face him, her eyes wide.

"You look beautiful," he said.

He heard a rustle of whispers behind him. And he gave her a knowing look.

"Thank you. So do you."

He knew she wasn't lying. She *did* think he looked good.

The heat between them was real.

It was all way too real.

Her mother looked between them. "I do wish we could've had a real wedding."

"You know why we have to do it quickly," Wren said.

"Nobody cares anymore if a woman is pregnant at her wedding, or if they have a baby in attendance," her mother replied.

"I care," Wren said.

"I was impatient," he said. "I just couldn't wait."

"Indeed," her older sister, Emerson, said, looking him in the eye with coolness.

"You don't approve of me?" he asked.

"I'm deeply suspicious of you. But then, I would be deeply suspicious of anyone marrying my sister."

"I hear tell that your husband is a pretty suspicious character, too."

"And Wren did her sworn sisterly duty by being skeptical of him."

Well, that was fair enough.

It was the youngest sister, Cricket, who gave him the kind of open, assessing look that made him feel actual guilt.

"You had better be good to her. Our father was terrible, and Wren deserves to be happy."

"I'll be good to her," he said.

He would be. Her happiness mattered. He told himself it mattered only because of their baby.

But somehow, he suspected it was more.

"Good," Cricket said. "Because if you aren't, I'll hunt you down and I'll kill you."

She said it cheerfully enough that he suspected she wasn't being hyperbolic.

They all filed into the courtroom, and he and Wren took their position up near the judge's bench. They exchanged brief pleasantries with the woman before getting down to business.

It was surprisingly quick. Pledging his life to another person. When the ceremony was stripped away, a wedding was just a business deal where you held hands.

Wren's voice trembled on the part about staying together until death separated them.

His own didn't. But maybe that was because he didn't feel like he was lying. He felt as committed as he could be to this. To her.

Maybe it was that simple for him because he didn't have other dreams of love, marriage or anything of the kind. He imagined that Wren, on some level, dreamed of romance. Most women did, he assumed.

He wondered what his sister would say if he leveled this theory at her. She would probably bite him. Honey didn't like to be what anyone expected.

And she would also be annoyed at him for having a wedding and not inviting her. Probably, she would be irritated at him for not telling her that he was going to be a father.

But Honey was a problem that would have to wait.

"You may kiss the bride," the judge said.

And this… Well, this was the part Creed had been waiting for.

He wrapped his arms around Wren and pulled her against him. The look in her eyes was one of shock, as if she hadn't realized they would be expected to do this. As if she hadn't realized that whether a wedding was permanent or not, in a courthouse or not, if you were trying to pass it off as something real to your family, you were going to have to kiss.

And so they did.

It was everything he remembered. Her mouth so soft and sweet. She was a revelation, Wren Maxfield.

And he tried to remember what it had been like when he wanted to punish her with his passion.

That wasn't what he wanted now. No.

Now what he wanted was something else altogether.

A strange need had twisted and turned inside him, upside down and inside out, until he couldn't recognize it or himself. He might not know exactly what was happening in him, but he knew desire. And desire flared between them whenever they touched. No question about it.

When they parted, her family was staring at them, openmouthed.

He shrugged. "There's a reason we had to get married so quickly."

That earned him a slug on the shoulder. Wren looked disheveled, and furious. And he wondered if he had set a record for husband who got punched soonest after the vows were spoken.

When it was over, they went to his truck, and sat there. Silence ballooned between them.

"I thought you weren't going to involve your family?" he asked.

"I… I didn't know what to tell them. I didn't want to tell them I was getting married to you just because of a legal thing. It felt stupid. And then it snowballed."

"Wren…"

"So, can I come to your house? Just for a while?"

She was making his whole seduction plan a hell of a lot easier than he had expected it to be. He had thought he would have to contrive a way to get her to spend their wedding night together, but it turned out she had walked herself into a situation where she was going to have to do it anyway.

"Gee, I think I can think of something for us to do."

"Creed…"

"You can't deny that it's real between us, Wren. Whatever else—the desire between us is real."

Wren stared at her new husband.

She had to wonder if all this time she had simply been lying to herself. By increments, stages and degrees. Lying to herself that they could be together and *not* be together, that they could somehow have a platonic relationship that wouldn't be affected if the other one ended up with a different partner. That they could be friends, and keep everything easy for their child.

But she realized now that perhaps the real issue in her parents' marriage had been honesty. And maybe it wasn't even honesty with each other, but honesty with themselves.

Wren didn't really know how to be honest with herself, that was the thing.

The realization shocked her about as much as anything else had since she'd started this thing with Creed. About as much as their kiss at the altar, and as much as how real the vows had felt.

It was just so different from how she had imagined. He was different from how she had imagined.

They were different together.

"Take me home," she said softly.

And he did.

The truck moved quickly around the curves as he maneuvered it expertly along the rural road.

"Did you ever want to do anything but work at the family winery?" she asked.

His eyes were glued to the road as he drove. "I have my ranch. Not a huge operation, because, of course, I'm tied up a lot of the time with Cowboy Wines. But I've found a way to do what I want, and what I feel like my responsibility is."

"So it feels like a responsibility to you?"

"Yes. It does. And more so in the years since my mother died."

Her heart went tight. "I'm so sorry. About your mother."

"I'm sorry about your dad," he said. "I know I wasn't very nice about it before. I'm not proud of what I said, Wren. But sometimes I get my head buried in the sand. I turned your family into an enemy, because you were competition, and because I was pouring myself into making our winery better. Since my mother died, I felt like I was on some crusade to make my dad interested in life. I lost sight of some things. But I'm good at that. I'm good at losing sight of things. Sometimes intentionally."

"Does that have to do with…"

"My son?"

"Yes."

"Trying to ignore that pain certainly didn't improve my disposition, let's put it that way. And it's a wound that hurts worse the older I get. The more I realize what I missed. What I can't get back. Kids always make you aware of how time passes, as I understand it. Mine comes with accompanying grief and regret."

She could see that. How that would work. At sixteen, everyone was short on perspective and long on time. But at their age… That's when a person realized how precious it all was, and that feeling only increased with the years. The desire to hang on to what was important.

Of course, she wasn't sure it was age that had given her that perspective.

"You know, losing my relationship with my father the way I did is what forced me to look at my life more critically," Wren said. "It's what forced me to ask myself why I was doing anything. And I think it's what made me feel ready for the baby. But even with those changes, there are so many things I still don't know how to navigate. So many things I'm not sure about. Because all these revelations are so very new and I..." She looked at him. "People like to be comfortable, don't we? We don't want to change. And usually, life doesn't ask us if we want to go through the things that most define us. We just have to go through them."

"I'm sure losing your dad the way you did is a lot like losing my mom."

She shook her head. "No. You can't see your mom anymore. I don't want to see my dad. It's a loss, Creed, but I wouldn't compare the two. My dad was never who I thought he was."

His truck pulled up to the long gravel driveway that led to the ranch. His house was so different from any she would have imagined herself living in before. Her place at Maxfield Vineyards was styled after the vineyard house itself, which was her parents' taste. Or maybe just her father's taste. Maybe what her mother wanted didn't come into it at all. Wren didn't know.

It bothered her, going from a house that had been decided on by her parents, straight to a man's house.

He stopped the car and looked at her. "What's wrong?"

"I've never had my own place. Not really. I don't know what I like. I don't know...who I am. I try to think of what kind of house I would choose and it's just a blank in my head."

"What *do* you know, Wren?" he asked.

"I know that I want you," she said, meeting his gaze.

Because that was one choice she had made in the middle of all of this, the one choice that had been down to her—kissing Creed Cooper in the first place.

They'd made a deal. A deal to not do this. But she

didn't think she could stick to the deal. Didn't think she could be near him, with him like this, and not have him.

So maybe just once?

Maybe just for their wedding night.

Whether it made sense or not, it was what she'd chosen.

That desire for him hadn't come from anywhere but inside herself. And there was something empowering about that.

Maybe the wedding had been his idea, but wanting him... She knew that was all her. Nothing anyone would have asked her to do. Nothing her family was even all that supportive of. Some might have argued it was a bad thing to have given in to, on some level, but it had been her own choice. And right now, sitting in a truck that wasn't hers, in front of the house that wasn't hers, having taken vows that weren't her idea, the desire between them at least seemed honest.

And wasn't honest what she really needed?

Yes, she was trying to be smart, whatever that meant in this situation. Yes, she was trying to do the right thing for her child, but if she didn't know what the right thing was for herself... How could she be a good mother?

She thought about her own mother. Soft but distant, somebody Wren had never connected with.

Because she didn't *know* her. She didn't know her mother, and Wren had to wonder if the other woman knew herself.

"Yes," she repeated now. "I want you. I want you, because I know that's real."

He threw the truck into Park and shut off the engine. Then he got out, rounded to her side and opened the door. He pulled her out and into his arms, carrying her up the front steps and through the door. Then he carried her up the stairs, set her down in his bed.

And when they kissed, she felt like she might know something.

Something deep and real inside herself.

She didn't have a name for it. But it didn't matter.

Because all she wanted to do was feel.

This was different from the other times they had been together. It wasn't fast or frantic. And when it was over, she drifted off to sleep. She had the oddest sensation that in his bed, without her clothes, without any of the trappings that normally made her feel like her... She was the closest to real that she had ever been.

Chapter 9

Wren began stirring in the late evening. They had skipped straight to the wedding night before the sun had gone down, and Creed was certain he would never get enough of her.

Then she had fallen asleep, all soft and warm and satisfied against him, and he would've thought that he'd find it…irritating. That he still wanted sex and the woman had fallen asleep.

But he didn't. Instead, he just enjoyed holding her.

It was amazing how much less of a termagant she was when she was asleep.

As soon as she began making sleepy little noises, he hauled himself down to the kitchen and put together a plate of cheese and crackers, and grabbed a bottle of sparkling cider, which he had bought a couple of days earlier.

How funny for Wren not to be able to drink wine. Wine was their business. It was what they were. But, of course, it wouldn't be part of her life for the next few months.

That meant it wouldn't be part of his either. No wine, but she got him as a consolation prize.

He imagined it was all a very strange turn of events for her.

He brought the food upstairs just as Wren was sitting up, scrubbing her eyes with the backs of her hands, the covers fallen down around her waist, exposing her perfect, gorgeous breasts.

"Happy wedding night," he said, holding up his offerings as he made his way toward the bed.

Her eyes took a leisurely tour of his body, and he could tell she enjoyed the view.

That she had ever thought the two of them could keep their hands off each other was almost funny.

Almost.

The problem was, he didn't find much funny about the way he wanted her. It flew in the face of everything that he was. Everything he knew about himself.

Everything he knew about keeping himself separate.

All the decisions that he'd made about his life eighteen years ago seemed… They didn't seem quite so clear when he was staring at Wren. The woman carrying his child.

The woman who was now his wife.

"Well, this is nice," she said.

"I can be nice."

She chuckled, and pushed herself up so she was sitting a little taller. The covers fell down even farther, and he set the food and drink down on the nightstand next to her, then yanked them off the rest of the way.

"Hey," she said.

But he was too busy admiring her thighs, and that sweet spot between them, to care.

"It's my payment," he said.

"I retract what I said about you being nice."

"If you keep showing me all this glory, I might go ahead and drop dead. And then you can do a little dance on my grave. I really would like to see you dance."

She smirked, then shook her hips slightly as she got up onto her knees, leaning over and taking a piece of cheese off the tray.

"Honestly, I would have married you a lot sooner if I'd known you came with room service."

"Room service and multiple orgasms," he said.

"You know, if you have to be the one to say it…"

"You know you're sleeping with a woman who has more pride than sense?"

"Nothing wrong with that," she said. "A little bit of pride never hurt anybody."

"Neither did a little bit of submission."

"That's where you're wrong," she said. "It hurts unless you want to give it."

"You say that as an expert?"

She shook her head. "Definitely not. Being totally honest, I've had a few *very* underwhelming boyfriends. And none of them have enticed me to do the kinds of things that you entice me to do. So there you have it."

"I haven't had girlfriends. None." He got into bed with her and stretched out alongside her, running his knuckles along the line of her waist. "I hook up. It's never about any one woman in particular so much as about my desire to get laid. That's actually vastly unsatisfying."

"Tell me more." She narrowed her eyes. "And this better end in a way that compliments me and makes me feel singular, magical and like a sex goddess."

"I can't keep my hands off you," he growled. "More to the point, I can't keep my mind off you. When I'm not with you, I want to be with you. And when you said you didn't want our relationship to be physical... I didn't know what I was going to do with that. I think about you, and I burn, Wren. Even if we weren't having the baby, even if we weren't together tonight because it was our wedding night, I think we would still be in my bed."

The frown on her face made his chest feel strange.

"We don't like each other," she said.

"I think we're both going to have to let go of that idea. Because obviously it's more complicated than that."

"We don't mesh," she said.

"We seem to mesh pretty well."

She poured herself a glass of the sparkling cider and took another slice of cheese, leaning back against the headboard, sighing heavily. "My parents' marriage has always mystified me. They don't really talk. It was very civil, but very distant, and I think I always imagined that's what marriage was. I tried to find a similar thing with the men I dated. This kind of external compatibility. We never fought. And anytime I ever broke up with someone... It just sort of fizzled out. Like I would notice it had been a while since we'd seen each other and I didn't really care. Or we were still going to events together, but not even bothering to have sex after. Or worse, we did have sex and I basically spent the whole time thinking about which canapés I liked best at the party, and not about what we were doing. I knew I didn't want that in a long-term relationship. Boredom before we got to forever, you know?"

"Sure."

"But there was never *this*. There was never any fighting, there was never any passion. I just thought passion was for other people."

"Why did you think that?"

She sighed. "It's stupid."

"Look, Wren, you know all about the worst thing that's ever happened to me. You tell me why you can't have passion."

"I never think about it. It's one of those things usually buried in my memory. You know when you're a kid you think you're going to be all kinds of different things. From a unicorn on down the list. For a while, I even fantasized about being a police officer. Chasing bad guys, solving mysteries. And then I realized that I don't like to run, and I never want to be shot at, so that kind of takes being a cop off the table."

He snorted. "Yeah, I can see how that would be an issue."

"But when I was a little bit older, I thought... I got really good grades in math. I really liked it. I also really liked art, and a teacher at school, at the boarding school I went to, told me that combination was sort of rare. She said it made me special, that I could think creatively and wield numbers the way that I did. She talked to me about the kinds of things I could do with a talent like that. One of the things we spoke about was architectural engineering. I was really fascinated by it. By the way you could put different materials together. Marrying form and function. Art with practicality. My father said it just wasn't what he saw me doing. He said my brain would be useful for the brand, and that I needed to remember the school that I went to, the clothes that I wore, everything that I was, came from the winery. Which meant I needed to invest back into the winery. I understood that. I really did. And I just didn't think about architectural engineering anymore after that. I got my degree in hospitality and marketing. And I've found that I really love my job. But I've just been asking myself a lot of questions lately. About who I might've been if my whole life hadn't felt so rigidly *decided*."

"Do you want to go back to school?"

"I have to take care of the winery. Cricket doesn't have any interest in it. Emerson is awesome, but she does a very particular thing, this kind of global brand ambassador stuff that requires lots of computer savvy. She's brilliant. It's actually a very similar kind of skill set as the one I have. She's so good with algorithms, but she's also great at finessing public branding. Doing posts that are visually appealing and that have a result. I mean, I get to use my gifts in my job. It's just every so often I wonder if I had known who my father was back then, would I have worked so hard to make him happy?"

"I don't think you can know that. The same way I can't actually know what kind of father I would've been. The honest truth is, Wren, I can get myself really angry about what was taken from me, and when I do that... Well, in my head I'm the best damn teenage father ever. I give up everything for my kid. Women and drinking and partying and being carefree." He paused, working hard to speak around the weight that settled over his heart. "But I didn't do any of that, I didn't have to. Louisa did. So did Cal. *They* are the ones who ended up sacrificing. They're the ones who gave my son a family. They're the ones who gave him his life. Yeah, in hindsight I can make myself a hero. But I don't know that I would've been. We can't actually know what we would have done. We can just do something different now."

As soon as he said those words, he realized how true they were. And they made his chest feel bruised.

He looked at Wren, and he felt a sense of deep certainty. "From this day on, Wren Maxfield, you can be whoever you want. You've chosen to be the mother of my child, and I appreciate that. Whatever else you want to be, I would never hold you back from it. I'd support you. If you wanted to quit working and just take care of the baby, I'd be fine with that. If you wanted to go back to school, I'd be fine with that, too. Whatever it is you need, I will help make that a reality."

"Why?" she asked.

"Because I've had more what-ifs in my life than I care to. And this… This gives me the chance to answer a lot of my greatest ones. Getting to be the father that I've wondered if I could be… I want to be a father. Everything else… Everything else doesn't matter as much."

"You don't expect to hear that from men," she said.

"Maybe not. But most men didn't lose out on the chance of fatherhood the way that I did. So for me… If you're going to get a second chance, you gotta be willing to pour everything into it. And that includes caring about your happiness, Wren. I want you to stay my wife."

"Creed…"

"Like I said, be whatever you want along with that. I'll support you. I swear it."

He had assumed so many things about her. He had looked at her and seen the glitter and polish, had associated her with her father and the kinds of things her father had done, and Creed had imagined her to be avaricious and shallow, because it was so much easier to reduce people to stereotypes. Because it was easier to do that than to see her as a person.

Because now that he saw her as a person, he had to contend with the complicated feelings she created inside him. And he knew he had been avoiding that. Avoiding it because something in him had recognized a connection to Wren the moment they first met.

He had no doubt about that.

And he had been running from complicated since the first time emotional entanglements had bit him in the ass when he was sixteen.

But he hadn't known anything then. And he hadn't known anything for a lot of years after because he had simply clung to his anger at Louisa and used it as a shield.

But age forced him to see everything with a hell of a lot more nuance, and being in this situation again demanded the same thing.

He was having to contend with the fact that Louisa didn't seem like such a villain anymore. And that the fact didn't make the past hurt any less for him.

Having to contend with the fact that there was a lot

of mileage between just sex and whatever this was between him and Wren.

And whatever their feelings were, whatever they could be, they were having a baby. And he wanted this child to have the benefit of everything his son had.

If there was one good thing about Creed never busting into his son's life, it was that he'd given him a family. He'd honored and respected that.

But now, Creed wanted the same kind of family for this child.

So he would give Wren anything. Absolutely anything.

"I don't know what I want yet," she said, looking almost helpless. "I'm not sure that I can make that decision while I'm still in the middle of this big…change."

"It's okay," he said. "I understand. Maybe it's not the best time, but my offer stands no matter when you take it."

"Thank you." She looked at him again. "For now, can we just focus on cheese and sex? Because those are decisions I feel like I can make. I would like both."

"And I can accommodate."

And that was when he pulled her into his arms again, and they quit talking about the future, about anything serious.

Because there was a whole lot of uncertainty out there, and in the future. But there was no uncertainty of any kind between them when it came to their mutual desire. It was certain, and it was real. And it made everything else seem manageable. Like it might be the easiest thing in the world for them to find some way to make this marriage and parenthood work.

Creed was determined in that.

If sheer stubbornness could will something into being possible, then he knew he and Wren would succeed.

Because they were two of the most stubborn people on the planet.

He just had to hope they could do it without deciding they wanted different things. Because in the end, that would end up tearing both of them apart.

She and Creed had been living together for two months.

She'd wanted a wedding night... She was getting a full-on honeymoon.

She'd wanted to do all this with a clear head. Had wanted to make plans for the baby, for how they would conduct themselves...

She'd wanted to do it all in a lab-like environment. As if they were talking heads who could divorce feeling and desire from everything else.

But they couldn't do that.

He'd set something free inside her and she didn't want to deny it. Didn't want to put it back. He'd asked for permanent and she didn't feel like she could answer him.

Was afraid to.

But she'd be lying if she said she wasn't fantasizing about it.

They had been sleeping together, talking to each other, eating cheese in bed. They'd talked about Christmas, and not just in the context of the event they were planning.

Their memories of it. The way they liked to decorate.

She liked it sparkly. He liked it homespun.

She liked a full turkey dinner. His mom had always made spaghetti, lasagna and bread.

They opened a present on Christmas Eve. He was scandalized by the idea. Christmas morning only.

She liked fake trees because they were perfect and didn't shed.

If he'd had pearls, he'd have clutched them. He'd been subjected to the virtues and tradition inherent in going to the woods and getting your own tree.

Another discussion they'd tabled for later, in terms of how they'd raise their child.

It was so difficult for her to reconcile the man that she was involved with now with the one she had first kissed all that time ago.

She could hardly remember hating him. She didn't hate him now. Not even close. She *couldn't* hate him. Her feelings were starting to get jumbled up, and it was frightening, to be honest.

But no more frightening than when she came home and saw that a real estate sign had been put up at his ranch.

"What is this?" she asked.

"I'm selling this place. Because I want us to pick out our own place."

"What?"

"You heard me. Wren, you told me you didn't know who you were. And that you were going from a house designed to your father's taste to one better suited to mine. I don't want you to feel that way. I don't want that for you. I don't want that for us."

"So you put your house up for sale without talking to me about it?"

"I didn't go out and buy a house without talking to you. That would have defeated the purpose."

She looked at him, and boggled. Because as much as she was coming to feel affection for him, he was still a big, stubborn, hardheaded fool.

And she cared about him an awful lot.

"I can't believe you would do this for me. This is your place. Your ranch."

"That's the only requirement I have," he said. "I do need to have property, or I need to be close enough to property I can lease."

"Don't be silly. That would be inconvenient."

"I don't care about the house," he said. "It can be whatever you want it to be. We could build too if you want, but that would take a lot of time."

"We need a place sooner than that."

They didn't waste any time. They started to house hunt after that. They went overboard looking at places, and Wren felt giddy with the independence of it.

That she was choosing a place. A place to call her own. One that would be shaped around this life she was sharing with Creed and…

She wondered when she had accepted it. That they were going to make a try at this together.

That she wasn't going to leave him after a year. Or when the baby was born, or whatever she had told him all those weeks ago.

Because she knew now that she wasn't going to do that. That there was no way. Because she knew now there would be no separating the two of them. They were forming a unit, as strange as it was.

And somehow, Wren found that their unit didn't compromise her desire for independence. Rather, it supported it.

He supported it.

There was a strange sort of freedom, having this giant brick wall on her team. She couldn't fully explain it. But there it was. True as anything.

The house that stole her heart surprised her.

It was a white farmhouse with red shutters, new, but styled in a classic way. She could see how their Christmas styles might even meet here. A little glitter, a little rustic.

The kitchen had gorgeous granite countertops and white cabinets. Light and airy, but not too modern. Perfect for Christmas Eve lasagna, and Christmas turkey.

She loved the layout of it, the great big living room that she could imagine being filled with baby toys, and a big old Christmas tree.

Fake or real, it suddenly didn't matter.

The way the bedrooms were configured, with one just down the hall from the master bedroom that she knew would make the ideal nursery, was perfect. More than she had ever dreamed. For a life she hadn't been able to imagine before, but could now, so vividly that it hurt.

"What do you think?" he asked.

"This is it," she said.

A life that was theirs. A life that didn't belong to anyone else.

"Yes," she said. "I think this is going to work."

* * *

Let it never be said that Creed Cooper was a coward, but he had been avoiding having meaningful conversation with his family for far too long. They were all dancing around the issue of his marriage, and his impending fatherhood. And it was obvious that whatever leash had been holding Honey back had just broken.

He was in his office, finalizing details for the upcoming joint winery event, when Jackson, Jericho, Honey and their father walked in. Or rather, Honey burst in, and the others came in behind her.

"Are we just not talking about this? About the fact that you got married?"

"I mean, there's not much to say."

"You married a Maxfield."

"I did," Creed said.

"She's pregnant."

"Honey, do I have to walk you through how that happens, or did you get sex ed in school?"

"I'm good," Honey said, her tone dry. "Thanks, though. My point is, what exactly is going on?"

"I got her pregnant. I married her. That's what a gentleman does."

Honey rolled her eyes. "I was under the impression a gentleman waited until he was married." She looked like she was deciding something. Then, decision made, her lips turned up into a smirk. "Or at the very least used a damn condom."

"Can you not say the word *condom*?" Creed asked.

"Why? I would assume you'd prefer to think that I was using them rather than not."

"I would prefer not to think about it at all."

"You've given *me* no such luxury. Since you clearly had *unprotected sex*. Like a ...horny goat."

"Are you just here to lecture me on protocol or...?"

"Do you love her?"

"What does love have to do with anything?" And the words sat uncomfortably in his gut. Because he felt something for Wren, sure as hell. He was selling his ranch for her, moving into another house.

As if she could read his mind, Honey's gaze sharpened. "Is she *making* you leave your ranch?"

"No," he said. "I suggested we get a place that's more about the two of us."

"You...*did*?"

"It was the least I could do. Considering I basically forced her to marry me."

"You didn't," Honey said.

"I did," he responded.

His sister stared at him, and he could feel his older brother mounting a protective posture. At him? That was ridiculous.

"Honey," Jackson said. "Maybe just leave it alone. Like we told you to when you were ranting a few minutes ago."

"You guys are terrible bouncers," Creed said, addressing his brother and Jericho. "You let her come right through the front door."

"I just don't get it," she said. "Why you would marry somebody you're not in love with."

"There's a lot of reasons to get married, sweetheart," he said. "And they often don't have anything to do with love."

"Then what?"

"Well, lust comes to mind."

"You don't marry somebody just because you lust after them. That's silly."

"Fine. The pregnancy."

"I still don't understand how you could be so stupid. You're not a kid."

"Honey, I pray that you always keep your head when it comes to situations of physical desire."

She tossed her pale brown hair over her shoulder. "I would never get that stupid over a man."

The three of them laughed at her. Well, chuckles, really, but Honey looked infuriated.

"Spoken like a woman who's never wanted anyone," Jericho said.

Honey's face went up in flames. "You don't know *anything*," she said, planting her hand on his chest and shoving him slightly.

"I know plenty enough," he responded.

"Did you guys just come to my office to bicker? To yell at me about something I can't change?"

"They're our rivals," Honey said. "That's what I don't get. Now you're married, and did you do anything to protect the winery when you made that deal?"

No. They hadn't signed a prenup of any kind. And in hindsight that probably wasn't the best decision. But all he'd been thinking of was making sure he was protecting his rights as a father.

He hadn't thought to protect his monetary assets at all.

"Everything will be fine," he said.

"How could you be so shortsighted?"

"I was only thinking about one thing," he said, his patience snapping. "I'm really glad that you can sit there on your high horse. But virgins don't get to talk about what it's like to be carried away by desire. I've made this mistake before." That made his sister look shame-faced, shocked. "And the woman took the kid from me, okay? I missed out on eighteen years of raising my son because I didn't make sure my rights were protected, and I wasn't going to do it again. I did what I had to do. My kid was more important than the winery."

Finally, his father spoke. "You compromised the win-ery for this marriage?"

"There are things that are more important than a winery, Dad. I would think you would know that."

He couldn't read the expression on his old man's face. "I protected the winery all this time," he said. "It was my…new dream after it became clear I wasn't going to get the first thing I wanted. And I never com-promised for it."

"No," Creed agreed. "You didn't. Down to not want-ing to make too big of an incident out of me getting a girl pregnant when I was sixteen. Yeah, Dad, you pro-tected the winery. But I protected my son. Can you say you did the same?"

Suddenly, Creed was done. Done with all of it. Done with all of them.

It was easy for them to pass judgment, but they didn't know what they were talking about.

His father had gotten everything he wanted in his life. He'd had a wife, had his children.

And then the old man had withdrawn into himself when his wife had died and let his children take over the running of the winery.

Yeah, he'd used them to protect the winery. At the expense of everything else. His father had asked endless sacrifices of Creed.

Creed was out of damn patience for his family.

"All of you spare me your lectures," he said. "A virgin and an old man who don't know what the hell they're talking about." He shook his head and walked out of the building, breathing in the sharp early-morning air.

He wasn't going to justify his decision to marry Wren. His course was set.

And whatever Honey thought, love did come into it. The love for his child. Nothing else mattered.

Chapter 10

The big cross-vineyard event was tonight, and Wren could hardly keep the nerves from overtaking her.

She got tired much more quickly than usual these days, and her midsection was beginning to get a bit thicker, which made the dresses she normally wore to things like this slightly tighter. She had spent countless hours trying on gowns in hers and Creed's bedroom, until he had grabbed hold of her and said very firmly that he loved her body like it was, and that absolutely everything looked good on her, or off her.

That had ended in him nearly destroying her makeup with his kisses, and she had scolded him roundly about the fact that they didn't have any time to get busy.

She had been filled with regret about that decision, however. And the fact that making love to him seemed a whole lot more interesting than readying herself for something she was supposed to be excited about irritated her.

As she slipped into the formfitting green dress she'd decided on, she tried to tell herself she was irritated simply because having a baby was such a big deal.

It was harder and harder to care about other things right now. She was consumed with the fact that in six and a half months she and Creed were going to be parents.

And for some reason, it kept sticking in her mind even more that they were still going to be husband and wife, for six more months and longer.

The baby was supposed to be what mattered.

And first, this event.

Her family was acclimating to the fact that she and Creed weren't rivals anymore. That they had to be friendly, to an extent, with Cowboy Wines. But it wasn't smooth sailing.

Not entirely. For some reason, Cricket was being difficult about playing nice. And while Wren had a lot of patience for what they were all going through under the circumstances, her sympathy still didn't make it easy to accept Cricket's behavior.

All dressed and ready, Wren kissed Creed goodbye and told him she needed to get to Maxfield Vineyards early.

He grumbled about being reluctant to let her go, but she pointed out that she hadn't been back home since they'd moved. Not to the house, anyway. She'd gone to the winery itself, to the public areas, the tasting rooms. There had been weddings and dinners and other things since she and Creed had gotten married. But she hadn't actually been in the house.

For some reason, she felt like she needed to do that today. And she felt like she needed to do it alone.

Nerves overtook her when she realized part of the reason she felt an urgency to visit was that she hadn't actually been alone with her mother, Cricket and Emerson altogether since the wedding.

When Wren arrived at the house, her mother looked impeccable, but stone-faced, and Emerson looked as radiant as ever. Cricket was wearing jeans and a T-shirt.

"What are you doing, Cricket?" Wren asked.

"Oh, I'm not going," Cricket said.

"Why aren't you going?"

"Because I don't want to," she said defiantly.

"But it's a family event."

"No, it isn't," Cricket said. "It's an event for the winery, and I don't have to be there. There's absolutely no reason for me to get dressed up and parade myself around. I'm not really part of anything that happens with the winery. It's never been me."

Wren was shocked, but she had to wonder if she would feel the same way had she been Cricket's age when their family had fallen apart.

"I'm divorcing your father," her mother said.

"What?" Wren asked.

"I'm divorcing him," she said. "I haven't seen him in months. What's the point of staying married? What was the point of any of it?" Her mother, who was often so quiet, sad even, seemed…not herself.

"More and more I question the point of any of this. I have this beautiful house, but your father never loved me.

I have you girls. The only good to have come out of my life in the last thirty years. Everything else is shallow. Pointless. I thought this winery mattered. This house. The money. It doesn't."

"And if it doesn't matter to her," Cricket said, "why should I pretend that it matters to me?"

"I'm all for bids of independence," Wren said. "And I'm not going to say I haven't been on a soul-searching mission myself these last few months. But save your breakdowns so they're not right before my big event?"

"Sorry it's not convenient for you," Cricket said. "You getting married and abandoning me wasn't great timing either."

Wren had a feeling that was directed at both her and Emerson.

"Cricket," Emerson said. "You don't have to go if you don't want. But if you're upset, maybe we should talk."

"We should talk now," Cricket said. "Because this family is a mess, and Wren is just making the same mistakes Mom did. Marrying Creed because she's having a baby, when they don't even love each other. You can pretend all you want but I don't believe you magically fell in love with him. It's going to end like this. Big house, lots of money. Maybe a winery conglomerate. Sad adult children and divorce."

"That's enough," her mother said. "I judge myself for the decisions I made for money. For comfort. For... for turning away from somebody who did love me for somebody who never could." Wren stared at her mother for a moment, not fully understanding what she was talking about. "But the one thing that I'm at peace with is anything I did for the sake of you girls. Wren made a decision for the sake of her child's future. And Creed Cooper isn't your father."

"No," Wren said, her tone firm. "Creed is a good man. He loves this baby. So much. You have no idea."

"Well, I don't have to participate in any of this."

Cricket turned and walked out of the room. Emerson put her hand on Wren's shoulder. "Don't worry about her. She doesn't know what she's talking about. She doesn't know what it's like."

There was something in Emerson's gaze that scared Wren, and she couldn't pinpoint why.

Didn't know what *what* was like? Relationships?

That she would believe. Her sister had led a cloistered life on the vineyard, and hadn't gone away to school the way Wren and Emerson had. In many ways, it had felt like their parents had given up by the time they'd gotten to Cricket. For all that the expectations of their father had been hard on Emerson and Wren, Wren suspected there had been no expectations at all of Cricket.

And that the low bar hadn't done her any favors.

But Wren didn't think that's what Emerson was talking about. And the alternative possibility made her stomach feel tight.

"Mom," Wren said, turning to her mother, deciding to reject any thoughts she was having about herself and deal with her mother instead. "What did you mean about 'someone who could love you'?"

"The Coopers are good men," her mother said. "If Creed is anything like his father, he has a lot more honor than James Maxfield ever did."

Wren's whole world felt shaky, and she decided not

to press the issue, because she didn't think she could take on any more right then.

Instead, Wren and Emerson went down to the grand event hall, which was decorated and lit up, overlooking the valley below. It was all pristine glass, floor-to-ceiling windows and honey-colored wood beams. A huge fake Christmas tree was at the center, lit up, merry and bright.

It looked elegant and perfect, and stations for each winery were beginning to come together. Lindy Dodge, from another local winery, was there, setting out samples and arranging small plates of food, her big, cowboy husband, Wyatt, helping with everything. The sight of those two people, so very different from each other— Lindy, petite and polished, and Wyatt, big, rough and ready—did something strange to Wren's insides. Made her long for something she didn't think was even possible.

She turned away from the couple, and made a show of looking at some of the displays put up by the other wineries before busying herself with the fine details of their own.

And when Creed arrived, her world spun to a halt. Just looking at him made her mouth run dry. Made everything in her go still, and her sister's words echoed inside her.

She doesn't know what it's like.

Not a relationship. No, nothing quite that simple. Not attraction either. Because that was not deep enough.

No, what Cricket didn't understand was what happened when a man entered a woman's life, who was wrong in every way, but fit so beautifully.

Who seemed to take all the jagged pieces and press

them together, turning something ordinary into something new. Making each fractured line seem a beautiful detail rather than a fatal flaw.

What Cricket didn't understand was the miracle involved in loving someone she shouldn't.

Loving someone who made no sense. And the way that it rearranged one's life into something unrecognizable.

What Cricket didn't understand was that love was a storm.

Wren had always imagined that loving somebody was civil. That it was something she could pick out, like selecting the perfect wine in a refined cellar.

But no. That wasn't how it was with Creed.

He was a brilliant and glorious streak of lightning, shooting across the sky, a low, resonating boom of thunder that echoed in her heart. He was nothing she would have ever looked for, and everything she was beginning to suspect she needed.

And that need wasn't comfortable.

Because just like a storm, she couldn't control it, didn't know how much damage it might cause, didn't know what the landscape would look like after it was finished raging.

Feelings like this, they could uproot trees. Reorder the slopes of mountains.

Damage her heart irrevocably.

She didn't know what to do, because she couldn't unthink all these things. Couldn't unknow the feeling that made her heart squeeze tight when she looked at the man. That made her want to mess up her hair and makeup and make love to him on the floor before an important event.

That made her want to test all his rough against her soft. That made her feel enamored of their differences, rather than disdainful of them.

The reason she had fought with him from the beginning was because she had been desperate to keep him at bay. She could see that now, with stunning clarity.

It was the wrong time to be realizing all of this. Any of this. Because she had to focus on this event. It mattered. It was the reason they were together in the first place, these initiatives.

Is it?

Or had she been unable to see a way forward without Creed because she had been desperate to spend more time with him?

Desperate to make him a part of her life and part of her business.

Honesty.

Hadn't she dedicated herself to finding honesty in who she was and what she wanted?

Her heart felt tender as she gazed at the tall, striking figure of her husband across the room, at a different winery station from her.

She didn't even know how that was going to work. They were separate. Though they were married.

And it wasn't just because they worked at different places. But because there was a very deliberate barrier between them when it came to emotion.

Creed had made it plain he wanted the marriage to last, but she knew that he was motivated by a deep, feral need to keep his child close to him.

It had nothing to do with her, and he'd never pretended it did.

It does, a little bit. He doesn't want anyone else to have you.

It was true. But was that the same as wanting her? Really wanting her?

She didn't know.

And she didn't even know why it mattered.

Why it suddenly felt imperative that there be love between them.

Because other than your sisters, have you ever felt like anyone really loved you?

The question bit into her, and she tried hard to keep on doing her job while it gnawed at all she was.

Eventually, she was unable to keep herself away from Creed any longer.

"This is looking good," she said.

"It is," he responded. "It's good."

She wanted him to say that he was proud of her.

But wanting his praise made her feel small and sad.

Because was she ever really going to be different? How could she ever be new? When she was still just simpering after the approval, the love, of a man who wasn't going to give it back?

Maybe he will. Maybe you just need to ask him.

She looked at his square jaw, at his striking features that seemed as if they were carved from stone.

He had been hurt. Badly. But did that mean he couldn't feel anything for anyone anymore? She knew that he loved their unborn baby. That he was intensely motivated by that love in everything he did.

Although, he had never said those words exactly. He didn't talk about love. He talked about opportunities, responsibility. He talked about not wanting to miss anything. But he had never said the word *love*. That didn't mean he didn't feel it, but it did give her questions about just how much he knew his own emotions.

Considering her own were a big giant news flash to her, she didn't think it was outrageous to suspect that he might not be fully in touch with his own.

He held himself at a distance. She looked down at his left hand, at the ring he wore there.

He was her husband. And it wasn't a secret. She closed the distance between them, kissing him on the cheek. "I'm glad that we did this."

The look in his eyes was unreadable.

"Me, too."

She didn't know if she had meant the event. The pregnancy. The marriage.

How could she feel something so deep for this man? This man she had thought she felt only antagonistic things for a few months ago. Well, she felt chemistry with him, but she hadn't known him. Hadn't known that deep wound that he carried around. The intensity with which he cared about things.

And whether or not he knew it was love, she did.

He had been ready to set everything aside at sixteen and become a father.

He bled responsibility. He was everything her father wasn't.

And then he had let her choose their house, had sold a place that meant something to him. His own house, so they could build a life together. He'd asked her about her dreams, and he'd said that what she wanted was important.

No one had ever said those things to her. No one had ever offered the things to her that Creed had.

All that, and it came with the kind of intense passion she hadn't even known existed.

How could she not fall in love with him? How could she have ever not loved him?

She swallowed hard and leaned against him, pressing her face against his suit jacket and inhaling his scent. "Thank you for dressing up for me again."

"It was appropriate," he responded, his voice hard.

She could feel him pulling away, not physically, but emotionally. And perversely it only made her want to cling to him even more tightly.

She couldn't help herself.

She was supposed to be focusing on the triumph of the evening. A few months ago, she would have been. It would have been all-important to her. Because she would have gotten approval out of it. Approval from her father.

It was such a different thing to be doing something for herself. She still cared about the winery. It was just that she already knew she approved of the job she'd done. She wasn't waiting for recognition. She was good at what she did, and she didn't question whether or not she could execute something like this.

It freed up her mind to worry about other things. It made all of this less all-consuming. Less important. Because it wasn't an essential part of her happiness. Wasn't an essential part of who she was.

She did this job for the winery. But she was also a sister. A daughter. A wife. Soon to be a mother.

She was interested in other things, and Creed had reminded her of that.

This event, and what happened at the winery, was no longer the highest-stakes thing happening in her world.

She wondered what kind of mother she would be. And she was worried about being a good wife.

About her husband's feelings for her.

This was satisfying. And it mattered.

But it didn't feel half so important or potentially fatal as it would have only a few short months ago.

And suddenly she thought maybe the transformation she'd been going through wasn't so much about becoming a different version of herself, but expanding what it meant to be Wren Maxfield.

Wren *Cooper.*

A woman who could want more than one thing, care about more than just her father's good opinion and this winery.

A woman whose definition of love could expand to accommodate a storm.

A woman who could be proud of what she had done all by herself.

It was a relief.

Because she had been worried. Worried that she might have to break all that she was into pieces and scatter them over the sea, bury them there, so she could become something completely and entirely new and foreign to herself.

But she didn't have to do that. She didn't.

She could just be.

She didn't have to worry about whether or not Cricket approved, or if it made any sense to anyone else that she had married her business rival.

That she loved him.

Her life belonged to her now. And she imagined it would change shape a great many more times before it was over.

But they would be shapes formed by her hands, her heart.

And the people she loved.

No, she couldn't anticipate the landscape and how it would look in the end.

But whatever it was, she knew she would find a way to navigate it, and if necessary, find ways to change it again.

Because she wasn't easily broken.

She was strong.

And she was trying to find a way to make her bravery match that strength. Her instinct was to continue to protect herself, but she didn't think the answers lay there. After all, it had been the strangest choices, the bravest choices, that had brought her here to begin with.

From deciding to join forces with her enemy, to kissing him. Deciding to raise her baby. Agreeing to marry him.

There was that honesty again.

Honesty took so much bravery.

Not fearlessness, but bravery indeed.

The party was packed full of people, and everything went wonderfully. She could feel the bonds she was building between her family business and these other wonderful family-run operations here in Gold Valley. She felt connected. In the same way she had felt disconnected that day she'd driven to town and realized all the things she had missed here, she could feel herself growing roots in the place that she had been planted from the beginning.

A place she had always felt might not be for her.

She had anticipated this cross-promotion being a boon for her business, but she had never expected all of this could matter so much to her personally.

Emerson was standing at the station for Maxfield, with her extremely handsome husband, Holden, at her side. Lindy was still standing with her husband.

And Wren made a decision, then and there.

Rather than going over to the station for Maxfield Vineyards, she went to the one that had been designated for Cowboy Wines. And she took her spot next to Creed.

She had no loyalty to a label.

She had a loyalty to this man. To all that he was, and more than that, all that they were together.

Yes, Maxfield would always be her family winery.

But Creed was her family now.

Creed was her heart.

Such an easy decision to make. Because now, she knew exactly who she was.

Chapter 11

Creed didn't know what the hell had gotten into Wren to-night, but it was as unsettling as it was arousing. She had been glued to his side the entire evening, tormenting him in that emerald dress that clung to her expanding curves. He loved the way her body was changing. The way her waist was getting thicker, the slight roundness low on her stomach speaking to the life growing inside her.

And, of course, he was enjoying the fullness in other parts of her curves.

She was beautiful in every way, but he was especially enjoying her current beauty because he was responsible for the changes. There was something intensely sexy and satisfying about that. But there was also a look in her eye that he was afraid he couldn't answer, and he didn't know what to make of it.

She had driven over to the winery on her own, but she left with him.

There was a determined sort of gleam in her eye, and it made his heart thunder, low and heavy.

Echoing like thunder inside him.

Like a storm.

She gave him a little half smile as they got into the house. And then she took his hand and led him over to the couch. He sat down, his legs relaxed, his palms rested on his knees.

Her eyes met his, and she reached behind her, unzipping that dress that had been torturing him so, and letting it fall from her curves.

His heart stopped. Stilled.

Everything in him went quiet. He couldn't breathe.

They'd made love countless times. Hadn't been able to keep their hands off each other these last few months. It was a storm of sensation and desire that had been building between them for years, and now that they lived together, now that they shared a bed every night, neither of them ever bothered to resist. But there was something different about tonight. There was an intent to her expression, a dare glimmering in her eyes.

Wren was never shy about sex. She was bold, and she was adventurous, but this was something else altogether. Still wearing her high heels, she unclipped her bra, removed it from her shoulders and let it fall to the floor. She did the same with her panties, standing there looking like a heavenly, dirty pinup that, thank God, was within arm's reach.

He didn't have to confine himself to just looking. He could touch.

He didn't know why he held himself back. Except that it was her show, and part of him was desperate to see exactly what she was going to make of it.

She pressed her hands to her stomach, slid them up her midsection and cupped her own breasts, teasing her nipples with her thumbs. Her eyes never left his.

"You know," she whispered, "you were my most forbidden fantasy. I tried to pretend that I didn't dream about you. About your hands on my body. But sometimes I would wake up from dreaming about you, wetter than I ever was from being with one of my other lovers."

"You have no idea," he ground out. "The dirty dreams I used to have about you."

"Is that why sometimes you were so mad at me when you would come and see me at work? Because you'd been dreaming about me naked, on my knees in front of you?"

And then she did just that.

Dropped to her knees in front of him, her dark hair cascading over her shoulders, the look of a predator etched into her beautiful face.

She pressed her hand over his clothed arousal, stroking him before opening up the closure on his pants. And then she leaned in, licking him, slowly, from base to tip, before making a supremely feline sound of satisfaction.

"I want you to know, I've never fantasized about doing this. But with you... I used to think about getting on my knees and sucking you to make you shut up. I could get off thinking about putting you in my mouth. That's not normal. Not for me."

And then she licked him again, and his world went dark. There was nothing but streaks of white-hot pleasure behind his eyes. Nothing but need. Nothing but desire.

She was a wicked tease, her mouth hot and slick and necessary.

How had she become *this*? He had thought her spoiled. Silly. Insubstantial.

You never really believed any of those things.

He closed his eyes and let his head fall back as she continued to pleasure him with that clever mouth that he had loved all the times it was cutting him to shreds, and now as it sent him to heaven.

No, he'd told himself those things. Because it was easy to disdain her, but much, much harder to have the guts to give in to a connection like this. A need like this.

Because this had nothing to do with the right thing, the good thing. With a pregnancy, or being a good father. It had everything to do with Wren. With his deep desire to wrap her in his arms and never let her go. With the intense possessiveness he felt every time he looked at her. And now, every time he looked at her and thought *wife*.

His wife.

His woman.

He hadn't asked for this. Hadn't wanted it. Had worked as hard as he could to avoid it, but all that work had been for nothing. Because here he was, and the inevitability of Wren, and his desire for her, suddenly seemed too big to ignore, too great to combat. And he was struck by his own cowardice. He had told himself so many stories about this woman that he had now seen weren't true, so many different things about the way he felt for her, that he could have easily examined and found to be lies.

He could tell himself he hadn't wanted this.

Because intensity had led to ruin all those years ago, and because he had failed.

Had failed as a father. Had failed as a man.

All because of desire. All because of wanting. The wrong woman. The wrong time.

But this was the *right* woman. The *right* time.

He gritted his teeth, rebelling against that thought as Wren's hand wrapped tight around the base of his arousal, squeezing him, sending his thoughts up to the stars and making it impossible for him to concentrate on anything else.

Impossible to do anything but feel.

She was a study in contradictions, so delicate and feminine as she destroyed his resistance with a kind of filthy poise he'd never imagined might exist.

He'd had sexual partners in the past. But he hadn't had a lover. Not really. Wren had become his lover. She'd learned his body, learned where to touch him and how, though he wondered if all these paths had been blazed by her hands, by what she wanted, by what she liked, because she seemed to conjure up sexual necessity out of thin air, make it so he couldn't breathe.

Couldn't think.

Wren had a spell cast on him that was unlike anything he'd ever experienced.

He had been smart to avoid it. Smart to try to turn away from it.

But he couldn't anymore. Not now.

Because she was here, and she was his wife. And everything she did was dark velvet perfection that took his control and ground it into stardust, glittering over the blank, night sky of his mind until she was all there was.

And without her, there would be only darkness.

And then what would he be?

Pleasure built low inside him, and he could feel his control fraying to an end.

"I need to be inside you," he ground out, lifting her up and away from his body, pulling her into his lap. Her knees rested on either side of his thighs, that slick, hot heart of her brushing his arousal. He brought her down onto him, over him, the welcome of his body into hers like a baptism.

Like something that might be able to make him new. Make him clean.

Even as he lost himself in a hedonistic rhythm, he knew many wouldn't call this salvation. But he did. Because the shattered glory he felt was the closest thing to pure he'd ever had.

And he reveled in it. Needed it.

She flexed her hips and rode him like an expert, and he was enrapt as he watched her. Watched her take her pleasure, watched her give pleasure to him. Her head thrown back, her breasts arched forward, the burgeoning evidence of her pregnancy echoing with deep, primal satisfaction inside him.

And when she came apart in his arms, her orgasm making her shiver and shake, he couldn't hold back anymore. He gripped her hips, pounding his need into a body that felt created for it. Created for him. Until the rush of release roared through him.

Then she collapsed over him, her hair falling over them like a curtain, her heart pounding fast against his.

"Creed," she whispered. "I love you."

* * *

She could feel it, the tightening of his muscles, the resistance in his body. What she'd said was the last thing he wanted to hear.

He wasn't happy to hear her say the words at all.

It was what she had been afraid of, except worse.

Because she had hoped... She had hoped that even if he wasn't going to say them back right away, he wouldn't resist them, or reject them.

That he would at least accept what she was offering freely, that he would let the words reach him, let the emotion touch him.

But the way those muscles went taut, it was like he had built a brick wall between the two of them.

A shouted rejection could not have been any louder.

With a firm grip, he set her away from him, putting her naked on his couch, the chill in the air feeling pronounced after she had been cradled so close to the warmth of his body only a moment before.

"It was a nice evening," he said. "Please don't spoil it."

"Oh," she said, feeling mutinous and angry. "Me being in love with you spoils the entire evening? Because I have news for you. I've been in love with you for longer than just tonight. It's only that tonight I realized just how deeply I felt about you."

"Wren, it's not the time."

"Why not? Why isn't it the time? We're married. We're having a baby."

"And I have a suspicion that you're trying to make a fairy tale out of all of this. And I get the appeal. Because you've been Rapunzel, locked away in a tower, and you seem to think I might be able to save you, or that I *did* save you. But that's not true. We're just two people who had unprotected sex. We have chemistry, or we wouldn't have done what we did in the first place. The first time I did it, I had the excuse of youth. But this time? You and I have something explosive. We both know that. We're not kids. We're not inexperienced. But because of our age, you should know that chemistry isn't love."

"Why would I know that?" she asked. "Why would I know that chemistry isn't love? I've been in a lot of relationships, and there was nothing like what we have. Shouldn't you want this? With the person you're going to spend the rest of your life with? Shouldn't chemistry be part of it? Maybe it's not love all on its own, but I think it definitely indicates we are the kind of people who could fall in love with each other. And I did. I don't need you to say you love me, I really don't. But I'd like it if you could take my words and at least…at least accept them. Let them sit inside you. See what they could heal. Creed, loving you has fixed so many things inside me. It's amazing. It's more than I ever expected. If you let it, love could heal you, too."

But she already knew he wasn't going to allow it to happen. Not here. Not now. She already knew he was going to say no, because refusal was written in every line of his body. And she knew him.

Knew him like she'd never known another person, and to an extent she had to wonder if she knew him so well because now she knew herself. Because of all that honesty.

She was really beginning to dislike honesty.

She was really beginning to resent this journey she'd

gone on to peel back the layers of herself and expose everything she was. Not just to the world, but to herself.

Because one thing she hadn't appreciated about the life she'd had before all this was the protection she'd had. Because she had been able to hide in plain sight, and tell herself she was doing everything she needed to do, when in reality, following that prescribed path presented little to no risk at all.

And now, here she was, on the path she was blazing for herself, standing in front of a man and exposing the very deepest parts of herself.

It hurt.

It was hard.

And this was why Wren understood—without knowing any of the details—that her mother had chosen a safer life. The one with borders and boundaries and limits.

Because these feelings didn't have limits. And there was no guide for how to proceed.

Because Wren felt simultaneously the most and least like herself in this moment that she ever had.

This was bravery.

And she was leaning into it while he was running scared.

"I love you," she repeated. "Isn't that a good thing?"

"I don't want to hurt you," he said, his voice low. "God knows you've been through enough. But that's not what I was in this for. It's not."

"Me either. I didn't kiss you that day down in the wine cellar so I could fall in love with you. So I could marry you and have your baby. But here we are. This has been the strangest journey, and it was the one I needed.

Because it *was* a journey to me, a journey to us. Because it was somehow absolutely everything we were ever going to be. It's all right here. You're the only person who has ever looked at me and asked what I wanted to be. And said that no matter what that turned out to be, you would support me…"

"That's not love," he said. "It's convenience. I want access to my child, and I want the marriage to be mutually beneficial so you don't leave it."

"Well, your generosity created love in me. Love for myself and my life, and for you. I didn't know that I could love you. I *hated* you. And I realize now the reason I hated you so much was that you called to something in me I wasn't ready to reveal. I didn't want my life to change. And something in me knew that you could change it. Just by existing, you could change everything that I was. Everything that I am. That you would drag me out of my comfort zone. Out of my safety. I wasn't ready. So I fought you. I pushed back against you. Until I couldn't anymore. My life was at a crossroads that day. I felt like an alien in my hometown, an alien in my skin, and it wasn't until I gave in to you that things started to feel right."

"That's good," he said. "And that has to be enough."

"That's the problem," she said softly. "It's not. Because I realized something tonight when we were at the party. When everybody was at their stations with their husbands, and I had to make a choice. What family was I going to join? I realized that my place was beside you. But it's not because of a piece of paper, and it's not simply because I'm carrying your baby. It's because of love. And it's… I've been chasing that my whole life, Creed. I tried to be the best that I could be, but I was looking for love and acceptance from a man who could never give it. I made myself acceptable for my father, and I lost myself. And I can't hide what I am anymore. Who I am. What I feel. Least of all with you. Please don't ask me to go back to hiding."

"Wren," he said. "I can't love you."

"Can't? Or won't?"

"Something broke in me a long time ago," he said. "I failed. I failed at the most important thing a man can fail at. I'm not a father to my son. And I created an enemy to take the blame. I wanted to blame Louisa. But now I realize… I can't."

"Why not? Why can't you blame her, but you can blame yourself?"

"She must have known. She must've known that I wasn't going to do the job that Cal did. And she did what she had to do to protect her life, her child. But it was my responsibility to be better, to do more, and I couldn't. I didn't."

"Because of that you can't love me now?"

"I…"

"Will you love our baby? Or is what you feel for him or her all tied up in the boy you can't have? Because it seems to me that's awfully convenient. To have put all your emotions into something that you lost eighteen years ago. Of course you love your son. I understand that. It makes sense to me, even though you don't know him. I get it. I do. But at a certain point, you're just self-fulfilling a prophecy. You've decided that you'll fail the people who love you, and you've gone ahead and made sure you will by deciding you're not able to give again.

You let that first loss decide how the rest of your life is going to go. Not just for you, but for me, for our baby."

"I want to be there," he said. "I want to take care of you both…"

"I grew up in a house that was quiet. That was half-muted with secrets and emotional distance. I have my sisters, and I love them dearly. But our parents… They didn't love each other. My father couldn't love anyone but himself. My mother is just defeated. I won't put our child in that place."

"I'm not your father," he said. "I would never hurt you. I would never hurt our child. I would never hurt another woman…"

"I know you aren't our father. But I still can't face a life without love. A house without love for me and for my baby. That kind of home was my whole existence before. You can't ask me to make it my life again. I finally found myself. All of myself. But I did that through loving you. And this woman I've become isn't going to accept less than I know that we can have. If I didn't think you could love me, then maybe I would take this. But the problem is… If I accept what you're offering now, then I'm going to be robbing us both, robbing our child. Of the life we can have, of the home we can have. Of everything we can build together."

"I gave you a house," he said. "I gave you vows. What more do you want from me?"

"Only everything," she said quietly. "Just everything that you are, everything that you ever will be. Your entire heart. That's all. And I'll give the same back, but you have to be willing to give to me. And if you can't, then… We'll share custody of the baby. I would never take this child from you." She paused, considering. "And you know what, if at this point you can't believe that I will keep my word about custody, then we really shouldn't be together."

"Wren," he growled.

He reached out and grabbed hold of her arm, pulled her to him, pressing her naked body against his. And then he kissed her. Deep and wild and hard.

But with fury.

Not love.

And she so desperately wanted his love.

Because she had come through the clearing, come through the fire, come through the storm. And she was willing to stand through it, whatever the risk.

And because she'd found a way to be brave and honest, she wanted him to do the same.

Because she loved him more than she had ever thought she hated him, and she desperately needed to know that he loved her, too.

She pulled away from him, even though it hurt. Pulled away from him, even though it felt like dying.

It would be easier to stay. Whether he ever said he loved her or not. It would be easier to just stay. But then he would still be in hiding.

And she would be out in the storm alone.

And he would never know…

He would never find this freedom that she'd found. The sharp, painful, beautiful freedom that made her all she was.

Love meant demanding more from him.

Love meant she had to push them both to be the best

they could be. She could not allow him to hide, not allow him to remain damaged but protected.

She wanted him to feel whole in the same way that she felt now. Glued back together, those cracks glowing bright because they were pressed together by love.

"I need you to love me," she said. "I need you to find a way. And if it takes years, I'll still be here waiting for you. But I won't live halfway. I won't live in a house with you without love. I won't share your bed without love. I won't take your name without love."

"You're ruining us," he ground out. "Over nothing."

"No, over everything. And as long as you think it's nothing, that difference is not something we can ignore."

Her dreams started to crack in front of her like a sheet of ice. Dreams of a shared life. A shared Christmas. Those Christmases she thought they might have here in this house, starting with this one.

But it was gone now.

Hope.

She whispered that word to herself.

Just keep your hope.

Wren collected her clothes and dressed slowly.

"Your car isn't even here," he said.

"No," she said. "I know. But my sister will come and get me." She stopped. "If you can't fight me now as hard as you did over the winery business, then... I don't know, Creed. I just don't know."

She went outside then. And it wasn't Emerson who ultimately came to get her, but Cricket.

"What happened?" Cricket asked.

"Oh, my heart is only broken," Wren said, pressing her face against the glass in the car.

"Why did you marry a man you hate?"

"Because I never really hated him. I was just afraid of loving him." She sighed heavily. "Because loving him hurts. Really badly."

"That's stupid," Cricket said. "Love isn't supposed to feel like that. It's not supposed to be that close to… this. All these bad feelings."

"The problem is," Wren said slowly, "when someone has been hurt, it's not that simple. And he's been hurt really badly."

"Well, now he's passed it on to you. And I don't think I can forgive him for that."

"I can," Wren said. "If he wants me to."

Cricket scoffed. "Why would you?"

"Because some people are like Dad," Wren said. "They're toxic. They don't love people because they are too busy loving themselves. But some people are wounded. Creed is wounded. What he has to decide is if he wants to stay that way. Or if he's going to let himself be whole."

"It all sounds overrated to me."

Wren thought back to the last few months, the journey that she'd been on, the one that had ultimately led here, which was so very painful. And she realized she would do it all again. Every time. Exactly the same.

Because however it came out in the end, it had led her to this place, where she had decided to be brave and honest. Where she had decided to heal regardless of what he chose to do.

"Someday you'll understand."

"No. I'm not interested in that kind of thing. And

when I am, I'm going to choose a nice man who has nothing to do with any of this."

"With any of what?"

"I want to leave the vineyard," Cricket said. "I realize this isn't the best timing. But I want to tell you… I want my own life. One that's totally different from this. I never wanted to be here. Mom and Dad never cared about what I did and…"

"I think Mom does care," Wren said softly. "But I think, like Creed, she's wounded. And sometimes she doesn't know how to show it."

"I'm not wounded," Cricket said, defiant. "I'm going to find a place with people who aren't. Present company excluded. It has nothing to do with you and Emerson. I might want a ranch. I want you to buy out my share."

Disappointment churned in Wren's chest. The idea of Cricket leaving the winery was painful. Another loss, but…

Her sister needed her chance. Her chance to find herself, like Wren had found herself.

"It's okay, Cricket. You have to find a place that makes you happy. You have to find your path."

Privately, Wren knew that it wouldn't be as smooth as her sister was imagining. But she also knew Cricket would have to find it for herself. And maybe… Maybe Cricket would find a nice, simple relationship. An easy kind of love. But somehow Wren doubted it. Because Cricket was too tough and spiky to accept anyone soft. To accept anything less than the kind of love that moved mountains inside her.

And that kind of love didn't come easy.

But if Cricket needed to believe she could find a love

that *did* come easy, then Wren wasn't going to disabuse her of the notion.

Because just like Wren's own situation, no one could do it for Cricket. She would have to fight her way through on her own.

"And what's your ideal man?"

"One who isn't half as much cowboy drama as yours and Emerson's dudes. I'm going to get a job at Sugar Cup. I've already decided. I'm going to serve coffee while I build my ranching empire. And I'll meet a nice guy."

"I didn't think you were interested in meeting anybody."

"I'm not," Cricket said.

"So there's nobody in particular that you like?"

"We shouldn't be talking about me."

"I prefer it to thinking about myself," Wren said.

"No," Cricket said. And she sounded so resolute that Wren wondered if she was lying. "I think love should make you feel sweet and floaty. I don't think that crushes should make you angry."

"Oh," Wren said. "Sure."

Sweet summer child.

But again, her sister was going to have to figure all this out for herself. Just like Wren had.

And honestly, even though Wren felt like she had figured a lot out in the last few months, she also didn't know how her story was going to end.

But she supposed that was the real gift. She had learned, through this series of changes, that while chapters of one's life would come to a close, there was always a chance to make herself new. To make her life into the best version that she could.

And she would carry that hope with her.

As long as she was here, she would have a chance to change for the better. The hope of better was what made one brave. It was what made everything worth it. And so, she would continue to hope, no matter how dark it seemed.

If that realization and her baby were the only gifts she could ever get from Creed, then she supposed they would have to be enough.

Chapter 12

"All right," his brother's voice came behind him. Creed braced himself for what would come next. "What the hell is the matter with you?"

He turned toward Jackson and scowled. "What's it to you?"

"Plenty. Because it's beginning to impact on my life, and I don't like that. You've been scowling around here for more than a week. It's a pain in my ass. Does it have something to do with your wife?"

He gritted his teeth. "She left me."

"What the hell did you do?"

"It's complicated."

"Try me."

"She said she loved me."

Jackson made a choking sound. "What a travesty. Your wife is in love with you. However will you survive?"

"That's not what this was supposed to be about."

"Oh, your marriage isn't supposed to be about love? What the hell is it supposed to be about, then?"

"I told you. It's complicated."

"I'm all ears."

"And why exactly do you think you're an authority on any of this? It's not like you've ever been in a real relationship."

"Maybe I'm not an authority on relationships, but I'm an authority on you. And you're miserable. Which means you need to sort it out."

"There's nothing to sort out. Nothing changed on my end. I offered her everything that was always on the table. I bought her the house she wanted, I told her she could do whatever she wanted when it came to work, and we set fire to the sheets. I don't know why the hell she thinks she needs more."

"It's this weird thing where people tend to want to be loved. Weird, I know. Especially since it's never been a major priority for either of us. But I think maybe it's not astonishingly strange."

"I don't understand why she needs it."

"I don't understand why it's a problem for you. Hell, you seem like you're in love with her."

"It's impossible. I can't do that. I already... Look, I wasted all my emotion. I can't love her."

"You can't? Or you won't?"

"She asked me the same question. But it amounts to the same thing."

"What's the real problem here? Because I don't get your resistance to this."

"The problem is that I didn't... I didn't get to love

my son the way that I was supposed to. So now I'm just supposed to move on? Just make a new family, make a new life? I thought I could. For a little while, I thought I could. But I can't. It's wrong. I can't just decide to get a do-over. I wanted to, but it's killing me. The guilt of it."

His brother just stared at him. "What do you mean you didn't love your son? It wasn't your choice not to be with him. Not to be around him. Louisa chose that for you."

"I could've fought harder. I've seen him around."

"Yeah. And you loved him enough that you didn't go crashing into his life and make it about you. You loved him enough that you let him have the family that he knows. Loving somebody doesn't just mean being in their lives every day. And I never would've thought of that if it weren't for you. But I've never doubted that you love that kid. Because I saw what it did to you all those years ago. It tore you up. But you had to make a choice not to make his life a war zone, and you made that choice. And every time you've ever seen him at an event, including the one a few months ago, you've made the choice to put his happiness above your own. That is love, Creed."

"It hurts," Creed growled.

"No one ever said love didn't hurt. Hurt makes sense. But not guilt. You've got nothing to feel guilty for."

The problem was, his brother's words rang true.

And if there was no guilt… Then there was nothing standing in his way. It was all a matter of being brave enough to step forward. Brave enough to allow Wren to have all of him.

Even though his emotions had been savaged, his heart torn to pieces.

He didn't know if he was brave enough.

But what's the alternative?

Another life spent with so much distance between himself and the people who held his heart.

No, he'd never gotten a chance to be a father before. Not in the way he wanted to be.

But he had the chance now. And not just to be a father, but to be a husband.

It was all well and good to fantasize about how well he'd do those things, but entirely different to take the steps toward *being* those things.

"It's terrifying," he said. "I've been so certain all these years that I would've been great at this, but... What if I'm not?"

"Well, then you're not. That's just part of life. Sometimes you're bad at something, and then you learn to be better at it. Was Dad perfect?"

"Hell no," Creed said. "He's still not."

"Do you love him?"

"Of course I do."

"Well, there's your answer. Did you need perfect, or did you need a father?"

"I'm going to be there for my kid, it's just..."

"Remember what Dad said? That he loved a woman who chose easy over him? That leaves scars. Are you going to leave Wren with those kinds of scars? Are you gonna leave yourself with them?"

"There's no easy answer, is there? There's no pain-proof way to do this."

"No. Life is tough. Nobody gets out alive."

Creed didn't like that reasoning. At all. He also couldn't argue with it.

Because that was just it. There were no guarantees. He just had to be brave.

And with sudden, stark clarity, he saw Wren as she had been. Standing there open and vulnerable and naked. Beautiful, demanding that he love her. And he realized that he'd failed her. He'd been a coward. An absolute, complete coward.

She had been so brave, after the betrayals she had experienced in her life. And he was... He was hiding behind his own hurt. Using his pain to shield him from more pain.

But it wasn't going to work. And in the end, it wasn't worth it. How could he choose safety at the cost of what could be the greatest joy he would ever experience?

He was hit with a blinding flash of truth.

If you wanted to have everything life could offer, you also had to risk your heart.

Just like Wren had said.

She wanted only everything.

And nothing else would do.

He understood that now.

Everything was the only answer. Everything was the least he could offer.

"I have to go talk to her," he said, his voice rough.

"Yeah," Jackson replied. "You do."

"I'll return the favor when you're in the same position."

"I won't be," Jackson said, chuckling, the sound sharpened by an edge that surprised Creed. "I'm happy for you. It's plain to anyone looking at you that you love her. And that you ought to be with her."

"I hope so."

She'd said she would wait. She'd said he could change his heart.

But he wondered. And he almost wouldn't blame her if she wasn't waiting. Because she had stripped herself bare, and he had offered her nothing.

He had rejected her.

"I just have to hope that she'll still have me."

Wren was wretched, and no amount of trying to ensure herself that standing in her truth, standing strong in what she needed, was making her feel any better.

Emerson was deeply sympathetic, having been through something similar with Holden. Cricket seemed like she didn't know what to do with her.

And a surprising source of support and sympathy came from her mother.

"I know it's hard to believe," she said, "but I know what it's like to have a broken heart."

"You're going through a divorce," Wren said. "I don't think it's hard to believe."

"Not your father. My heart broke slowly over the choices I made, but he didn't break it. I was in love once. And I'm the one who walked away from it. It makes such a deep scar. I hope Creed realizes it before it's too late. Because you can't protect yourself by turning away from love. You just sign yourself up for a life of…less."

"That's why I left… I wanted him to love me. To find it in himself to admit that he does. Because if he can't find it in himself to admit it, then the alternative would be something terribly sad."

"It is," her mother said. "Believe me. And it's taken me years to get to a place I could have been in a long time ago if I had just done the work on myself back then. But instead I hid. I hid in a marriage that didn't have love. I hid behind money. I hid here in this house, because it was what I chose. Status. Wealth."

"Mom," Wren said slowly. "Were you in love with Law Cooper?"

But she didn't get a chance to hear the answer because Cricket came running into the room. "I told him to go away," she said fiercely.

"What?"

"Your husband," her sister said, her lip curled. "I told him to go away. But he's still here."

"Oh," Wren said, springing out of her chair and bounding toward the door.

"Forget about him," Cricket said. "He's not worth it."

"He is," Wren said. "And when you're in love you'll understand."

And there he was, standing in the entry of their grand home, looking out of place in his blue jeans, T-shirt and cowboy hat, his face bearing the marks of exhaustion, of sadness.

"You look like I feel," Wren said, staring at him.

"I feel like hell," he said. "It's been…the worst week of my life."

"Mine, too."

"Wren," he said. "I'm so sorry. I thought… I was so comfortable punishing myself for what happened with… Lucas. My son's name is Lucas. And I don't know him. And I've used that pain to drive me. I told myself all the things I would have done differently for him. And I made myself feel confident in this hypothetical version of me. And at the same time, I used the guilt to keep me safe. To convince myself that I never had to love again, because I had already loved and lost it. But I was just using that guilt to protect myself. Because it was easier than maybe being hurt again.

"I never loved Louisa," he said. "But what she told me was that I might not be good enough, and I let that sit inside me. But I want to be good enough. For you. I want to be everything for you."

"Creed," she said. "What you did for me... You brought me on a journey to myself. And it was the thing I needed most, when I needed it most. I spent my life protecting myself, so I understand how compelling that is. I know what it is to live your life feeling like you might not be enough. But we were just trying to be enough for the wrong people. When we're already more than perfect for each other."

"Wren," he said, his voice rough. "I love you."

"I love you, too," she said, flinging herself into his arms and kissing him with everything in her heart. "I love you so much."

"This isn't just a second chance," he said, putting his hand on her stomach. "It's our chance. And I'm so damn grateful."

"Me, too."

Wren Maxfield loved Creed Cooper more than anything. He was a cocky, arrogant pain in the butt, and he was hers. And suddenly, even with all the twists and turns in the road to get here, Wren knew she was living her life, the best life.

She knew who she was.

She was Creed's and he was hers.

And nothing could ever be better than that.

Epilogue

Creed was the proudest father around. Matched only by how proud of a husband he was.

He loved watching his son grow, and he loved watching Wren learn, as she went through the process of getting her degree so she could become an architectural engineer.

The people he was blessed to love astounded him in every way.

He astounded himself, because he never really imagined he would enjoy a one-year-old's birthday party. But he did. It had been the best day, down to watching his son's pudgy little fingers smash the cake they'd had made especially for that purpose.

His fascination a few months earlier with their Christmas tree—fake because Wren wanted a very particular spectacle, and Mac would eat fallen pine needles—had been just as cute. Though they'd had to anchor it to a wall so he didn't pull it down on himself.

But it was the knock on the door after the birthday party that led to the most unexpected thing of all.

Wren was the one who answered it. And she came running to him, where he was sitting on the floor with Mac, only a few moments later.

"Creed. You need to come here." Wren swooped down and picked up Mac, and then stepped back as Creed made his way to the door.

Standing there, outside, was his oldest son.

"You don't know me," the kid said. "But... My mom told me the whole story. Everything, a few months ago. And she said what I did with it was up to me, but... I thought it was time I came to meet you."

Creed's heart slowed as Lucas looked past him. The color drained from the kid's face. "Oh, I hope I didn't cause any problems."

"No," Creed said. "You didn't. I just... I never wanted to go crashing into your life and cause any problems for you. But there's always been a place for you in my life. And there always will be."

"I guess my dad always knew," Lucas said. "You know. My..."

"He's your dad," Creed said. "He's the one who raised you. But I'd like the chance to be something to you."

Because that's what love did. It grew, it expanded, it changed. And it left no room for resentment.

And Creed was damned thankful that he had a woman who understood that. Because Wren accepted Lucas into their lives with as much ease as he could have asked from her.

And sometime down the road he realized it wasn't love that caused hurt. It was fear.

And his family made a rule not to operate from fear. But just to grow from love.

And that was what they did. From then, until forever. They just loved.

And they were happy.

* * * * *

In Gold Valley, Oregon, lasting love is only a happily-ever-after away. Don't miss any of Maisey Yates's Gold Valley tales, available now!

Gold Valley Vineyards
Rancher's Wild Secret

Gold Valley
A Tall, Dark Cowboy Christmas
Unbroken Cowboy
Cowboy to the Core
Untamed Cowboy
Smooth-Talking Cowboy
Cowboy Christmas Redemption